Sam Dundee saw Jeannie Alverson fall....

He cut through the crowd like a machete slicing through untamed jungle.

"Who the hell do you think you are?" someone asked.

"I'm the cavalry to the rescue," Sam proclaimed, the deadly curve of his mouth an easily understood warning. Bending on one knee, he gently lifted Jeannie into his arms. She looked even more delicate, more fragile, than she had six years ago.

Jeannie gazed into Sam's eyes, and a hard knot of fear formed in the pit of his stomach. He remembered those warm, loving, compassionate eyes.... "Everything will be all right, Jeannie. I'm here now."

"Thank you." Her voice was sweet and unintentionally sultry. A slow, honey-coated Southern drawl. Her fingers touched the nape of Sam's neck. A soft, tender touch.

Sam's nerves screamed.

His body tensed.

His world would never be the same....

Dear Reader,

We've got a terrific lineup of books to start off the New Year. I hope you'll enjoy each and every one. Start things off with our newest Intimate Moments Extra, Kathryn Jensen's *Time and Again*. This book is time travel with a twist—but you'll have to read it to see what I mean. One thing I can promise you: you won't regret the time you spend turning these pages.

Next up, Marie Ferrarella's cross-line miniseries, The Baby of the Month Club, comes to Intimate Moments with *Happy New Year—Baby!* Of course, this time we're talking *babies* of the month, because Nicole Logan is having twins—and it's up to Dennis Lincoln to prove that a family of four is better than a family of three. Sharon Sala's *When You Call My Name* brings back Wyatt Hatfield from her last book, *The Miracle Man*. This time, Wyatt's looking for a miracle of his own, both to save his life and heal his heart. Beverly Barton continues her miniseries, The Protectors, with *Guarding Jeannie*, Sam Dundee's story. Alexandra Sellers gives the ever-popular secret-baby plot line a whirl in *Roughneck*, and I know you'll want to come along for the ride. Finally, welcome new author Kate Hathaway, whose *His Wedding Ring* will earn a spot on your keeper shelf.

Until next month—happy reading!

Yours,

Leslie J. Wainger
Senior Editor and Editorial Coordinator

Please address questions and book requests to:
Silhouette Reader Service
U.S.: 3010 Walden Ave., P.O. Box 1325, Buffalo, NY 14269
Canadian: P.O. Box 609, Fort Erie, Ont. L2A 5X3

GUARDING JEANNIE

BEVERLY BARTON

Silhouette®

INTIMATE™MOMENTS®

Published by Silhouette Books

America's Publisher of Contemporary Romance

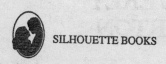

SILHOUETTE BOOKS

ISBN 0-373-07688-6

GUARDING JEANNIE

Printed in U.S.A.

Books by Beverly Barton

Silhouette Intimate Moments

This Side of Heaven #453
Paladin's Woman #515
Lover and Deceiver #557
The Outcast #614
Defending His Own #670
Guarding Jeannie #688

*The Protectors

Silhouette Desire

Yankee Lover #580
Lucky in Love #628
Out of Danger #662
Sugar Hill #687
Talk of the Town #711
The Wanderer #766
Cameron #796
The Mother of My Child #831
Nothing But Trouble #881

BEVERLY BARTON

has been in love with romance since her grandfather gave her an illustrated book of *Beauty and the Beast*. An avid reader since childhood, she began writing at the age of nine and wrote short stories, poetry, plays and novels throughout high school and college. After marriage to her own "hero" and the births of her daughter and son, she chose to be a full-time homemaker, a.k.a. wife, mother, friend and volunteer.

When she returned to writing, she joined Romance Writers of America and helped found the Heart of Dixie chapter in Alabama. Since the release of her first Silhouette book in 1990, she has won the GRW Maggie Award, the National Readers' Choice Award and has been a RITA finalist. Beverly considers writing romance books a real labor of love. Her stories come straight from the heart, and she hopes that all the strong and varied emotions she invests in her books will be felt by everyone who reads them.

To my husband, the father of my children,
the love of my life, Billy Ray Beaver,
and to every woman who has ever wished
she possessed the ability to take away a loved
one's pain and willingly suffer it for them—
a child, a husband, a parent, a lover, a friend.

Prologue

The man lay facedown in the sand, the water lapping at his feet. From where Jeannie stood on the knoll above the beach, she could make out very little in the moonlight, only that he was quite large and he wasn't moving.

Who was he? From where had he come? A boat hadn't docked at Le Bijou Bleu in over a week. Had the man fallen overboard out there somewhere in the Gulf and his body washed ashore?

Leaning heavily on the simple wooden cane she relied on in order to walk, Jeannie made her way down the hill, slowly, carefully. If the man was dead, there was no hurry; if he was alive, she would be of little help to him if she fell and injured herself.

Maneuvering on the sand wasn't easy for Jeannie. Her heavy limp hampered her movements. As she neared the prone figure, her hands trembled. If he was alive, what would she do? Did she dare touch him, a stranger whose injuries she might not be able to discern?

Sticking her cane in the sand, she lowered herself onto her knees, all the while saying a silent prayer for assistance. *Help me do the right thing.*

Reaching out, she held her hand over the man's head. The moonlight revealed the width of his huge shoulders. His wet white shirt stuck to his muscular back. His thick blond hair lay plastered to his head and neck. With every ounce of willpower she possessed, Jeannie forced herself to touch him. The heat from his body seared her. She moaned softly. Threading her fingers through his damp hair, she closed her eyes and allowed the energy from his body to begin its journey into hers.

He was alive! Dear Lord, he was alive—but just barely. She could save him. She knew in her heart that she could.

He groaned, the sound a deep growl in his throat. When he moved his head to one side, Jeannie caressed his face, her hand cradling his cheek and jaw. For one incredible moment, she couldn't breathe, so intense was the power emanating from his big body.

She jerked her hand away, but could not stop looking at his face. Pale, haggard, and yet devastatingly handsome. Fresh blood dripped from a wound at his temple.

Did she have the strength to save him? Could she keep him alive until they got him to the mainland, to a hospital? Was he too powerful, his pain too great? She had learned from past experiences that her body and mind could accept only so much pain before the transference endangered her own life.

But she couldn't let him die, could she? Jeannie had no idea who he was, but one thing she knew—fate had ordained that he wash up on her beach, placing him in her care. This man had been sent to her. She believed that as surely as she believed the sun would rise in the morning.

With her heart beating rapidly and her stomach twisted into knots, Jeannie released her cane, which she had been holding on to with one hand, and sat down in the sand.

The man groaned again, louder, harsher, and moved his body slightly, as if he were trying to turn over. Jeannie ran her hand down his arms, soothing him, comforting him. He rolled over onto his side, opened his eyes for a split second, then passed out again.

"You're going to be all right," she told him as she lifted his head onto her lap and took his face in her hands.

She felt the first faint trickling of energy again leaving his body, the pain a delicate fluttering. Now, before the pain overwhelmed her, Jeannie surveyed what she could see of his body, searching for any other injures besides the gash on his forehead. An enormous scarlet blot stained his shirt from armpit to waist. Had he been shot? Stabbed?

"Oh!" Jeannie cried out when the pain increased. Hot, searing pain, doubling her over. She clutched at the man's shirt, holding on, trying to make her hands lie flat against the surface of his chest.

He groaned loudly, opened his eyes and cried out, rending the night air with the sound of his agony.

Help me, Jeannie pleaded. His pain was so great. She screamed when the fullness of his torment filled her. Sweat broke out on her face. Rivulets of perspiration trickled down her neck, dripping inside her blouse, leaving a moist trail between her breasts.

He manacled her wrist with his big hand, but she did not feel the pressure of his grip. All she felt was the pain she had taken from him, the torturous physical agony.

"Where... am... I?" His deep, husky voice huffed out the words, each syllable a strained effort. "Who... are... you? An angel...?"

Although she heard his questions, Jeannie could not answer him, could respond only with a wild look of helplessness in her eyes.

Now his mental and emotional pain entered her, and she screamed from the sheer misery of his thoughts. He blamed himself for someone's death. *All my fault. I was a fool. I should have been the one to die.* Oh, dear Lord, the guilt, the sad, bitter guilt. And the anger. The anger could destroy her quicker than the pain. She had to hold on, absorb it and release it. Negative energy was so destructive. It could kill her.

"What... what are you... doing?" He tried to lift his head, but the effort was too great. "I feel... I don't hurt..."

Releasing him, she fell down beside him, her face only inches from his. She was weak, so very, very weak. But she always was afterward—after she had absorbed another's pain, taken it into herself and shared an agony too great to be borne alone.

But this man would still die if they didn't get him to the hospital soon. She would have to go with him. When the pain returned, he would need to share it with her.

She had to summon Manton. The stranger was a big man, but Manton was far bigger. He would be able to carry the man to the boat, and if they hurried, they could get him to the mainland before he died.

With the remnants of the stranger's pain still radiating through her, Jeannie focused her mind on the task of summoning Manton. He was one of the few people with whom she was able to connect mentally.

Lying there in the sand, waiting for Manton to respond, Jeannie lifted her hand, then reached out and took the stranger's hand into hers. She looked into his eyes. They were a steely blue-gray in the moonlight.

"You're going to live," she said. "I won't let you die."

He didn't seem to have the strength to respond. He gazed at her for endless moments, then closed his eyes.

Jeannie didn't know how long she lay there. She, too, had closed her eyes and slept. But now Manton stood towering above her, his round bronze face and bald head shining in the faint glow of the moon.

He helped her to her feet, then glanced down at the man still lying on the beach.

"We have to get him to the hospital in Biloxi as quickly as possible." Jeannie spoke slowly, so that Manton could read her lips. She was too exhausted to speak to him telepathically, having used so much of her energy in saving the stranger. "Do you think you can carry him to the dock?"

Manton nodded, then bent down on one knee and lifted the big, unconscious man. Grasping her cane, Jeannie jerked it out of the sand and followed Manton up the beach and toward the dock where their boat was anchored.

She cradled the man's head in her lap on the journey from the island of Le Bijou Bleu to Biloxi. Each time he started to bleed again, she stopped it. Each time his pain returned, she removed it, taking it into herself, suffering it for him.

Chapter 1

Whipping her tan Lexus around the corner, Jeannie raced up the driveway and came to a screeching halt at the side entrance of the antebellum home she shared with her foster father. She hoped Julian was still at the hospital board meeting. If he saw how upset she was, he would worry. Not that he wasn't already worried enough to give himself another heart attack.

Checking in the rearview mirror, she sighed with relief. Somehow she had lost the reporter who'd been following her since she left the Howell School. Tory Gaines had been waiting for her when she walked out the door. The aggravating man was bound to show up on her doorstep anytime now. After all, he knew where she lived. It seemed everyone in Biloxi, Gulfport and the surrounding towns knew where Jeannie Alverson lived, thanks to Gaines's eavesdropping and subsequent snooping into her past.

Jeannie opened the door, set the tip of her wooden walking cane down on the paved drive and eased out of the car. Leaning on her cane, she retrieved her briefcase from the front seat, then shoved the door closed with her hip. Oh, what she'd give for a cup of tea and a few moments of utter quiet.

For the past five days, ever since the story about her performing a miracle and saving a student's life had hit the newsstands, and Tory Gaines had revealed the ugly truth about her past, Jeannie's world had been turned upside down. Newspaper and magazine reporters from coast to coast called, wanting interviews. Television reporters from every network offered her the chance to tell her story to the world. And letters from across the country were pouring in, from people pleading with her to heal them from a thousand and one different ailments.

This couldn't be happening. Not again. Not after all these years of being so careful to use her extraordinary talents selectively and to keep her past life as a child healer on the revival circuit a secret.

Jeannie made her way around the hood of the Lexus, her briefcase tucked under her arm. A thin, sallow-faced middle-aged man walked out from behind the row of six-foot-high, neatly trimmed shrubbery that separated the Howell property from that of their next-door neighbor. Jeannie gasped. Who was this man? What did he want? He certainly didn't look like a reporter.

"Jeannie." His high-pitched voice sounded shrill to her ears.

"What do you want?" Remain calm, she told herself. He isn't going to harm you.

"I'm dying." He held out both hands to her, gesturing for her to come to him. "I—I have an inoperable brain tumor. You're my only hope."

"I'm sorry," Jeannie said. "I'm so very sorry. What's your name?"

"Jeremy Thornton." He grabbed Jeannie's free hand. "Please heal me. I'll give you everything I own, if you'll heal me."

Jeannie clutched her walking cane tightly. Her briefcase slipped down to her hip. She tried to catch it with her elbow, but Jeremy Thornton tugged her forward, and the briefcase fell to the ground.

"Mr. Thornton, if I could heal you, I would, but I can't. I'm not God. I don't have the power to do what you're asking."

The wild, deranged look of disbelief in Jeremy's eyes said he thought she was lying.

Jeannie squeezed his hand. "I can ease your pain... temporarily." She looked into his gaunt face, and her heart ached for him.

"I don't want you to just ease the pain," he said. "I want you to heal me. Make the tumor disappear."

"I can't do that."

"But you must." Tears welled up in his eyes. He gripped her by the shoulders, shaking her. "I don't want to die."

She focused her attention on the man's face for a brief moment, then closed her eyes. She felt the humming inside her head, the tingling current passing through her body. It would be so simple to ease his pain. All she had to do was accept it into her own body, drain it slowly away from him and experience the pain herself. So simple, and yet so devastating for her.

He shook her again, harder this time. "Help me! Everyone claims you're a healer, a miracle worker. Heal me, damn you, heal me!"

His hands tightened painfully on her shoulders, his bony fingers biting into her flesh. What could she say to reason with him? How could she make him understand the limits of her abilities?

"Ollie!" Jeannie cried the housekeeper's name at the top of her lungs, praying Ollie could hear her.

"No, don't call out for help. They're not going to take you away from me until you've healed me."

Just as Jeremy placed his hands around Jeannie's throat, she saw a lanky, sandy-haired man walking up her driveway. She didn't know or care who he was. She didn't even care if he was another reporter.

"Please, whoever you are, help me make this man understand that I can't heal him."

Jeremy's grasp around her neck loosened slowly as he turned around to face the man, who carried a white Bible under his arm.

"Brother," the man said, "you do not wish to harm this woman, do you? Her fate should be in the Lord's hands."

Jeremy slowly released Jeannie. Taking a deep breath, she stepped away. Her hands trembled. Her heart pounded.

"I want her to heal me," Jeremy said. "I can't—can't go until she heals me."

"I'm afraid you must leave. You heard her say that she cannot heal you. If you do not leave, we will have to call the police. You don't want that, do you?"

The sandy-haired man placed his hand on Jeremy's shoulder. "The Lord will heal you, if it is his will." He then turned to Jeannie, "I'm the Reverend Maynard Reeves, pastor of the Righteous Light Church. I have important business to discuss with you, Miss Alverson—the Lord's business."

The Reverend Reeves knelt down, picked up Jeannie's briefcase, then extended his arm to her. "May I escort you inside your home?"

Relief washed over Jeannie. Jeremy Thornton seemed to have calmed somewhat. Now was her chance to escape into the safety of her house, with the Reverend Reeves as an escort.

"Thank you, Reverend." She took her briefcase, accepted his arm and allowed him to lead her away from Jeremy, who stood in the driveway, dazed and unmoving, until they entered the house. "Please come down the hall and into the library with me. I'll have Ollie fix us some tea."

"Tea isn't necessary," Reeves said. "All I require is a few moments of your time."

"I suppose that's the least I can do to repay you for your assistance." Jeannie shuddered at the thought of poor, pitiful Jeremy Thornton's wild-eyed anger.

The inadequacy of her healing gave her the greatest grief. If only she could truly heal. If only she had the power to annihilate pain and suffering permanently, to put an end to all illnesses. People like Jeremy would not believe the truth, preferring to believe that she *could* heal them and was withholding that precious gift from them.

Jeannie laid her briefcase on the enormous oak desk that sat directly in front of the two floor-to-ceiling windows. "Please, sit down."

She relaxed in a tufted leather chair beside the empty fireplace. Reverend Reeves took the matching chair to her left.

"What is this important business you have to discuss with me?" Jeannie asked.

"I've driven in from New Orleans. That's where our church's headquarters are. But the Righteous Light Church has a faithful following here along the Mississippi Gulf Coast." Maynard Reeves smiled, showing a set of perfect white teeth—sparkling purity against a golden-tanned face covered with freckles. "We are greatly concerned about the gambling curse that has invaded this state."

"I don't understand." Jeannie slid her body forward, sitting on the edge of her chair. "What possible connection can I have to legalized gambling in Biloxi?"

Reeves laughed; the sound was hearty and jubilant. "I digressed. Forgive me. I simply wanted you to know that I am a man doing the Lord's work."

Where had she heard that before? All the years her stepfather dragged her from one revival meeting to another, forcing her to use her empathic abilities, he had told her they were doing the Lord's work.

"How does your work involve me?" Balling her hands into fists, she clutched them at the sides of her hips.

"I am here to offer you the opportunity to prove to me and to the world that you derive your powers from the Almighty and not from Satan." Reeves jumped to his feet. The loose jacket of his black suit swung open, revealing the gleaming silver cross hanging from his neck. "If your powers are from God, join me in my ministry, and together we will heal the sick and spread the holy message to the world."

Maynard Reeves was offering her the life she'd once known, the life that had destroyed her childhood and kept her in continual pain from the age of six until she was thirteen, when her mother's and stepfather's deaths had freed her.

"Am I to understand that you are inviting me to become a part of your ministry, to use my abilities to further the cause of your Righteous Light Church?"

"Indeed I am." Kneeling in front of her, Reeves stared at Jeannie, his eyes glowing, his face flushed with zealous eagerness. "Powers such as yours, psychic powers, empathic powers, have a supernatural source. Those who possess power from Satan must be destroyed, and those who possess power from God must use it in his service."

"I was born with my special talent, Reverend Reeves. I have been an empath since childhood." Being able to draw the pain from others and experience it herself had seldom been a blessing to Jeannie. In fact, most often it had been a curse. But she knew her talents had no sinister, evil source, and she did not need to join forces with some hellfire-and-brimstone fanatic to prove the goodness of her heart.

"Join me, sister. I offer you the chance to acquire glory and fame and wealth, all in the name of God."

When he reached out to touch her, Jeannie leaned back in her chair, not wanting any physical contact with this man. He rose to his feet, then held out his hand to her. She shook her head.

"I don't want fame and glory," she said. "And I am already a wealthy woman. All I want is to be left alone, to continue the life I've chosen for myself."

"You're refusing to join me?" The smile vanished from his all-American-boy face. "I did not want to believe you were a child of the devil."

"I am not a child of the devil." Lifting her cane into position, Jeannie stood. "I appreciate your helping me with that poor man outside, Reverend Reeves, but I'm afraid I must ask you to leave. I'm not interested in joining your ministry. The last thing I want is to have my empathic powers exploited again, the way they were when I was a child."

"You are either with me or against me!" Reeves raised his voice to a thundering bellow. "If you are my enemy, I will destroy you!"

Jeannie stood, bracing herself with her cane. "Reverend Reeves, I must ask you to leave. I'm not interested in joining your ministry. I have nothing to offer you."

Grabbing Jeannie by the arm, Reeves jerked her toward the window. "Come see what awaits you as Satan's daughter."

Dear God, by accepting the reverend's assistance, had she simply exchanged one danger for another? If this man didn't agree to leave, Jeannie thought, she would scream. Surely Ollie was in the house somewhere.

Lifting the edge of the sheer curtain, Reeves shoved her in front of the window and pointed outside. Jeannie gasped. A small crowd lined the sidewalk in front of the house, every person carrying a sign, each message a threat, ranging in tone from Refuse Evil, Choose God to Death to the Devil's Seed.

"I am not alone," Reeves said. "My disciples are prepared to do my bidding. Join us, Jeannie, and live life to its fullest. Refuse me, and prepare yourself to be a sacrifice to a vengeful God who will not abide your black magic."

"You're crazy." Jeannie tried to pull away from him, but he tightened his hold about her arm. "Let me go. *Now.* I'm not alone in the house."

"Choose, Jeannie Alverson. Choose the path of righteousness." Reeves's voice rose higher and higher with each word. "I offer you life or death! The choice is yours!"

"Just what's going on here?" Julian Howell, tall, slender, and regally commanding, stood in the open doorway. "Who are you, sir? And how dare you speak to Jeannie in such a manner?"

Releasing Jeannie, Reeves spun around, his captivating smile returning. "I am the Reverend Maynard Reeves, a servant of the Lord. Put on this earth to save the wicked and destroy those who will not repent."

"How the hell did you get into my house?" Julian's brown eyes turned black with indignation.

"Julian, please don't upset yourself," Jeannie said. "Reverend Reeves was just leaving." She glared at Reeves.

"You have not seen or heard the last of me," Reeves said. "I shall tell the world the truth about you. You are the devil's daughter. The Righteous Light brethren will help me destroy your evil."

"Get out of my house at once, sir, or I shall telephone the police!" Julian shook a long, slender finger at the reverend.

Reeves glowered at Jeannie. "You had your chance." He walked quickly by Julian, who followed their unwanted visitor to the front door and out onto the veranda. Jeannie waited in the foyer until Julian returned.

"This has gone too far." Julian ran a shaky hand through his thick mane of white hair. "Reporters hounding you day and night. Sick, dying people pleading for your healing touch. And now, some lunatic threatening to destroy you because he believes you're the devil's child."

Jeannie slipped her arm around Julian's waist. She loved him dearly. He had been a father to her since she was thirteen, and he was the dearest, kindest man in the world. "Calm yourself. He's gone."

"But we haven't heard the last from him." Julian shook his head. "I'm afraid for you, my dearest girl. Reporters we can deal with somehow. But there is no telling when some terribly ill soul in pain may turn on you. And Maynard Reeves is a man to fear. I saw the insanity in his eyes."

"I know you're right." Jeannie led Julian down the hall and into the library, then rang for Ollie, asking her to bring them a pot of tea.

"I've heard of this Reeves fellow," Julian said. "He and his followers have a reputation for being dangerous fanatics. His threats aren't idle threats."

"He frightens me, too." Jeannie squeezed Julian's hand. "I sensed his hatred when I refused to join him."

"You need protection," Julian said as he sat down on the oxblood-leather sofa. "I want to hire a bodyguard for you."

"A bodyguard? Surely that's not necessary. Perhaps the police—"

"The police won't provide you with twenty-four-hour-a-day protection, and that's what you need."

"Julian, do you realize what hiring a bodyguard would mean?" Jeannie asked. "We would have no privacy. This man would live in our house, share our meals, go with me everywhere I went."

"Exactly." Julian slapped his hands down atop his thighs. "And I know just the man for the job."

"You do?"

"Yes, I do. That fellow you and Manton brought in from Le Bijou Bleu a few years back. That big blond DEA agent who came by here to see you after he was released from the hospital. I can't remember his name." Clicking his tongue, Julian frowned. "What was his name?"

"Sam. Sam Dundee." Intense memories flashed through Jeannie's mind at the mere mention of his name.

Sam Dundee. In the six years since she'd found him lying on her beach at Le Bijou Bleu, she hadn't forgotten the man whose pain she had endured, whose emotional agony she had shared—the man whose very soul had joined with hers for a fleeting moment.

No, Sam Dundee would never return to Biloxi, not even for her. He might have promised that if she ever needed him, he would help her, but how could she hold him to that promise?

"I'm sure Mr. Dundee is far too busy to be bothered with coming to Biloxi," Jeannie said.

"Nonsense. The man sent you his business card when he opened his private security business, didn't he? He wouldn't have done that if he hadn't wanted you to be able to reach him if you needed his assistance."

"Why don't you call Mr. Deaton? Our lawyer should be able to line us up with a reputable security firm."

"I don't understand your reluctance to call this Dundee fellow. After all, he does owe you his life. I'm sure the man will want to pay his debt to you."

Jeannie had thought she'd never seen Sam Dundee again. There had been no legitimate reason to contact him. Over the years, she had come to realize that the link she'd made with Sam had not been severed, that in some strange way they remained connected. He was still a part of her soul. Such a joining had never happened to her, before or since, and admitting the strength of their bond, even to herself, unnerved Jeannie.

"Mr. Dundee won't come to Biloxi himself." She had known the day he came by the house to thank her and say goodbye that he had no intention of ever returning to the Gulf. What had happened to him on his last DEA assignment had changed his life forever and put him on the run from guilt and remorse. The day she found him on her beach, she had felt his emotional agony, as well as his physical pain.

"I'll call him all the same." Julian patted Jeannie's hand. "I'm sure he'll want to repay his debt to you. And if he can't come personally, I'm sure he'll send one of his associates."

"I wish you wouldn't insist on—"

"What's wrong, my dear? Is there something about Mr. Dundee I don't know? Some reason I shouldn't call him?"

"No, of course not. It's just that..." Jeannie groaned, then took Julian's hand into hers, instantly sensing his unease and his great fear for her. She shouldn't be arguing with Julian. He was an old man with a weak heart. If calling Sam Dundee would put his mind at ease, then she'd make the phone call.

"I'll call Mr. Dundee," Jeannie said.

Julian smiled. "Yes, yes, by all means, call the man. Ask him to fly down as soon as possible. Tonight, or tomorrow at the latest. We should have him here before your press conference tomorrow."

Jeannie hugged Julian, then kissed his weathered cheek. "I still have the business card Mr. Dundee sent me. It's upstairs in my address book. After we have our tea, I'll call him in Atlanta and let him know I need his help."

"Your Mr. Dundee is the answer to my prayers," Julian said. "You know I'd give my life to protect you, but I'm an old man, and do well to take care of myself. As a surgeon, I've spent my whole life helping other people, and now I can't help the person I love most in this world."

"You *can* help me, and you do, just by loving me."

And Sam Dundee could help her. He could provide what Julian could not, the protection she so desperately needed. Now, after six long years, she would see him again—the man who haunted her dreams and possessed a part of her soul, the man whose power over her she feared far more than she feared Maynard Reeves.

Sam Dundee loosened his black-and-gray silk tie, then flipped through the stack of newspaper articles piled on top of his desk. Jeannie Alverson stared up at him from the black-and-white photograph some determined reporter had snapped of her as she was leaving her home several days ago. Hell! The woman had become front-page news across the country.

They were calling her a miracle worker. A healer. A psychic. An empath with unlimited powers.

A tremor shook Sam's shoulders. For six years he'd told himself that he had imagined what happened on that beach, when an angel of mercy held him in her arms. He had pretended he'd been delusional, that she had not drawn his pain from him. He had not wanted to believe she had delved into his mind and eased the torment he had felt—still felt— knowing he'd been responsible for the deaths of others. But here the truth was—in print. Or was it the truth? Hell, it couldn't be. No one possessed those kinds of powers.

Sam picked up the remote control, switching on the videotape of the newscasts from the past several days—the ones dealing with the Mississippi empath who had once been touted throughout the south as a child healer.

He froze the picture the moment the camera zoomed in for a close-up shot of Jeannie. Jeannie. She was as hauntingly lovely as her name. Even though Sam knew the woman's strength, had experienced it firsthand, he saw the sadness in her eyes, the vulnerability in that soft, endearing face.

Jeannie Alverson had somehow bewitched him six years ago, leaving him unable to forget her. He owed her his life. There was no doubt about it. He had felt compelled to see her after his release from the hospital, to find out if what he remembered had really happened. But once he looked into her hypnotic brown eyes, all he'd wanted was to get away from her before it was too late. His gut instincts had warned him that if he ever became involved with Jeannie, he would never be able to escape.

Sam stopped the VCR tape. Damn, what was he doing to himself? Jeannie was a part of his past, a part of that dark, devastating misery he had endured in Biloxi. He could not remember Jeannie without remembering all the rest. Perhaps that was his punishment, never being able to put the past behind him.

Several quick taps on his closed office door brought Sam's head up and focused his vision on the opening door. His secretary peeped in.

"I'm leaving early, Sam." Gertie Saunders waved her ring-clad fingers at her boss. "Everybody's out except J.T. He said to tell you he'll bring in some sandwiches for the two of you in about five minutes."

"Thanks, Gert. Have a nice dinner."

"I will," the attractive grandmother of three said, a flirtatious smile on her face. "My gentleman friend is taking me somewhere special."

"Well, in that case, feel free to come in late tomorrow morning."

Gertie had worked for Sam since he'd opened his Atlanta office, nearly six years ago. A recent widow, with two sons in college, she hadn't worked outside the home in twenty-five years, but hiring her was the smartest thing Sam had ever done. She ran his office like a well-oiled machine, and she knew how to keep him and his partners in line. No one intimidated Gertie Saunders, not even J. T. Blackwood, and J.T. could intimidate the devil.

The telephone rang just as Gertie was closing the door. "You want me to get that?" she asked.

"No, I'll get it," Sam said. "You don't want to keep your gentleman friend waiting."

Sam picked up the receiver. "Dundee Private Security. Dundee speaking. How may I help you?"

"Sam?"

Every nerve in his body froze instantly. He hadn't heard that voice in over six years, but he would never forget it. He heard it in his dreams, whispering his name, comforting him, reassuring him.

"Jeannie? Jeannie Alverson?"

"I suppose you've read about me in the newspapers and seen the stories on television."

"You're headline news."

"My whole world is topsy-turvy. My life's a mess. I can't go anywhere or do anything without being followed by reporters, and people begging me to heal them, and now..."

"And now what?" She wasn't calling him to discuss the details of her life that he'd seen on television for the past few days. No, there had to be something wrong, terribly wrong, for Jeannie Alverson to contact him.

"There's a man named Maynard Reeves. He's the minister of a group who call themselves the Righteous Light Church."

"Never heard of him."

"He's based in New Orleans, but he has a congregation in Biloxi," Jeannie said. "He's claiming I received my powers from Satan, and he's threatened to destroy me. I believe he's fanatical enough to kill me if he has to."

"Are you calling to ask for my help?" *No, don't ask me to come back to Biloxi. Don't ask me to face the demons that have haunted me for six years. Don't ask me to become personally involved in your life.*

"Yes. Julian and I agree that I need a bodyguard until all this hullabaloo dies down and we are certain Reverend Reeves isn't a real threat to me."

"Who's Julian?" Sam asked before he even thought, then suddenly remembered what he'd read about Jeannie having been raised by foster parents—Dr. and Mrs. Julian Howell.

"Julian is my father. My foster father."

"So you and your father think you need a bodyguard." *But not me,* Sam thought. *I'll send you my best man. I'll make sure you're safe, but I will not come back to Biloxi.*

"Of course, we'll pay you your regular fee. It isn't a question of money."

Sam swallowed hard. It wasn't a question of money for him, either. It was a matter of preserving his sanity. If he went to Biloxi to guard Jeannie, he would have to come to terms with his past. Jeannie Alverson would probably want to help him. He didn't want to be helped. He had become accustomed to living with the anger and guilt, had accepted it as his punishment.

"I'll send J. T. Blackwood to Biloxi tomorrow. He's one of my partners and the best at what he does." Sam heard the indrawn breath, then the silence on the other end of the line. "I don't take bodyguard assignments myself. Not anymore."

"Oh, of course, I understand. By sending your best man here to guard me, you'll still be keeping your promise to me."

Why had he ever made that stupid promise? *If you ever need me, all you have to do is ask.* He supposed he'd thought she'd never need him. Hell, he'd prayed she'd never need him, that he'd never have to deal with what had happened between them.

"What difference does it make whether I come myself or I send someone just as capable?"

"It doesn't make any difference," she said. "I understand. Believe me, I do."

"Ms. Alverson, I owe you my life." Blowing out an aggravated breath, Sam clutched the telephone fiercely. "I want to repay you, but...Biloxi holds a lot of really bad memories for me."

"You still haven't forgiven yourself, have you?"

"I don't know what you're talking about."

"I need help, Sam Dundee. My life could be in danger. If you feel you can't return to Biloxi, that you don't have the strength to face your ghosts, then send Mr. Blackwood. But ask yourself one thing. Do you really want to put my life in another man's hands?"

Bull's-eye. She'd hit the mark. Jeannie Alverson knew that for any other man the assignment would be nothing more than a job, but for Sam it would be personal.

"When do you need me?"

"Now," she said. "By tomorrow at the latest. I'm holding a press conference at the Howell School tomorrow, and I really need—"

"You're doing what? Where?" Sam hollered at her.

"I'm holding a press conference at the Howell School, in the gymnasium."

"What's this Howell School and why the hell would you agree to hold a press conference there?"

"The Howell School was founded by Julian's wife, Miriam, to help children with physical and mental challenges that make it difficult for them to receive the help they need in regular schools. I work at the school as a counselor. My degree is in psychology." Pausing, Jeannie took a deep breath. "Julian and I decided to hold a press conference where I'll have the opportunity to explain to everyone the exact limitations of my powers. We think it's a wise course of action."

"You're crazy if you hold a press conference anywhere," Sam said. "But especially in a school gymnasium. You'll be too confined. It's a stupid idea. Don't do it."

"I disagree," Jeannie said. "The press conference is already set for ten tomorrow morning. Can you be here by then?"

What the hell was the matter with her reasoning? And with Julian Howell's? Didn't they realize that the press would eat her alive? "I'll fly my Cessna down first thing in the morning and meet y'all at the Howell School."

"Thank you, Mr. Dundee. I knew I could count on you."

"Goodbye, Ms. Alverson." Sam slammed down the telephone. "Dammit!"

J. T. Blackwood stood in the doorway, holding two roast beef sandwiches in his hands. It looked like Sam was in rare form this evening.

His partner of over four years had become his best friend. Oddly enough, the two men had found they had a lot in common, despite the vast differences in their backgrounds and present lifestyles. J.T. admired Sam Dundee more than anyone he knew. Sam was a man you could trust with your life, a man you could count on to be a tower of strength.

Like J.T. himself, Sam didn't make friends easily. Of course, he could be a mean bastard at times, but that was part of his charm. And one more thing the two of them had in common. In any fight, J.T. would want Sam on his side.

A lot of men disliked Sam, but J.T. didn't know one smart man who wasn't just a little bit afraid of Sam Dundee.

"Got a problem?" He walked into the office, laid the sandwiches on top of the stack of newspaper clippings and sat down on the edge of the desk.

"Nothing I can't handle." Sam glanced at the sandwiches. "Roast beef?"

"What else?" J.T. eyed the coffee machine on the low shelf in the corner. "I take mine black."

"What?"

"My coffee," J.T. said. "I brought the sandwiches. I figured you'd fix the coffee."

"That stuff's been sitting there for a couple of hours. It'll probably grow hair on your chest."

"I'll take my chances."

Sam scooted back his chair, walked across the room and poured two cups of strong, well-aged coffee. "Here." He handed J.T. a bright red mug.

"So, are you going to tell me or not?" J.T. asked.

"I've got to fly to Biloxi in the morning. I don't know how long I'll be gone. A week, two, maybe more."

"Biloxi, huh?"

"Yeah, I know. I said I'd never go back there."

"What changed your mind?" J.T. unwrapped his sandwich, took a bite, then washed it down with the coffee.

"Jeannie Alverson."

"Who's Jeannie—? Hey, you mean the woman on the news, the healer who saved some kid's life after she'd been wounded in a drive-by shooting?"

"Yeah, that Jeannie Alverson."

"You're taking a bodyguard assignment? You haven't done that in years. Why now?"

Sam lifted his mug to his lips, tasted the bitter coffee and frowned. "I should have made us a fresh pot."

"Is there something personal between you and this Jeannie Alverson?"

"Yeah, you could say that. She's the woman who saved my life six years ago, when the DEA sting I was involved in went sour."

"So you owe her."

"Yeah, I owe her. I promised her that she could demand payment in full anytime she needed me."

"And she's called in your marker."

"Something like that."

There was more going on here, something Sam wasn't telling. J.T. had known the man for nearly five years, he considered him his best friend, but there was a lot the two of them had never discussed. Oh, they shared old war stories… Sam's days in the marines and the DEA… J.T.'s own stint in the army and his life as a Secret Service agent. He had explained to Sam why he wore the black eyepatch, had told him all about how he'd lost the vision in his left eye when an assassin's bullet lodged in his head. But he'd never told Sam about his childhood, had never told him about his Navaho mother. J.T. twisted the silver-and-turquoise ring on the third finger of his right hand.

A man usually didn't share the demons in his soul, those personal demons that kept him raw and bleeding inside, long after old wounds should have healed.

J.T. had known, when Sam told him the bare-bones details of his last DEA assignment, that something had happened during that time to change Sam's life forever. J.T. wondered if that something had anything to do with Jeannie Alverson.

Chapter 2

Sweat coated the palms of Jeannie's hands, beaded across her forehead and trickled between her breasts. Her heartbeat roared like a runaway train, the sound drumming in her ears, pounding in her chest. Her legs weakened. She gripped the curve of her wooden cane. Nausea rose in her throat, bitterness coating her tongue.

Why wouldn't they leave her alone? She had tried to answer their questions, had tried to make them understand. But they circled her like vultures waiting for the moment of death. They shoved microphones in her face. They bombarded her with questions so personal her cheeks flamed with embarrassment. Flashes of light from their cameras blinded her.

If only she could escape. But there was no escape from the media—from the frenzied crowd of reporters determined to get a story out of Jeannie Alverson. Nor did there seem to be any escape from Maynard Reeves and his followers. At least a dozen of the reverend's disciples were there this Thursday morning, dispersed throughout the crowd, their Die Witch posters held high for everyone to see.

How could this have happened? She'd been so careful for the past fourteen years, revealing the truth to no one, using her abilities to only a limited degree, so that others would not suspect.

The day Cassie Mills was shot, how could Jeannie have known that by helping her, she would doom herself to a living hell? Poor Cassie, in all her childish innocence, had told the police exactly what had happened, and neither she nor the police had realized a snoopy reporter could hear their conversation at the hospital. Tory Gaines had not been content to exploit the present facts. No, he had dug into Jeannie's past—a past she had prayed would never return to haunt her.

"When did you realize you possessed the ability to heal, Ms. Alverson—or should we call you Ms. Foley?"

"Do you claim to work miracles for God?"

"How much money did your mother and stepfather cheat people out of by passing you off as a faith healer?"

"What religion are you, Jeannie?"

"The people we've questioned who were present when you supposedly worked your magic on Cassie Mills claim that you seemed to go into shock, taking away the child's pain and stopping the bleeding from her gunshot wound. Is that true?"

Dr. Julian Howell wrapped his arm around Jeannie's shoulders. She desperately wanted to lean heavily on the man who had been her foster father since she was thirteen, but Julian was a very old man, and his health had been failing these last few years. Jeannie realized she had to be strong as much for him as for herself. But she wasn't sure how much longer she could endure the endless questions, the clamor, the noise, the bodies that pushed closer and closer.

Dear Lord in heaven, help me, she prayed. Agreeing to hold this press conference had been a terrible mistake. She should have listened to Sam Dundee. He'd tried to warn her. Why, of all places, had she chosen the gymnasium of the Howell School as the location for this debacle? There was nowhere to run, and no one to help her and Julian.

Tory Gaines shoved his way through the throng of reporters, his tall, gangly frame towering over the others. His dark eyes focused on Jeannie.

"I understand that since the truth was revealed about you, Jeannie, you've been flooded with requests from terminally ill people begging you to heal them."

"Is it true that a man you refused to help actually attacked you?" a red-haired TV news reporter asked.

"Please, listen to me." Jeannie couldn't bear the way they were looking at her, the way they were treating her. As if she were some freak, some alien creature. "I do not possess the power to heal people. I never have. I have certain...abilities...as an empath. I can feel the pain of others. What I do for people is temporary. That's all—"

"You can't only feel their pain, you can take it away." Tory raked back a long strand of black hair that had fallen over his right eye. "You can remove both physical and psychological pain, can't you, Jeannie?"

"I am not a true healer." Jeannie glanced down at her wooden cane. "If I could heal others, why wouldn't I heal myself?"

Julian's arm, clasping her shoulder, trembled. Jeannie sensed her foster father's frustration at not being able to protect her.

"I'm all right, Julian," she whispered. "Please don't worry. All this stress isn't good for your heart."

"We have answered every question we can," Julian said, facing the crowd, his voice strong and authoritarian. "Jeannie has told you everything. There is no more. Please, allow us to leave."

When Julian, aided by Marta McCorkle, the supervisor of the Howell School, tried to assist Jeannie through the crowd, the media closed in around them, pushing and shoving. Julian and Marta flanked Jeannie, slowing their pace to accommodate Jeannie's hampered gait.

"I had hoped he would be here by now." Julian leaned down, directing his conversation to Jeannie. "When you spoke to him again early this morning, he promised he would arrive in time for the press conference, didn't he?"

"He'll be here soon." Jeannie saw the microphone as it came toward her face. She stopped dead, aware that the young female reporter for the local television station was not going to move aside.

"Is it true, Ms. Alverson, that the deacons from the Righteous Light Church here in Biloxi have condemned you as a fraud, and their minister, Reverend Maynard Reeves, has gone so far as to claim you are a witch, a devil worshipper?" The reporter glanced meaningfully at the Die Witch signs held high in the air by Reeves's avid disciples.

Jeannie tried to turn her head, wanting to avoid answering the question. But the reporter was persistent, stepping closer, inserting one of her feet between Jeannie's feet, pressing the microphone a hairsbreadth from Jeannie's mouth.

"Let us pass," Julian commanded, unaccustomed to people disregarding his orders.

"I've called the police." Marta pointed her index finger at the persistent reporter.

"Are you a fraud, Jeannie? Or are you a witch?" the reporter asked.

"I'm neither."

The reporter's foot slid into the side of Jeannie's walking stick. Jeannie gripped her cane, but to no avail. The cane tumbled from her hand. Her knees gave way. She clutched at Julian's sleeve, but her clammy hands slipped off the soft material of his jacket. Marta cried out, reaching for Jeannie, her fingers just touching her hair as she toppled over, landing roughly on her knees.

Sam Dundee saw Jeannie Alverson fall, accidentally tripped by the overzealous redhead harassing her. Sam cut through the media horde like a machete slicing through untamed jungle. The reporters stared at him, whispers rising from the mass, questioning the big man's identity.

"Who the hell do you think you are?" a bearded middle-aged tabloid photographer asked.

"I'm the cavalry to the rescue." Sam proclaimed, the deadly curve of his mouth an easily understood warning to others.

Sam reached out, grabbing the red-haired reporter who had tripped Jeannie Alverson. Manacling her arm, he glared at her, noting the shock in her green eyes. When he released her, she backed away, the surrounding swarm following her lead.

Sam stared down at the woman whose face had been plastered on the front page of newspapers and across every television screen in the country for the past few days. Jeannie looked even more delicate, more fragile, in person. Bending on one knee, Sam gently shoved Julian Howell aside and lifted Jeannie into his arms. She gazed into his eyes, and a hard knot of fear formed in the pit of Sam Dundee's stomach. He remembered those compassionate eyes. Those warm, compelling brown eyes.

Jeannie clung to Sam, draping her arm around his neck, resting her head on his shoulder.

"Everything will be all right, Ms. Alverson. I'm here now. I'll take you to safety. I had a limousine pick me up at the airport. It's waiting outside."

The crowd watched in stunned silence while Sam Dundee carried Jeannie Alverson through their midst. Once the pair had exited the building, the reporters followed, taking little note of Dr. Julian Howell or Marta McCorkle.

Sam told himself not to look at Jeannie Alverson again, to simply carry her out to the waiting limousine. Her fingers touched the nape of his neck. A soft, tender touch. Sam's nerves screamed. His body tensed.

"I prayed for your help." Her voice was sweet, and unintentionally sultry. A slow, honey-coated southern drawl. "Thank you, Mr. Dundee. I appreciate your coming in person."

Against his better judgment, Sam looked at her then. She smiled—a closed-mouth, half-formed smile. Jeannie was not classically beautiful. Her features were too large—her big eyes a gentle, faded brown, her full lips a pale pink, her round cheeks flushed with emotion. Despite the frailty of her appearance, she felt sturdy and solid in his arms. And at that moment, Sam knew without a doubt that her fragile facade was an illusion, that behind her delicate feminine softness existed an incredibly strong woman. Jeannie Alverson was a survivor. And yet she possessed a quality so totally feminine, so genuinely genteel, that Sam wanted nothing more than to protect her, to keep her safe from all hurt and harm.

He forced his gaze away from her face.

The chauffeur held open the limousine's door. Sam slipped inside, depositing Jeannie on the seat.

"Where's Julian?" she asked, tugging her billowing skirt over her legs.

"I'm sure he's fine. The reporters aren't interested in him. Only in you," Sam said, then turned to the driver. "Take the route I mapped out for you. That should take care of some of our followers."

"Where are we going?" Jeannie took a long, hard look at her rescuer, and her breath caught in her throat. This big, strong man, who had carried her through the crowd as if she weighed nothing, was the man she had found dying on the beach at Le Bijou Bleu six years ago. She had saved his life then; now he was here to protect her and repay the debt he thought he owed.

"I'm taking you home." Sam sat back in the seat, his gaze focused out the side window. He was not going to be suckered by this woman, despite her aura of sweet innocence. She was a job, and nothing more. *Liar!* His conscience screamed at him. He should have sent Blackwood or Roarke. *But this was Jeannie Alverson.* He had no choice but to handle the job personally.

He owed her his life. If she hadn't found him six years ago, he would have died. And nothing she asked of him would be too great a price to repay her for his life.

Jeannie didn't mean to stare at Sam, but she couldn't stop herself. She had dated several men over the years, but hadn't allowed herself to become close to any of them. She knew she never could give herself to a man without first being honest with him about her past, about who and what she was. And she had been able to control her sexuality all her life. So why couldn't she handle the attraction she felt for Sam Dundee?

She wanted to reach out and touch his hard, lean face. She wanted to say or do something that would make him smile. He looked as if he seldom smiled. His face had set into a

sensually beautiful aloofness, every feature blatantly, irre-
sistibly male.

His thick, wavy blond hair was styled short in the back
and sides, with more length left on the top. His heavy brown
eyebrows hooded a set of intense blue-gray eyes.

Sitting at his side, Jeannie could feel the power and
strength of the man. She felt safe and protected, and at the
same time she was vividly aware of the danger Sam Dundee
posed to her.

In six years, she had not been able to forget him. He had
remained a vivid image in her mind, a smoldering passion
in her heart.

They sat alone in the back of the limousine, neither of
them speaking. Sam continued gazing out the window.
Jeannie closed her eyes in silent meditation, praying for the
strength to live through this ordeal, to be able to resume her
normal life and find a way to bring peace to Sam Dundee's
tortured soul.

When they arrived at Julian's home, the limousine slowed
to a snail's pace as the chauffeur turned into the driveway.
Crowds of people—reporters, curiosity seekers, true believers and accusers—lined the driveway, filled the front
yard and spilled over into the street.

"Damn!" Sam cursed under his breath.

"What's wrong?" Jeannie peered out the tinted side
window. "Oh, dear Lord!" There were more people surrounding her home than had overrun the Howell School.

"Don't worry. I'll try to get things under control before I
take you inside." Sam glared at her, his look a warning in
itself. "Stay here. I'll come back for you in just a minute."

Jeannie nodded her head. She clutched her hands together in a prayerlike gesture, trying not to think about
anything—not the past, not the present, not the future.
Summoning all her willpower, she forced herself not to look
out the window, not to check on what was happening. If she
and Julian were going to survive this ordeal, they would
have to allow Sam Dundee to do his job. After all, he was a
trained professional who was ready to lay his life on the line
to protect her.

She heard voices outside, a mixture of questions, shouts and pleas. Closing her eyes, she tried to concentrate on emptying her mind, on blocking out everything except the serenity within her own soul. Someone threw a brick at the limousine, shattering a side window. The loud crash jarred her from the moment of peace she sought.

The door flew open. Sam Dundee reached inside, dragged Jeannie across the seat and lifted her into his arms. "We're going in the side entrance. The housekeeper will open the door the minute we approach."

"What about all these people?" Jeannie asked, holding on to Sam's neck as he carried her up the sidewalk, the crowd closing in around them. "Why won't they leave me alone?"

Sam knew that he couldn't hold back so many people for long without using his 9 mm Ruger. He had to get Jeannie inside as quickly as possible.

"Just hang on tight." Sam broke into a slow run, carrying Jeannie directly to the side porch.

The housekeeper flung open the door the moment Sam's feet hit the porch. When they were safely inside, he didn't turn, but continued down the narrow hallway. Ollie Tyner shut and locked the side door.

"Bring her on in here to the back parlor." Ollie, a short, plump, gray-haired woman, darted in front of Sam, sliding back the panel doors. "She can't walk without her cane, so don't put her on her feet."

Sam looked directly into Jeannie's faded brown eyes and wished he hadn't. He couldn't shake the feeling that his very life depended on protecting this woman, this gentle, helpless woman. No, not helpless. Even if she couldn't walk without her cane, she would never be helpless. Her eyes told him that she was strong, that she would endure whatever came her way. And her eyes told him that she knew he would help her.

Sam eased Jeannie down onto a red velvet settee in front of an empty fireplace. She slipped her arms from around his neck slowly, never taking her eyes off his face.

"Thank you, Mr. Dundee."

"You're welcome, Ms. Alverson. I was just doing my job."

"Won't you sit down?" Without waiting for his reply, she turned to Ollie. "I would very much like some tea. Mr. Dundee, would you care for anything?"

He shook his head, indicating that he didn't. Ollie exited the room quickly.

"I'm worried about Julian," Jeannie said. "He has a heart condition, and all this excitement isn't good for him."

"I'm sure Dr. Howell is fine. He probably left right after we did. I don't think he was in any danger. You were the reporters' target. They aren't interested in anyone except you at this point."

Sam glanced around the room, looking up at the high ceilings and the elaborate moldings, then down at the antique furniture. "Where's the telephone?"

"On the desk. There." Jeannie pointed to the gold-and-white mock-antique telephone perched atop the small cherry desk.

"The police need to clear out this crowd around the house," Sam said. "We've got a near-riot situation on our hands."

"The emergency numbers are listed there by the phone." Jeannie rubbed her forehead with her fingertips, massaging the ache in her temples. "Thank you, Mr. Dundee. I appreciate your arriving when you did. I don't know how I would have gotten away from the school without your help."

Sam glared at her. "Why the hell did you agree to a press conference? You should have known what would happen. I tried to warn you. Why didn't you listen to me?"

Jeannie sat up straight, stiffening her spine. She wasn't used to being spoken to so harshly. "We... Julian and I thought that if we met with the press, we might be able to reason with them."

Sam grunted. "Lady, nobody is that naive. You're news, big news, and those vultures aren't going away for a long, long time. Not until something or someone else comes along that is bigger news."

He scanned the pad on the desk, dialed the police department and demanded to be put through to a senior officer. After explaining the situation and being assured that the police would disperse the crowd, Sam hung up the phone and paced the room. Glancing at Jeannie, he noticed the strained look on her pale face and wondered if she was in pain.

Jeannie rubbed her thigh. Even thirteen years after the car wreck, after several surgeries and endless therapy, the pain never completely left her. But it was a bearable pain, a pain she had become accustomed to, unlike the pain of being exposed to the world as Jeannie Foley, child faith healer. She thought it ironic that she could share the pain of others, vanquish it from their lives temporarily, but had to endure her own pain alone.

"Are you all right?"

"Yes, I'm ... I'll be fine. Thanks to you. I feel safe, here at home."

"Well, the safest place for you, for the time being, is going to be inside this house. You don't want a repeat performance of today's events, do you?"

"I can't allow my life to be disrupted this way," she said.

"I'm afraid you have little choice in the matter." Sam took the biggest chair in the room, a floral-tapestry wing chair. "The best I can promise you is to keep you safe, to protect you from the press and anyone else who won't leave you alone, especially this fanatical minister you told me about when you called."

"I will not let my life become the three-ring circus it was when my mother and Randy Foley were alive." Knotting her hands into fists, Jeannie held them in front of her. "From the time I was six years old and Randy persuaded my mother to take me to a revival meeting, until I was thirteen and they were both killed in a car crash, my life was a living hell."

"I've read all the newspaper accounts," Sam said. "The recent ones from the past couple of days, and the old ones from when you were a child. Your parents made a lot of money off of you, didn't they? They must have died millionaires."

Ollie knocked at the door, then entered, carrying a silver tray. She placed it on the marble-topped mahogany table in front of the settee.

"Thank you, Ollie. That will be all for now." Jeannie lifted the silver teapot.

"Ollie," Sam said just as the housekeeper started out the door.

"Yes, sir?"

"Keep watch at the side entrance," Sam told her. "We're expecting Dr. Howell."

"Yes, sir." Ollie left the parlor.

Jeannie added sugar to her tea, then lifted the china cup to her lips, sipping leisurely. She eyed Sam over the rim of her cup. "Randy Foley was my stepfather," she said. "And yes, my mother and Randy did die millionaires."

"Money they fleeced off suckers who believed that little Jeannie Foley possessed a special power from God that could heal them."

"Yes. Money that poor, gullible fools handed over to Randy eagerly, just to have me lay my hands on them and take away their pain, to give them a temporary healing." The cup in Jeannie's trembling hand quivered on the saucer. She set her tea on the silver tray.

Just to have me lay my hands on them and take away their pain. Was that what the woman who'd found Sam on the beach six years ago had done? Had she laid her hands on him and taken away his pain? Sam could remember those hours vaguely, could remember soft, caring brown eyes filled with tears—his tears, tears she had cried for him when she drew his pain out of his body and into hers.

Hell, it hadn't happened that way. It couldn't have. He had imagined the whole thing, hadn't he? He'd been burning up with fever and conscious only part of the time. For a few minutes, he'd thought he had died and that the woman who held him in her arms was an angel. Didn't that show how crazy he'd been? How totally out of his head?

"How long have you lived here in Biloxi?" Sam asked.

"Since I came out of the hospital, when I was thirteen. Julian and his wife, Miriam, became my foster parents."

A door slammed shut. Feet tramped up the hallway. The parlor door opened, and Dr. Julian Howell walked in, followed by Marta McCorkle.

Julian rushed to Jeannie's side. Sitting beside her, he took her hands in his. "My dearest girl, are you all right? There's an enormous crowd hovering around outside."

"I'm fine, Julian. Really I am. With Mr. Dundee acting as my protector, how could I be otherwise? Besides, Mr. Dundee has telephoned the police. They should arrive shortly and take control of that unruly crowd."

Marta McCorkle walked over to Jeannie and handed her a wooden cane. "I was able to pick this up before we left the school. I know it's your favorite, and I was afraid someone would take off with it."

"Thank you, Marta. You're right, it is my favorite cane. Miriam gave it to me."

Turning, Jeannie gazed up at Sam, her lips curving into a warm smile. Sam felt as if he'd been hit in the stomach with a sledgehammer. Dammit, this had to stop, and stop now! He couldn't allow himself to feel anything special for this woman, couldn't allow their relationship to become personal.

Who was he kidding? Their relationship was already personal, about as personal as a relationship could be without sexual intimacy. Sam shuddered, his big shoulders moving only slightly. His guts knotted painfully. When a man owed a woman his life, anything that happened between them was personal.

Standing, Julian offered Sam his hand. "I'm Julian Howell. I can't tell you how glad I am that you agreed to take this assignment yourself. I knew you were the only man for the job."

Every nerve in Sam's body came to full alert. Of course he was the only man for the job. No one else owed Jeannie as much as he did. No one else was as highly trained to protect her as he was, or as prepared to die for her.

"All of us who love Jeannie are grateful for your presence, Mr. Dundee," Marta said.

Turning to Julian, Jeannie squeezed his wrinkled, age-spotted hand. "I've told Mr. Dundee that I would like to continue living my life as normally as possible."

"And I've told Ms. Alverson that what she wants will be impossible," Sam said.

"Oh, my dear, Mr. Dundee is right." Julian shook his head, grunting sadly. "Until this scandal dies down, I believe the safest place for you is Le Bijou Bleu. No one could reach you except by boat or helicopter, and it's doubtful anyone would discover your whereabouts there."

"I will not be run out of Biloxi!" Jeannie jerked her hands out of Julian's grasp, positioned her wooden cane, then stood and confronted Sam. "I have my work at the school. The children need me. They're very special children, with special needs. You're going to have to find a way to protect me. Here in Biloxi. I intend to hold my head high and see this thing through to the end, without running away, without shirking my duties to the students at the Howell School."

Marta, who still stood at the side of the settee, reached out and patted Jeannie on the back. "If continuing to work at the school puts you in any danger, we can make do without you for a while."

Sam stared into Jeannie's eyes, those faded brown eyes that he would never be able to forget. Julian Howell had mentioned Le Bijou Bleu, the island where Sam had washed ashore. Memories of those hours when Jeannie Alverson had acted as his angel of mercy flooded Sam's mind.

"You're the boss, Ms. Alverson. We'll do things your way," Sam said. "But it won't be easy for you, and the minute things get out of hand, we start playing by my rules, no questions asked. Agreed?"

Jeannie was unaccustomed to men like Sam Dundee. Men who issued orders. Men who put their lives on the line to protect others. Men who carried guns. She had felt Sam's holster when he held her in his arms.

"I agree to your terms," Jeannie said. "We do it my way, and if that doesn't work, then we'll do it your way."

"All right." Sam turned to Julian Howell. "I'll need a room as close to Ms. Alverson as possible. At this point, I think the physical danger to her isn't life-threatening. The reporters will continue to hound her as long as they think the public is interested. My main concern is this Reverend Reeves. Fanatics are unpredictable, especially those who are under the false impression that God is on their side."

"The reporters are a nuisance," Julian said, "and I feel sorry for those poor people who are begging for Jeannie to heal them, but you're quite right—what concerns me most is that this Reverend Reeves has threatened her. He and his congregation have accused Jeannie of being the devil's daughter. Reeves told her that if she didn't join his church, he would destroy her."

"We can handle the threats," Sam said. "As long as these people don't act on them. If that happens, we'll be in for some real trouble."

"Maynard Reeves is the worst of his kind," Marta said. "He uses every opportunity possible to get himself on TV and in the news."

"Mark my words," Julian said, "Reeves will do more than make threats. Jeannie has sensed he wants to kill her."

Dammit, Sam thought, was Jeannie claiming to be telepathic, as well as empathic? He didn't believe she was a healer, but he might buy her being psychic. His niece Elizabeth was psychic. She'd had the uncanny ability to read people's minds and pick up on their feelings since she'd been a child.

"Are you telepathic, Ms. Alverson? Can you read people's minds, send and receive messages?" Sam asked.

"Only to a limited degree," Jeannie said. "But I am able to feel other people's emotions. When Reverend Reeves touched me, I felt a deep hatred. If I don't join his ministry, I think he plans to kill me."

"It will be my job to make sure that doesn't happen." Sam clasped Jeannie's elbow, uncertain what was true and real about this woman, and what was pure hype. "Why don't you give me a tour of the house, Ms. Alverson? I'll need to know what sort of security system y'all have here. And I'll want a list of the people who would normally visit you or Dr. Howell here at home."

"Fine." Jeannie led Sam to the door, then stopped and turned, smiling at her foster father. "Why don't you go upstairs for a nap before dinner? I'll take care of Mr. Dundee."

"Yes, very well," Julian said. "Put him in the guest room directly across the hall from your room. I'll have Ollie prepare it for him."

"I'll see Julian upstairs," Marta said. "I'm staying for dinner, if that's all right."

Jeannie nodded. "I'm glad you didn't allow what happened today to change your plans to dine with us tonight."

Sam cleared his throat. "Ready to give me that tour, Ms. Alverson?"

"Yes, I'm ready."

Nodding goodbye to Julian and Marta, Jeannie leaned heavily on her cane, the stress of the day's upheaval having taken its toll on her. She willed herself to stand as straight as possible. Sam Dundee was watching her closely, and she did not want him to think of her as helpless. He was the kind of man who would respect strength, not weakness, and she very much wanted Sam's respect. She dared not admit, even to herself, that she wanted far more than that from him, more than she'd ever wanted from any other man.

Chapter 3

Sam pulled back the green cotton velvet draperies in the room he had been given. The room's elaborate style wasn't to his taste, but that was of little importance. Over the years, he had discovered that he was equally restless or content, whatever his surroundings. Whether he slept on silk sheets or in a sleeping bag, Sam's state of mind was the only factor dictating his satisfaction.

And tonight he was greatly dissatisfied. His gut instincts told him that this case might well be his undoing. After six years of waiting for the inevitable, Sam was now back in Biloxi, with the one person on earth who knew the depth of his torment and guilt.

Six years ago, Sam had been a DEA agent on an undercover assignment. Foolishly, he had thought he had the upper hand, that the game would be played by his rules. He'd been wrong. Dead wrong.

Sam removed his coat, laying it across the chair where he'd thrown his tie. There was definitely something different about Jeannie Alverson. She didn't claim to be a healer; she professed to have only the power to take away a person's pain. Temporarily. But did he believe her?

His memories of Jeannie were all tangled up in his mind with the memories of his last DEA assignment and the tragedy that had almost ended his life. He wouldn't have met Jeannie, never would have washed ashore on her island, if he hadn't been trying to entrap a big-time drug dealer.

Jeannie was lovely and sweet and certainly the type of woman who made a man want to protect her. All feminine and fragile. What man wouldn't be attracted to her? It was only natural for a man to think about making love to her.

And Sam certainly didn't live a celibate life. But he did choose his sexual partners with great care. It was a proven fact that Sam Dundee had a heart of stone, and he always steered clear of permanent entanglements.

He had learned, the hard way, never to have an affair while working on a case. Any man who allowed his sexual needs to overrule his better judgment was a fool. Sam had been a fool once, but never again! And most certainly not with Jeannie Alverson. A man with a raging beast inside him didn't have the right to even think about making love to an angel.

Sam stormed out of the bedroom, slamming the massive wooden door behind him. Dammit, he hadn't allowed himself to truly desire a woman in a long time.

He could handle his attraction to Jeannie Alverson, but he couldn't forget how he felt about the woman who had saved his life. If he could separate the two in his mind, he didn't have anything to worry about. But what if he couldn't?

Jeannie sat at the antique secretary in her bedroom. Staring down at the blank page in her daily journal, she lifted her pen. She dated the page, then wrote.

Today he came back into my life. Sam Dundee.

Clutching the pen in her hand, Jeannie bit her bottom lip as she thought about the day's events.

For six long years she'd been unable to forget him, yet certain she'd never see him again. And now here he was, in her home, a few yards away, across the hall. He would be at her side, near her day and night, protecting her from the nightmare her life had suddenly become, keeping her safe from the outside world.

Why had this happened? Why had she become front-page news? For thirteen years, her past had lain dormant, and she'd prayed it would never awaken. She could not—would not—allow the painful memories to destroy her, any more than she would allow recent events to take away the life she dearly loved.

A soft knock sounded on Jeannie's door. Surely it wasn't Julian. He had retired shortly after dinner. Perhaps it was Ollie, saying good-night before she went to bed.

Jeannie lifted the pastel floral silk robe off the edge of her bed, slipped into it and, leaning on her cane, walked across the room. She opened the door, smiling, prepared to say good-night to Ollie.

Sam Dundee, all six feet four inches of him, stood in her doorway, the muted hall light turning his blond hair to dark gold.

Jeannie's smile faded as she gasped at the sight of the big man, who had discarded his jacket and tie and removed his gun holster. His shirt was partially unbuttoned, revealing his thick neck and a swirl of brown chest hair.

"I'm sorry to bother you, Ms. Alverson, but I'd like to speak to you for a few minutes."

Sam tried not to look directly at her, focusing his gaze over her shoulder. Her room was even larger than the one he had been given and, if it was possible, even more elaborately decorated. In quick succession, he noted the intricately carved mirrored wardrobe, the massive matching bed, the pale pink quilted bedcover and the light floral-and-striped wallpaper.

"Yes, please come in, Mr. Dundee." Jeannie stepped back, spreading out her arm in a gesture of welcome.

The only man who had ever been in her bedroom was Julian. She had to admit it felt odd having Sam Dundee enter her private feminine sanctuary.

"Won't you sit down?" Jeannie indicated the sitting area by the floor-to-ceiling windows where the rococo-revival sofa, armchair and marble-topped table had been arranged.

"No. Thanks. This won't take long." Sam felt like a bull in a china shop. Despite the sturdy appearance of the antique furniture, Jeannie's bedroom was totally feminine, as soft and delicate as the woman herself. He had the oddest feeling that if he walked too heavily, he would destroy the beauty of the room.

"What did you want to discuss with me?" Jeannie walked across the room, leaned on the bedpost and rested her cane against her side. Suddenly feeling exposed in her floor-length ivory silk gown and floral robe, she tightened the sash around her waist.

"As you already know, six years ago I was here in Biloxi on an undercover assignment for the DEA." Sam looked directly at her then, searching for some sign to indicate how much she really knew about him. She walked away from him, seating herself on the sofa. "I was shot, then thrown overboard off a barge. Undoubtedly I wasn't far from a small island. I don't have any memory of what happened until I awoke on the beach and found myself in the arms of an ... angel."

Jeannie's head lifted, and she gazed into Sam's steely blue-gray eyes. She was indeed his angel of mercy, and at this precise moment she looked like an angel, her long, wavy brown hair cascading down her back like a waterfall of dusty beige silk.

"I only remember bits and pieces about that night. I was unconscious most of the time." Sam sat in the chair beside the sofa. "I'll never forget your gentle brown eyes and your soothing voice. Or the enormous dark-skinned man who carried me to the boat."

"Manton," Jeannie said. "His name is Manton."

She had thought Sam Dundee remembered practically nothing about that night. After his release from the hospital, he had found her and thanked her for saving his life. He'd told her then that he remembered very little of what had happened after he was shot.

Did he know that, for one brief instant when she had borne his pain and cried his tears, their souls had been united? No, of course he didn't.

"Manton, huh?" Spreading his legs apart, Sam leaned forward and placed his hands on his knees. "When I came to in the hospital, after surgery, I was told that some huge bald man had carried me into the emergency room and then disappeared. If it hadn't been for that report from the emergency room staff, I would have thought I'd dreamed the whole thing. The island. The woman. The man.

"Lucky for me one of the emergency room nurses had a child enrolled in the Howell School, or I would have had a tough time finding you. Why didn't you and Manton stick around after he carried me into the emergency room?"

"We had done all we could do for you. There was no need for us to stay."

"Where is Manton now?" Sam asked.

"Manton lives on Le Bijou Bleu. He never leaves the island unless there's an emergency." Jeannie rested her trembling hands in her lap. "When my mother and Randy bought the island, Manton was the caretaker, so they kept him on. Manton is a deaf-mute, but he can read lips." *And he and I can speak to each other telepathically,* Jeannie thought.

"Then Le Bijou Bleu belongs to you?"

"Yes, it's mine. I go there whenever I want to escape from the world."

"Why did you protest so strongly when Dr. Howell suggested you go there now, until things settle down?"

"Because I will not be run off. I will not allow others to dictate my actions." Jeannie lifted her cane from the side of the sofa where she had placed it. "For years, Randy Foley controlled every moment of my life. Once I was no longer at his mercy, I swore that no one would ever again force me to do anything I didn't want to do."

Jeannie stood and walked to the windows. Noticing the way her shoulders quivered, Sam knew she was crying. He couldn't bear to see her hurting. Hell, why did he let her get to him this way? Women's tears usually had little, if any, effect on him.

Walking over to her, Sam placed his hand on her shoulder. She tensed. He draped his arm around her, then turned her slowly to face him, gripping her shoulders in his big hands.

"You saved my life that night."

She did not try to hide her tears from him, but she ignored them, allowing them to fill her eyes and fall onto her cheeks. "I did all that I could to keep you alive until we arrived at the hospital."

Sam let out a deep breath. "For six years I've wondered about you. Wondered if you were as pure and sweet and caring as I'd thought you were. Wondered if you really did take away my pain, or if I'd been delusional and just imagined the whole experience."

"You didn't imagine any of it. What happened between us was real."

"Tell me something."

"What?" Did he remember the moment when they had become one, the moment when she had prayed for his life and for her own, and the tears she had shed were the tears of two?

"Do you have the power to heal?" he asked, taking her chin in his hand and tilting her face.

She shook her head. "No, I'm not a true healer. I can't make the sick well again. Randy passed me off as a faith healer, but I've never had that kind of power."

"But you can take away pain? You draw physical and mental pain out of a person, and bear that pain yourself?"

"Yes. Julian and Miriam said that I was an empath, that I could experience another's pain. Somehow I reach inside people's minds, inside their hearts and their bodies, and feel what they're feeling. I can heal temporarily, but the pain returns, as does the injury or the illness. It usually returns in a few hours. Sometimes the results last for a few days. But that's rare."

He wiped the tears away from her face, their moisture coating his fingertips. "That's what you did for me six years ago on the beach, isn't it? You drew the pain out of me and experienced it for me? Is that why I felt practically no pain, although I was suffering from gunshot wounds and exposure?"

"You were almost dead," Jeannie said. "And you didn't want to live. You felt a tremendous guilt for someone else's death."

"You absorbed that guilt, too, didn't you? You took it away for a while."

"I had no choice. Otherwise you might not have willed yourself to live."

Releasing her abruptly, Sam backed away, his gaze riveted to her gentle face, her warm eyes, her caring smile. She lifted her hand, extending it toward him.

This woman had saved his life. There was no doubt about that fact. He remembered how the pain had left him, not only the physical pain from his wounds, but also the mental and emotional torment he'd suffered. Had she taken the burden of his pain, his guilt and his unspoken wish to die, and suffered for him, freeing him, saving him?

Did he dare believe her? Could he trust his own feverish memories?

Taking a tentative step toward her, Sam accepted her welcoming hand and pulled her into his arms. She gasped when their bodies touched. He released her, then cupped her face in his big hands.

"Jeannie." He said her name with reverence.

"Sam." The man she had dreamed of for six years, the stranger she had been unable to forget, was looking at her with a passionate, possessive hunger he could not disguise.

"I'll take good care of you, Jeannie." Lowering his head, he kissed her tenderly. A gentle, undemanding kiss. A kiss of gratitude. A kiss filled with promise.

Jeannie felt that sweet kiss in every nerve of her body, and for one tiny instant, she was tempted to ask for more. But now was not the time. Sam Dundee was confused about his feelings, about what was happening. She sensed his frustration, his doubts, his fears and the guilt that never left him.

Sam grabbed her by the shoulders, shaking her gently. "Don't misunderstand the reason I'm here. I'm not looking for healing and salvation. So don't go probing into my past. Maybe you really can take away pain. Maybe you took mine away. Hell, I don't know. But I do know I owe you my life. And I always pay my debts. Do we understand each other?''

He rushed out of the room, leaving her standing there staring at his broad back. Leaning on her cane, she made her way to the bed, removed her robe, folded it and draped it around the bedpost. She lay down, drawing the sheet up to her waist.

She willed herself to relax, to erase everything from her mind. Tomorrow she would have to face reality again. Tonight she needed rest, and if she didn't stop thinking about Sam Dundee, she wouldn't get any sleep.

Sam didn't even try to sleep. He had far too much on his mind. The past, the present and the future. He could never escape from the past. Where Jeannie Alverson was concerned, the present kept getting all mixed up with the past. She was a part of that horrible night when everything had exploded in his face and two people had died because of his stupidity.

Sam checked his watch. Almost midnight. He pulled out a chair and sat down at the kitchen table. Everything had been quiet for hours. The local authorities had patrolled the street for several hours after dark, and once the few stragglers still hanging around outside saw the police car, they had disappeared.

Sam entwined his fingers, then laid his hands on top of the table. He had no idea how long he'd have to stay in Biloxi. He knew he'd be here until Jeannie was no longer in any kind of danger. That could be weeks or even months, depending on how long the press continued making her front-page news, and if and when Maynard Reeves made good on his threats.

Sam owed Jeannie his life. He'd never told anyone except his niece Elizabeth about everything that had happened the night he washed ashore on Le Bijou Bleu. And he'd had no choice but to level with Elizabeth. Since she'd been psychic since childhood, she would have read his mind anyway.

Sam sat at the table in the semidarkness. The only light came from a fluorescent fixture over the sink. He was pretty sure he could handle things here alone, but if necessary, he'd send for J. T. Blackwood, one of his partners, or Hawk or Kane, the new members of his agency.

Sam grunted, the sound containing an element of humor. He recalled a female acquaintance once comparing him to J.T. She'd said that where Sam was Chivas Regal, J.T. was pure white lightning; they were as different as night and day, and yet both possessed the power to kick you on your butt.

Waking with a start, Jeannie lay in the darkness, listening to the sound of her own breathing. She had been dreaming—a sweet dream at first. But it had turned dark and frightening. She had been dancing in Sam Dundee's arms, not needing her cane, her legs strong and sturdy. She felt free and happy and totally safe. Then Sam had been ripped from her arms and she cried out, but no one heard her screams. And then Sam had returned to her, broken and bruised and writhing in pain, but he wouldn't allow her to touch him.

The dream had been so real. Too real. She wiped away the tears that had gathered in the corners of her eyes. Was the dream a premonition, or just the result of a traumatic day? Surely the latter, for she knew she would never dance in Sam's arms. And who could bring such a strong and powerful man to his knees? But then she remembered that Sam had been shot and dumped in the ocean six years ago. Sam was a strong, powerful man, but he was not invincible.

Slipping out of bed, Jeannie felt for her cane. Leaning on the wooden stick, she walked across the room, pulled back the curtains and gazed out at the dawn. Fingers of pale pink light wiggled across the charcoal sky. She glanced down into the courtyard at the back of the house and saw a shadowy figure standing against the wall, near the trailing red rosebush, barren in late summer.

The faint moonlight blended with the first tentative rays of sunlight. Pressing her face against the windowpane she sought a better look at the man. He stepped away from the

wall, and she knew instantly that it was Sam Dundee. Few
men were as big and tall as he; few possessed his broad
shoulders and tawny blond hair. She wondered what he was
doing up at this hour. Had he been restless and unable to
sleep? Had nightmares kept him awake?

Turning his head, he looked up at her window. Jeannie
sucked in her breath. Had he seen her? Yes, she knew he
had. He continued staring up at her and she down at him.
She laid her hand on the windowpane. He nodded his head.

What would it take, she wondered, to reach his soul, to
get inside him and free him from his pain and anger and
guilt? He would never willingly allow her to help him.

"Somehow, I'll find a way to save you, Sam Dundee,"
she vowed.

Chapter 4

Sitting at the mahogany table in the dining room, Sam glanced away from Jeannie Alverson, who was nibbling on a banana muffin and sipping her morning coffee. Sam stared at the ceiling, only half noticing the intricate plaster molding that complemented the graceful plaster detailing in the dado and cartouche panels. He had gotten very little sleep last night, but that didn't bother him. It took days of sleep deprivation before Sam felt the effects. Lack of sleep wasn't what was bothering him, nor the small group of people gathered on the sidewalk across from the Howell home.

What was bothering Sam was Jeannie herself.

He could not allow himself to become involved with Jeannie. A close relationship could be dangerous for both of them. For a woman like Jeannie, a delicate, tender-hearted, spiritual creature, he would mean disaster. Sam knew himself only too well. He was a hard-edged, tough re-alist who had nothing to give a woman except a brief phys-ical encounter. Jeannie would want more—more than he could ever give her. By keeping his distance, both physi-cally and emotionally, he'd be doing them both a big favor.

"Do you think there will be a problem for Jeannie leaving the house?" Julian Howell asked. "It's not even eight o'clock and already there's a crowd outside."

Sam glanced toward the head of the table, where Dr. Howell sat, his dark eyes filled with concern. "I can control the crowd temporarily. The limo will arrive shortly and I can whisk Ms. Alverson away without incident. Don't worry, Dr. Howell, I know what I'm doing. If I thought I couldn't handle the situation, I'd have already called the police."

"I wasn't questioning your abilities, Mr. Dundee. I was simply voicing my concern." Julian's long, thin fingers gripped his china cup, his hand quivering slightly.

"I understand," Sam said. "But rest assured that nothing is going to happen to Ms. Alverson."

"I spoke with Marta before I came down for breakfast." Jeannie looked at Sam for the first time since she'd walked into the dining room. She had deliberately avoided eye contact, knowing how difficult it would be to stop herself from trying to mentally connect with him, something he would resist. As far as he was concerned, he had come to Biloxi to do a job and repay a debt. She had to respect his desire to be left untouched by her empathic powers.

"What's the situation at the school?" Julian asked.

"Marta said that things are relatively quiet. There are only a few people waiting around outside." Sam's steely gaze surveyed her. She tilted her chin, continuing to stare directly at him. "You think going to the school is a mistake, don't you, Mr. Dundee?"

"I think you're asking for trouble by exposing yourself." Sam picked up his coffee, swallowed the last of the warm liquid and set his cup on the saucer. "My job would be a lot easier if you stayed at home. You would be a lot safer. By the time we arrive at the school, the crowd probably will have doubled."

"There are people counting on me at the school." Could she make him understand how important her job was, how essential helping the children was to her? "I can't allow the frenzy that has taken over my life to deprive the children of the guidance and comfort I give them."

"If you want to go to work today, then I'll take you to work." Sam scooted back his chair and stood. "But if anything goes wrong and I think you're risking your life, you'll take my advice. You'll do what I tell you to do."

Jeannie glared at Sam. She had to stop herself from making a biting retort. She wanted to scream that he wasn't going to tell her what to do, that she wouldn't allow him to order her around. Although Julian and Miriam had guided her gently through her teen years, they had been careful not to try to control her life, well aware of the scars left on her soul by her stepfather's domination.

Jeannie laid her napkin on the table, eased her chair back and stood, lifting her cane from where she had hung it on the chair arm.

"Will you check and see if the limousine has arrived?" She asked Sam, then leaned over and kissed Julian on the cheek. "Don't worry about me. I'm in capable hands."

Jeannie did not see Sam's body tense, but she sensed his reaction. Watching him exit the room, she marveled at the sensations coursing through her, at the pure sensual longing that came over her. These feelings weren't new, but they were unique. She had felt them only twice. Six years ago, with Sam Dundee. And now.

But why? Why, out of all the men in the world, did she respond only to this particular man?

Returning, Sam halted in the doorway. "The limousine is here. We can leave whenever you're ready."

Walking over to Sam, Jeannie took his arm. The moment she touched him, she sensed the anger and pain simmering inside him, just below the very controlled surface of his emotions.

He walked slowly, adjusting his long strides to her shorter, partially unbalanced gait. She curled her fingers around his forearm, tightening her grip when he opened the door and guided her outside.

Shouts from the group on the sidewalk bombarded them the moment they stepped onto the side porch. Cameras clicked, flashes blinded, voices rose higher and higher. In the background, the Righteous Light brethren chanted, "Witch!" as they held their posters high above their heads.

Sam hurried Jeannie into the waiting limousine, got in beside her and slammed the door. She touched his shoulder, then jerked her hand away and stared at him, into those blue-gray eyes that told her she shouldn't be surprised by what she had sensed. Jeannie shivered. Within Sam Dundee there existed a suppressed violence, a deep remorse, a guilt so great that it created a physical ache in him.

Dear Lord, how had he survived for six years with so much pain? If he would let her, she could help him. The emotions buried within Sam were slowly killing him, destroying him as surely as any bullet could.

And now the anger and pain and, yes, even the guilt, extended to her. Because she had helped save his life six years ago, Jeannie was tied to his past, had become a part of his torment. He would never allow her to help him, to reach inside his tortured soul and give him peace. And yet he longed to repay his debt to her, to keep her safe, to protect her from all harm.

The limousine made its way slowly past the milling crowd. Jeannie sat beside Sam, looking neither to the right nor the left, wanting desperately to shut out the intruding world. The silence within the limousine was somehow comforting, as was Sam Dundee's presence. There was something so powerful about the man; he radiated strength and control.

Surely there was some way she could help him, some way she could save him from himself, without running the risk of falling in love with him. Loving Sam Dundee would be disastrous. His inability to return her love would destroy her. If she was smart, she would accept him on his terms, allow him to act as her bodyguard and repay the debt he owed her. She dared not give him more, nor expect more in return.

Twenty-five minutes later, Jeannie opened the door at the side entrance of the Howell house and jerked away from Sam's hold on her arm. "I'll be in the front parlor, if anyone needs me."

"Dammit, there's no need to act this way," Sam said. "I couldn't allow you to go inside the school. The risk would have been far too great. Those idiots were throwing rocks at you, yelling, 'Stone the witch.' I told you before we left here that if anything went wrong, we'd do things my way."

"And that's exactly what we did." Jeannie stopped in the hallway, pivoted quickly and glared at Sam. "No discussion. No compromise. The minute we arrived and a few people threw some pebbles at the limo, you ordered the driver to turn around."

"A few pebbles, hell! I'll bet there are dents all over the limo. Those people meant business. Why do you suppose Marta McCorkle had called in the police?"

Gritting her teeth, Jeannie squinted her eyes and huffed, then turned around and marched down the hallway, the *tap-tap-tap* of her cane echoing in the stillness.

Sam followed her, although what he wanted to do was go to the airport, board his Cessna and fly home to Atlanta. "We need to talk."

"What is there to say?" Jeannie shoved back the panel door and entered the front parlor. "You overstepped your authority. You are my employee. I'm supposed to give the orders."

"You hired me to protect you, didn't you?" Sam stood in the doorway. "If you won't listen to my advice, how the hell am I supposed to save you from your own stupidity?"

"My own stu— Oh! It is not stupid to want to go to work, to want to help the children I love so dearly, to want my life..." Jeannie slumped down on the sofa, clutching her cane in her trembling hands.

Damn, was she going to cry again? He hated it when she cried. Other women used tears like a weapon, wielding them to make a man do their bidding. But Jeannie wasn't like other women. And that was *his* problem. He had to stop thinking of her as special and start remembering that she was just a woman—nothing more, nothing less.

"For the time being, you're going to have to stop worrying about everyone else and concentrate on yourself and your safety." Crossing the room, Sam stood in front of her, neither looking at her nor touching her. "I know you're upset because the media and the miracle seekers and Maynard Reeves have stolen your privacy."

"They've stolen my life!" Jeannie yelled.

Julian Howell rushed into the front parlor. "What happened? What's wrong? I could hear the two of you screaming at each other all the way upstairs."

"We weren't screaming at each other," Jeannie said. "We were having a slight difference of opinion."

Julian turned to Sam. "Why have y'all come back to the house? What happened at the school?"

"Ms. McCorkle had to call in the police," Sam said. "The place was crawling with reporters, and a huge crowd of Righteous Light brethren were marching, chanting and throwing rocks. The grounds outside the school were a madhouse."

"You didn't allow Jeannie to get out of the limousine, did you?"

"No! He most certainly didn't let me get out of the limousine!" Jeannie repeatedly tapped her cane on the floor.

"Oh, I see. So that's what this is all about." Smiling, Julian sat down on the sofa beside Jeannie, then looked up at Sam. "You see, Mr. Dundee, our Jeannie doesn't like to take orders. Give her a little time and she'll see that you did the right thing. She's too busy fuming over being told what to do to see the reason behind your actions."

Jeannie rested her cane against the edge of the sofa, leaned back and crossed her arms over her chest. "What are the children going to think if I don't show up? They won't understand."

"Marta will try to explain things to them, my dear," Julian said. "Until Maynard Reeves can be stopped, you must allow Mr. Dundee to take every precaution."

Jeannie glanced at Sam, who was looking not at her, but at some point over her head. "I'll allow Mr. Dundee to do his job. But in the future, I would appreciate his discussing his decisions with me, instead of issuing orders."

"If the situation warrants a discussion, we'll discuss it," Sam said. "Otherwise, you'll do what I say, when I say. Your life might depend on your following my orders."

"If you think—" The moment he looked at her, she couldn't speak. His cold, steel gray eyes issued a warning. "We'll discuss this later. I want to call Marta and check on the situation at the school."

The doorbell rang. Ollie, who had been dusting in the foyer, stuck her head just inside the open parlor door. "There's no need to call Marta. That's her at the front door, with some gray-haired man. And there's a couple of policemen with them."

"Let them in, Ollie," Sam said.

"Show them in, please, Ollie," Jeannie said, as if Sam hadn't already spoken.

Sam walked out into the hallway, standing just outside the front parlor and watching while Ollie opened the door. Marta hurried inside, not speaking to Ollie or acknowledging Sam in any way, and went straight to Jeannie.

"Are you all right? I've been so worried," the plump, petite Marta said. "I've never seen anything like it!"

"I'm fine. Just a little shaken. I had no idea it would be so bad," Jeannie said.

The two uniformed policeman stayed in the foyer, by the front door; a heavyset middle-aged man in a lightweight cotton suit walked up to Sam.

"I'm Lieutenant Rufus Painter. We've taken care of things at the Howell School. I left several men there to make sure things are safe for the staff." Painter held out his hand. "Good thing you got Ms. Alverson out of there as quickly as you did. That crowd was getting mean."

Sam shook the lieutenant's hand. "Sam Dundee. We spoke over the phone recently. I'm Ms. Alverson's private bodyguard."

"Well, Dundee, things are going to get worse before they get better. As long as Ms. Alverson is front-page news, people are going to hound her. She'd be better off if she stayed out of sight until things die down a little. And so would the whole town of Biloxi."

"Please come into the parlor, Lieutenant," Jeannie said, her voice a bit louder than usual.

Sam followed Lieutenant Painter, the two men coming to a standstill, side by side, in front of Jeannie. "Glad to see you're all right, ma'am," Painter said.

"How could I be otherwise, with Mr. Dundee taking such good care of me?" Jeannie smiled at Sam, then at the detective. "Would you care for some coffee, Lieutenant?"

"No, thank you, ma'am. I just came by to check on you, and to let you know we arrested several of those Righteous Light people."

"What about Reverend Reeves?" Julian asked.

"I'm afraid not," Painter said. "The reverend was gone by the time we arrived."

"Is there any way you can keep those people from blocking the school entrance?" Jeannie asked. "It's important for me to be able to go to work."

"Ma'am, all we can do is disperse the crowd and arrest anyone who isn't cooperative or is causing any harm." Painter shook his head. "I'm afraid we just don't have enough manpower to keep officers at the school all the time."

"Jeannie?" Reaching down, Marta took Jeannie's hand. "Most of the children didn't come to school today."

"What?" Jeannie stared up at Marta, who squeezed her hand.

"We had numerous parents call to say that they saw WXBB's morning newscast showing the crowd outside the school. They're afraid, Jeannie, and I can't blame them."

"This situation is intolerable!" Rising off the sofa, Jeannie lifted her cane. "Our children are being punished by that swarm of reporters and that picket line of so-called Christians. And it's all my fault. Because of me, the children can't even come to school."

"This isn't your fault," Marta said. "You've done so much good for the children. You've helped them in a way none of us can."

"But now my coming to the school will harm them." Jeannie walked over to Sam. "I thought I was doing the right thing going to school today, but I see now that as long as things stay the way they are, I can't continue my work at the Howell School. My presence would pose a threat for the children and the staff."

"The staff is one hundred percent behind you," Marta said.

Jeannie smiled that warm, gentle smile that tore at Sam's heart. He couldn't let her smile or her tears keep getting to him this way!

"Marta, you and the others will have to carry on without me. Until I have control of my life again, I can't come back. But I would appreciate being kept informed on each child's progress."

"I'll call you every day and fill you in on all the details." Marta gripped Jeannie's free hand tightly.

"Thank you." Jeannie closed her eyes for a brief moment, absorbing Marta McCorkle's fear and concern. "Don't be afraid. Everything will be all right."

"I know it will." Marta bit her bottom lip. Tears gathered in the corners of her hazel eyes. "I'll handle things." Marta glanced at Sam. "Please take care of her. She's very dear to all of us, you know."

Sam swallowed hard. Damn sentimental females! He nodded. What was he supposed to say? Hell, he owed Jeannie Alverson his life, and he was going to do whatever was necessary to keep her safe.

Jeannie looked at Sam. "I'm sorry I overreacted. You were right and I was wrong."

Sam didn't say anything; he simply nodded again. Maybe now she'd follow his orders without question. It sure would make life a lot simpler if she did.

One of the young policemen standing in the foyer called for Lieutenant Painter. "I think you'd better come here, Lieutenant. Take a look outside."

"Stay here," Sam told Jeannie.

"All right." Jeannie held on to Marta's hand.

Sam stood behind Lieutenant Painter, looking over his head, when the man gazed out the panel window on the right side of the front door.

"Damn," Painter said.

A live news team from WXBB had one camera aimed at the Howell house and another at a small group of Righteous Light brethren surrounding their leader. Reeves, his mane of sandy red hair glowing like fire in the morning sunshine, stood atop a folding chair in the midst of his followers, who waved their signs in the air and looked to Reeves for cues. A shout of "Repent, devil's daughter!" rose from the disciples.

"I ran a preliminary check on Reverend Reeves," Sam told Painter. "He talks a good game, and he appears to be a spellbinding speaker. I'd say he sees an opportunity for publicity and intends to use his damnation of Jeannie Alverson as a stepping-stone to national recognition."

"I'd say the man could be dangerous." Painter motioned to the two uniformed policemen. "Go outside and ask the reverend to take his band of merry men and women somewhere else before I have their butts tossed in jail."

"Yes, sir," the two men replied in unison.

Painter opened the door for his men. "Whatever you do, Dundee, keep Ms. Alverson inside."

Sam stood in the open doorway, watching Painter walk out onto the veranda. Suddenly a war cry of "Witch!" rose from the Righteous Light disciples. Reverend Reeves, sweat dripping from his flushed face, pointed a neatly manicured index finger toward the Howell house and demanded that Jeannie end her unholy alliance with the devil. The WXBB newswoman shared with her audience the hoopla surrounding the Howell home, where the Mississippi faith healer lived. The camera zoomed in on Reeves's face, showing plainly the righteous indignation of the evangelist determined to bring Jeannie Alverson to repentance.

Sam realized that Reeves considered himself a power to be reckoned with. His gut instincts warned him that the scripture-quoting evangelist was evil incarnate, a disciple of hate, not of love. And Jeannie was right. The man probably did intend to kill her.

What Sam needed was a complete, detailed report on Reeves's life. Somewhere there was bound to be a well-kept secret, a little flaw in the man's holier-than-thou armor. Sam hoped he could show the police proof that Reeves was a real danger to Jeannie before the man actually tried to harm her.

He had to find a way to stop Reeves. Even if that meant killing him to defend Jeannie. If it came down to that, he'd have no other choice. But what would she think of him then, gentle, tenderhearted Jeannie? Would she be able to understand the savage warrior in Sam, the primitive nature inside him that made him capable not only of dying to protect her, but also capable of killing, if need be, to keep her safe?

Sam shouldn't give a damn what Jeannie thought of him. But, heaven help him, he did.

Chapter 5

Later that Friday evening, Jeannie decided to face the mounting correspondence piled on her desk. She divided the letters into three separate stacks on top of the pale pink heirloom quilt that covered her bed. Every day, more and more letters poured in from across the United States, and now requests were coming in from Canada, Mexico, South America and Europe. In a week's time, her sane, sensible, orderly life had been completely destroyed. Poor little Cassie Mills, in all her sweet innocence, had opened a Pandora's box of problems for Jeannie.

"Why do you read those things? You should throw them in the trash." Sam Dundee stood just inside the open door, pure masculine beauty in his tailored gray pin-striped suit and coordinating burgundy-and-gray silk tie.

"I divide them into categories." Jeannie patted the stack directly in front of her. "These I throw away—" she pointed to the stack on her left "—and these, too."

"Let me guess." Sam closed the heavy wooden door behind him. "The throwaway letters are from journalists requesting interviews and from crackpots condemning you as a witch."

Jeannie looked up at Sam, standing by her bed, his steely blue-gray eyes piercing in their intensity as he stared at her. Her heart skipped a beat. "These—" she cleared her throat "—are from people asking for my help." Lifting the large stack of letters in her hands, she pressed them to her bosom. "They break my heart. So much misery and suffering, and I can't even offer them hope."

Tears gathered in the corners of her eyes. Sam looked away, not wanting to see her cry. Why the hell did she care so much about people she didn't know? And why weep over the fact that she couldn't permanently heal the whole world of its illnesses? Because Jeannie was that kind of person. She cared too much, and that caring caused her great pain.

He realized there was a lot he didn't know about Jeannie. And he wanted to know everything, yet at the same time he was afraid to find out more.

Sam walked over to the window and looked outside. Early-evening shadows, violet blue and cool, wavered in the August twilight. He kept his back to Jeannie, hoping she wasn't crying and hoping she didn't realize what he was thinking. Sam Dundee was a man who'd seldom been afraid of anything, and yet Jeannie Alverson frightened him in a way nothing and no one ever had.

In some ways, she reminded him of his niece Elizabeth. Both of them were unique women, born with special talents. But there was a vulnerability in Jeannie that Sam had never seen in Elizabeth. A sadness that ran so deep in her that he instinctively knew that only an abundance of love could ever lessen it.

The telephone on the nightstand rang. Jeannie reached out to answer it; Sam grabbed the phone.

She glared at him. "I don't like not being able to answer the phone in my own home."

He thrust the phone at her. "Here, answer it!"

Snatching the telephone out of his hands, she scooted to the center of the bed and turned her back on him. "Hello. Oh, hi, Julian." She cut her eyes in Sam's direction. He looked at her, his expression unreadable. "No, no, you musn't come home for dinner on my account. Ollie's prepared us a nice light chicken salad. You go ahead and take Marta out for dinner.''

Sam hated it when Jeannie confronted him with her displeasure over his specific orders. One of his rules was to always let Ollie, Julian or him answer the phone if she chose not to let the answering machine get it. He'd also strongly advised her to allow him to take care of her mail, without her ever having to see it. But she was so damned stubborn. She didn't like having her routine disrupted and seemed to resent his suggested changes, changes meant to protect her.

Jeannie replaced the telephone on the nightstand. ''Who did you think it was, Maynard Reeves? I doubt he has our new number, since it's unlisted.''

''There are ways to get unlisted numbers.'' Sam stuffed his hands into the pockets of his trousers, lifting the edges of his jacket, revealing the hip holster that held his Ruger.

Jeannie shivered at the sight of the gun. She hated guns, hated weapons of any sort. But she understood the necessity of Sam carrying a gun. There were bound to be times when a man in his line of work would have to rely on more than brute strength.

How difficult it must be for him, Jeannie thought, to protect others, to carry the burden of their security on his wide shoulders. She could not imagine a man more suited for the job, a man more capable. Despite his cool and aloof attitude, his hard, ironclad exterior, Sam Dundee possessed a golden center of gentle strength and loving compassion. He would deny its existence, perhaps didn't even know of its existence, but Jeannie knew. She knew because she had once tapped into that golden core, had touched the secret heart and soul of this man.

She knew she shouldn't be fighting him at every turn, repeatedly refusing to follow his orders. No, not *orders,* exactly. Perhaps *directions* was a better term. He didn't make suggestions to irritate her, even though they did; no, he made suggestions he thought would protect her.

''You're right about these letters. There's really no need for me to go through them.'' She mixed together the three piles of correspondence, scooped them up in her hands and placed them in the curve of her left arm. Bracing herself with her cane, she walked into the sitting room and tossed the letters into the brass wastepaper basket near the mahogany writing desk. "From now on, you can handle all the mail. And I won't answer the phone again."

"Such easy compliance, Ms. Alverson." Sam's lips twitched in an almost smile. "What brought about this sudden change of heart?"

"It wasn't sudden," she admitted. "I've been thinking about all the suggestions you've made, and I realize that if I continue being stubborn, I'll make your job more difficult. I don't want to do that."

"I appreciate your cooperation." Dear God, how he wanted to pull her into his arms, kiss those full, sweet lips and hear her sigh.

Jeannie avoided eye contact with Sam, sensing a growing hunger within him. She had never before been confronted with a man's needs—needs that she wanted to fulfill. She knew very little about male-female relationships, had distanced herself from the sensual side of her nature, but Sam Dundee made her want to explore that unknown.

A soft knock on the door came as a welcome relief. Sam opened the door to Ollie, who came bustling in, carrying a cloth-covered silver tray.

"I've brought your supper up here, just as you requested," she said to Jeannie, who willed herself not to blush. "Just leave everything on the tray when you're finished, and I'll take care of it in the morning."

"Thank you." Jeannie smiled at Ollie, then turned her attention to the silver tray that the housekeeper had placed on the Battenburg-lace-covered round table.

Ollie excused herself, leaving Jeannie and Sam alone. Lifting the cloth covering the tray, Sam surveyed the contents of their meal. Chicken salad, croissants, fresh fruit and cheese.

"Sit down, please." Jeannie lifted her eyes and glanced directly at Sam.

"Ladies first." He pulled out her chair and seated her, his hand brushing her shoulder. He sat across from her, watching while she poured hot tea into the delicate Lenox cups. Her hands quivered ever so slightly. Sam glanced down at the china plate containing a mound of freshly prepared chicken salad lying on a bed of crisp lettuce.

He made her nervous. Sam found that realization strangely reassuring. Obviously he wasn't the only one experiencing an unnerving, unwanted attraction. Since arriving in Biloxi yesterday, Sam had felt unbalanced, as if his equilibrium were a bit off center. Jeannie Alverson had that effect on him.

With emotions he usually had no trouble keeping under control gone haywire, Sam had no point of reference in how to deal with what he felt. He was torn between his desire to protect Jeannie at all costs and to repay the debt he owed her for saving his life, and another, equally strong desire. The desire to claim her, body and soul . . . his primeval masculine need to possess. Heaven help him if he ever acted on his desires—heaven help them both.

"You aren't eating." Jeannie's smile trembled, her brown eyes questioning his silent absorption in his dinner plate.

Picking up his fork, he lifted a small portion of salad to his mouth and ate. He nodded, then glanced at Jeannie. "It's delicious."

But not as delicious as her mouth last night, when he'd taken one tender kiss. Being with her, wanting her so desperately and knowing he was totally wrong for her, only added to Sam's confusion. He had never known a woman like Jeannie, and he'd have bet his last dime that she'd never known a man like him. They were poles apart, opposite ends of a spectrum—a physical man and a spiritual woman.

He had once run away from his past, from the painful memories and the woman who had saved his life. Now he was trapped by a promise he'd made, captured by his own deepest, most primitive needs. Needs that could destroy him if he didn't keep them under control.

They ate in silence, each sneaking occasional glances at the other. The room was utterly, devastatingly quiet, the steady tick-tock of the grandfather clock in the hallway and the clink of silver against china the only sounds.

If the silence continued much longer, Jeannie thought she might scream. How had this happened, this long stretch of tense stillness? They were aware of each other to such a heightened degree that Jeannie began to sense Sam's thoughts. The moment she realized he was fighting the desire to kiss her, she immediately withdrew, ending the connection.

Jeannie's telepathic abilities had always been extremely limited. She and Manton could converse, and in the last days of Miriam's life, they had been able to connect. But Sam was the only other person with whom she had shared this rare joining, and he would not admit it, even to himself.

Scooting back his chair, Sam stood, then tossed his linen napkin down on the table and glared at Jeannie. "You were doing it again, weren't you? Trying to get inside my head."

Tilting her chin defiantly, she looked up at him. "I couldn't have made the connection without your cooperation. You were connecting with me, too. That's why I was able to sense what you were feeling."

He rounded the table so quickly that when he hauled Jeannie to her feet, she cried out in alarm. She clung to his arms, feeling the bulging muscles beneath his jacket and shirt.

"Don't do it again! I don't want any connection, any 'spiritual joining.' Got it?"

"You want to kiss me," she said. "That's why you're so angry. You don't like my knowing how much you'd like to kiss me."

"What?"

"I'd like to kiss you, too."

"Lady, are you out of your mind?"

"Maybe I am, but I've never been truly kissed by a man, and the thought of your kissing me intrigues me."

"You're paying me to be your bodyguard," Sam said. "Not your lover."

She covered his lips with her fingertips. "Shhh. I'm not asking you to make love to me, just to kiss me. What's wrong, Mr. Dundee, are you afraid to kiss me?"

With one hand, he tightened his hold around her waist, and with the other he grasped her chin. "All right, if you're sure it's what you want. Just remember that it doesn't mean anything. I've kissed a hundred women before you, and will probably kiss a hundred more before I die.''

"Then I expect you're very good at this, at kissing, aren't you?"

Her eyelids fluttered. She clutched his arms. Drawing her up against him, Sam slipped his hand under the wavy fall of her hair and gripped her neck. His heartbeat roared in his ears like the hum of his Cessna's twin engines.

A steady, throbbing ache spread through him, threatening to overpower his restraint. When he lowered his head, his lips just making contact with hers, she seemed to melt into him, to become a part of him. He felt her surrender, her eager compliance, in every cell of his body.

Of all the women he'd known, all the pretty faces, all the luscious bodies, not one had ever sent him into a panic. But then, he had never wanted anyone the way he wanted Jeannie. And it was that need, that raging, all-consuming need, that frightened the intrepid Sam Dundee.

"I'm no good for you," he warned her. Or was he warning himself? "So don't let this kiss give you any ideas."

Slipping her arms around his neck, she closed her eyes and welcomed his kiss. Her soft, sweet, giving lips met his. Innocent and untutored, she gave herself over completely to his mastery, absorbing the undeniable pleasure he was experiencing, realizing that she felt their shared enjoyment in the kiss.

Opening her mouth on a sigh, Jeannie accepted the tender thrust of his tongue, the sensual probing. Her body tingled with excitement. A slow, steady throb of desire began to build inside her.

Sam deepened the kiss. He cupped her buttocks, shifting her body, lifting her up and into him, so that his arousal pulsated against her femininity. She moaned loudly, then slid her tongue inside his mouth, exploring him the way he had her. He ached. She ached even more. He groaned deep in his throat, the power of Jeannie's nearness rendering him helpless against his own masculine needs.

Jeannie cried out from the hot, pounding hunger and demanding desire raging inside her. Sam's hunger. Her desire. She felt them both, and felt them simultaneously.

She scratched his back, her short, rounded nails clawing fiercely at his cashmere jacket. Her body undulated against his, feeding his hunger, fanning the flames of her desire. She was on fire with their combined passion, and was no longer in control of her actions. Sam's needs dictated hers. The greater his desire was for her, the more she desired him.

She overpowered him with the fervor of her response, momentarily stunning him. Slowly ending the kiss, he lifted her into his arms and carried her out of the sitting room and directly toward her bed, then lowered her on top of the quilted pink coverlet. Her arms still draped around his neck, she pulled him downward. With his lips almost touching hers, he braced his hands on each side of her.

He had never expected her to go wild in his arms, had never imagined that sweet, innocent Jeannie possessed the power to bring him to his knees with nothing more than a smoldering kiss.

He looked down at her face, flushed with arousal, her lips red, damp and slightly swollen. "Jeannie?" He wanted to take her and make her his. He wanted to remove her clothes and cover her naked body with his own. He wanted to bury himself deep inside her and find the ecstasy he knew awaited them. But he could not, would not, take advantage of her. He sensed that she had never before felt this way, that she was experiencing sexual desire for the first time in her life.

Suddenly the truth hit him, like a bullet between the eyes. This really *was* the first time for her. The first time she'd ever been kissed. The first time she'd ever been aroused.

"Sam? Is it…is it always like this?" Was it possible that what they were feeling was what normally took place when a man and a woman shared a passionate kiss?

"You can feel what I'm feeling, can't you?" Suddenly he pulled away from her, easing her arms from around his neck as he stood up beside the bed. "Your empathic powers obviously include sharing your partner's arousal."

Jeannie sat up on the bed, looking at Sam, a mixture of wonder and uncertainty in her eyes. "Does it bother you that I—"

"That you're not only inside my head, but my body, as well, when I'm making love to you? Yeah, it bothers me.

You actually felt everything I felt!'' Sam loosened his tie, then ripped it off his neck and clutched it in his big hand.

She had not only known how much he wanted her and how out of control he'd been, but had felt those exact same emotions. But how could that be?

Jeannie Alverson really was an empath, Sam admitted to himself. To what degree, he wasn't sure, but he knew for certain that she'd somehow felt exactly what he had felt.

"You sensed what I was feeling, too, didn't you?'' she asked, scooting slowly toward the edge of the bed. "Has that ever happened to you?''

"Hell, no! And it didn't happen this time, either.'' Sam crammed his silk tie into his pocket. "When I have sex with a woman, the only way I know what she's feeling is in the way she responds. And no woman has ever been able to experience what I'm feeling.''

Jeannie slid her legs over the side of the bed. Sam stepped out of her reach. "Then what just happened between us was very special, wasn't it?''

"All we did was kiss!'' Sam raked his hand through his hair, disheveling it.

She held out her hand to him, bidding him to come to her. "Yes, all we did was kiss.''

He stared at her hand. Small, soft, delicate. Did he have the courage to accept what she was offering? All Sam had ever wanted, all he'd ever expected, from a woman was a mutually satisfying, uncommitted relationship.

Jeannie Alverson was a forever kind of woman, a woman who'd want to know everything about a man, a woman who'd want to save his soul.

"I'm in your life again because I want to repay a debt,'' Sam said. "I'm not here because I want anything from you. I don't want your healing. I don't want your sympathy. And I sure as hell don't want your love.''

"You're afraid of me.'' Her voice held a breathless tremor. "You don't want to share yourself with anyone. You think you deserve to be unhappy and alone for the rest of your life. You see it as your punishment. And you're afraid I have the power to change all that.''

"I told you that I'm no good for you. I am the wrong man for you. You deserve—"

"I deserve a man who will truly love me."

"That man isn't me. Not now. Not ever."

Tilting her chin defiantly, Jeannie looked directly at Sam, her bottom lip quivering slightly. Sam glared at her, wishing he'd never kissed her, wishing he wasn't obligated to stay in Biloxi and guard her.

Several sharp taps on the door snapped Jeannie and Sam out of their silent confrontation. Ollie rushed into the room, oblivious to Jeannie's position on the bed. "You gotta come downstairs right now, Mr. Dundee. And hurry!"

"What's wrong, Ollie? You're white as a sheet," Jeannie said.

"I found a package on the front porch. It's a small brown-paper-wrapped package. I don't know where it came from, but it's addressed to Jeannie."

"No one delivered the package?" Sam asked. "You just found it lying on the porch?"

"It could be a present for her, you know." Ollie wrung her hands together. "But what if it's... I mean, there could be something dangerous inside. A snake, or a—"

"A bomb," Jeannie said.

Ollie gasped.

"Where did you put the package?" Sam asked.

"Where did I—? I didn't put it anywhere. I left the thing on the porch."

"Good girl." Sam patted Ollie on the back. "You stay up here with Jeannie. I'll go take a look at our little gift."

Jeannie called out to him. "Sam?"

Halting in the doorway, he turned and looked at her.

"Please, be careful," she said.

"I always am," he told her, then walked out into the hall.

The minute Sam was out of sight, Jeannie turned to Ollie. "Get my cane for me."

"Why do you need your cane? Mr. Dundee said we were to wait up here."

"Ollie, don't ask questions. Just get me a cane. Please."

Obeying, Ollie handed Jeannie a walking stick, then grabbed her by the arm when Jeannie stood and headed straight out the bedroom door. "He'll be furious if you go downstairs."

"I won't get near the package," Jeannie said. "I promise. But I can't sit up here not knowing what's happening."

"Oh, all right. I'll go with you. But I won't take the blame for this. If Mr. Dundee gets all fired up—"

"I take full responsibility."

The package was just as Ollie had described it. Small, brown-paper-wrapped and lying on the front veranda, only a few inches from the steps. Well, it might be nothing more than a gift from an admirer of Jeannie Alverson. But then again, it might be a bomb. No use taking any chances, Sam decided.

He went back into the house and phoned Lieutenant Painter. "I'll keep an eye on the package until your boys get here," Sam said. "Tell them to make it quick. I don't know how long this thing has been out here, and if it's a bomb, it could be timed." Sam replaced the receiver.

"You really do think it's a bomb, don't you?" Jeannie stood in the library doorway, Ollie at her side.

Sam jerked around, glaring at her. "What the hell are you doing down here? Didn't I tell you and Ollie to stay upstairs?"

"I would have gone crazy staying up there, wondering what was happening, not knowing if you were all right or not."

"Ollie, take her out the back door and keep her there, even if you have to sit on her."

"Come on, Jeannie." Ollie tugged on Jeannie's arm. "Mr. Dundee's right. If it's a bomb, it could explode any minute now."

"Sam, please come and tell me the minute you know for sure." Her warm brown eyes pleaded with him. "Be very careful. Let the police handle things."

"That's just what I intend to do," Sam said.

After he'd made certain Jeannie and Ollie were out back, he returned to the front porch to wait on the Biloxi police. The wait was short; Lieutenant Painter arrived with the bomb squad in ten minutes flat.

"You think someone left a little present for Ms. Alverson?" Lieutenant Painter asked, stepping around the square-shaped object lying so innocently on the veranda.

"I have no idea, but my gut instincts are scaring the hell out of me." Sam leaned back against the closed front door, bending his knee and bracing the tip of his left foot on the floor. "If this package is from Reeves, then it's obvious the man means business. But what do you want to bet that there will be no way to trace the package and whatever's inside to the good reverend, or anyone else?"

Sam and Rufus Painter watched from afar while the bomb squad took every precaution unwrapping the package and then opening the box within.

One of the policeman laughed, another grunted and cursed. Sam and Lieutenant Painter walked off the porch and down the sidewalk.

"What have you got there, Ivey?" the lieutenant asked.

"You're not going to believe this one," Ivey said. "Come take a look, Lieutenant. This is a new one on me."

When they approached the policemen hovering around the opened package, Ivey turned around and held out a brand new white Bible.

"What the hell?" Painter shook his head.

"A Bible," Sam said. "A white Bible. Maynard Reeves's trademark. But my guess is there isn't a fingerprint on it, other than your men's."

"Yeah, if it is from Reeves, he's too smart to leave fingerprints," Painter said. "Besides, there's no law against someone sending someone else a Bible, is there?"

"Take a look inside," Ivey said. "Just flip it open where the bookmark is."

Painter eased the pages back. "Hell! Take a look, Dundee."

"I wish I didn't have to show this to Jeannie, but she won't give us any peace until she knows," Sam said. "Any reason why she shouldn't be shown the Bible?"

"No reason I can think of. We can go ahead and show it to her." Lieutenant Painter clasped the Bible in his hand. "I'll go with you and reassure Ms. Alverson that everything's all right. Then we'll take the Bible downtown and have the lab run some tests.''

Jeannie met them at the door leading into the kitchen. ''Was it a bomb?''

''No bomb,'' Sam said.

Sam moved out of the way as Jeannie entered the kitchen, Ollie following. ''What was it?''

The lieutenant held out the white Bible. ''I believe this is yours.''

Jeannie stared at the Bible.

''Why, it's the good book,'' Ollie said. ''And you were worried somebody sent Jeannie something to harm her.''

''Do you want to see this?'' Sam asked Jeannie.

She looked at him, realizing the import of his question. There was more to the gift than the obvious. She nodded. He handed the Bible to her. A white satin ribbon marked a page near the beginning. Jeannie opened the Bible to the specified page and noticed that the white ribbon was dotted with dark red spots. One short verse had been smeared with the same red liquid that dotted the marker.

Jeannie read the verse silently. She swallowed hard, then read it aloud. ''Thou shalt not suffer a witch to live.''

''Who'd send such a thing?'' Ollie jerked her head around in Sam's direction, and when he didn't respond, she looked back at Jeannie.

''It's a warning, isn't it?'' Jeannie asked.

''What do you think?'' Sam lifted the open Bible out of her unsteady hands. Placing the marker and the page to his nose, he sniffed, and then he scratched at the red spots on the marker with his fingernail.

''What are you doing?'' Ollie stared at him, perplexed by his actions.

''The stains are blood, aren't they?'' A knot of fear formed in Jeannie's throat, threatening to cut off her breathing.

''Yeah, they're blood,'' Sam said. ''But not necessarily human blood.''

''Just what are the police going to do about this?'' Ollie asked. ''Folks don't have the right to be sending blood-stained Bibles to other folks and as good as accusing them of being a witch."

"Ollie, there's nothing you can do about this," Jeannie said. "Lieutenant Painter will handle the matter—won't you, Lieutenant?"

"I'll be glad when all this business with the reporters and the sick folks and that crazy preacher comes to an end." Ollie continued mumbling to herself as she walked over to the kitchen cabinet. "I'll fix us all some coffee. I doubt we'll be getting any sleep tonight."

"I'll give y'all a call if we find out anything," Lieutenant Painter said.

"Please let me know if the blood is human or animal," Jeannie said.

Sam grabbed the Bible out of her hands. "There's no way we'll be able to prove Maynard Reeves is the gift-giver, but I don't have a doubt that this—" he snapped the Bible shut "—is the good reverend's handiwork."

"He's doing more than accusing me of being a witch." Jeannie shivered, the reality of the warning hitting her full force. *Thou shalt not suffer a witch to live.*

"He's threatening your life." Sam handed the Bible to Lieutenant Painter. "We have to find some sort of evidence against Reeves and put a stop to him before—"

"I know Maynard Reeves wants me dead," Jeannie said. "He's going to try to kill me."

"We'll do everything we can to help." Painter held the white Bible securely in both hands. "But without some hard evidence, our hands are tied." He nodded, smiling sadly at Jeannie, who returned his smile, then he left the kitchen.

"Coffee is nearly ready," Ollie said. "Dr. Howell will be home soon, and when he finds out what happened tonight, he's going to be terribly upset."

Jeannie sat down at the kitchen table. "There's no need to worry Julian about this until tomorrow." She looked up at Sam. "Maynard Reeves *is* going to try to kill me, isn't he?"

Sam knelt down in front of Jeannie. Taking her face in his hands, he looked her directly in the eye. "The truth?" he asked.

"Between us, always," she said.

"Since you refused to join his ministry, Reeves has convinced himself that your empathic powers came from the devil. He sees it as his duty to destroy the evil, and the only way he can do that is to kill you."

Jeannie gasped several times, repeatedly sucking in gulps of air. Sam put his arm around her. She laid her head on his shoulder, accepting his comforting caress.

"I won't let him succeed, Jeannie. I promise. I'll keep you safe. I'll guard you with my life."

Jeannie closed her eyes. One tear caught in her eyelashes, another trickled slowly down her cheek. Unconsciously she began absorbing the rage inside Sam. The hatred and anger centered on Maynard Reeves, but spread out in tiny waves toward anyone who meant Jeannie harm.

Sam was prepared to kill to protect her. Jeannie had never felt that type of hatred. Not even when she longed to be free from her stepfather's cruelty had she wished him dead. Jeannie wasn't sure she was capable of killing, even to defend her own life. There was a gentleness in her soul that longed to ease pain and suffering, to eliminate hatred and fear. Could she ever understand the barbaric ability to kill?

Safe in Sam's arms, the cruelties of the world far away, Jeannie delved into her soul, into that minuscule spot where a fragment of Sam's soul remained from their joining six years ago. Such a fragile link, one she knew Sam would sever if he was aware of its existence.

He kissed the side of her face, his lips brushing it tenderly, as he stroked her shoulders and back, soothing her with his touch.

In an instantaneous flash that left her as quickly as it had come, Jeannie knew exactly what Sam was. Sam Dundee, her protector, was a unique creature. He was an elegant savage, a compassionate warrior, and only if she was strong enough to become his equal could they ever truly be united.

Chapter 6

"No. Absolutely not." Crossing his arms over his chest, Sam Dundee gave Jeannie his killer glare, the look that had made many a formidable opponent quake in his boots.

"Yes! Definitely yes." Jeannie didn't glance up from the task at hand, transferring the contents of her shoulder bag to a beige leather purse.

"It's out of the question." What would it take to get through to this woman? Didn't she realize that every time she went out in public, she was exposing herself to danger?

"I have not missed church in years. I'm not asking to attend the regular service the way I usually do. All I'm asking is for you to take me to the early-morning prayer service. There won't be many people at church." Jeannie snapped her purse shut, then smiled at Sam. "Now, I'm ready to go whenever you are."

"I'm not ready."

Jeannie surveyed him from head to toe, leisurely inspecting every inch of his massive body. She drew in a deep breath. Shivers of remembrance rippled through her, memories of a kiss that had rocked the very foundation of her life, memories of being held lovingly, protectively, in those enormous arms.

Sam was devastatingly handsome, and the very picture of a successful businessman in his navy blue double-breasted suit, a gold Rolex his only piece of jewelry.

Any other man Sam's size would look like a muscle-bound gorilla in a suit, but not Sam Dundee. His tailored clothes fit him to perfection, his thick blond hair styled by an expert and his massive hands recently manicured. He possessed an air of unpretentious sophistication, one Jeannie felt certain he had cultivated over the years.

But inside the expensive clothes lay the finely honed body of an athlete. Beneath the polished exterior beat the heart of a primitive male. Chip away his refined facade and you'd find brute strength. Sam Dundee had the soul of a warrior.

"Like what you see?" His mouth curved into a smirk. "Thinking about staking a claim?"

Jeannie willed herself not to blush at his comment. He'd caught her shamelessly assessing his physical attributes. "Actually, I was noticing that you look like you're ready to go to church."

"I advise you not to attend services today."

"I'm going to church," Jeannie said. "Are you going with me, or do I have to go by myself?"

"Doesn't Dr. Howell go to church?"

"Julian is a Catholic. He's going to Mass with Marta before they go out for lunch."

"You're damned and determined to do this, aren't you?" Sam shook his head, frustration boiling inside him, threatening to overflow. He wanted to make Jeannie stay at home, where he knew he could keep her safe and protect her from a threatening world.

"I've looked outside the house, and there's not one reporter or protester in sight." Clutching her purse in her hand, Jeannie laced her arm around Sam's. "And I don't think we have to worry about Reverend Reeves today. After all, this is Sunday, and he'll be preaching to his Righteous Light brethren."

Accepting defeat, Sam eased his arm around Jeannie's waist. "Yeah, he's probably firing them up with a sermon on witches. No doubt quoting from the Old Testament."

"Exodus," Jeannie said, knowing she would never be able to forget the Bible verse marked in blood, blood she prayed the police lab would find to be animal and not human. "You're right, of course, Sam. Just because I'll be safe from Maynard Reeves at my church, that doesn't mean he isn't inciting his followers to condemn me as a witch."

Sam tightened his hold around Jeannie's waist, wanting to pick her up in his arms, carry her upstairs and lock her away from the evil she could not escape in the outside world.

Jeannie walked slowly, carefully, always aware of her limited abilities to maneuver and her dependency on her cane.

Sam adjusted his gait to Jeannie's step-by-step movements. His gut twisted into knots as he watched her struggle with the simple task of walking. It would be so easy for him to carry her to the car and then carry her into the church when they arrived. But Jeannie would never allow it. She was fiercely, stubbornly proud. Sam marveled at her strength and determination.

The late-August morning held a hint of autumn, especially in the refreshingly cool breeze blowing in off the Gulf waters. The sun's early warmth blended with the wind, creating perfect weather.

Sam seated Jeannie on the passenger side of her Lexus. She had insisted he dismiss the limousine, telling him she felt uncomfortable riding in the big gray Cadillac.

He reached for the shoulder harness at the exact moment Jeannie did. Jerking her head up, she looked into his eyes, and he knew she saw clearly what he was thinking. His hand covered hers; she didn't pull away. With quick precision, he snapped her seat belt in place, stood up straight and closed the door. Jeannie's gaze focused on her clasped hands, placed atop the purse in her lap. Sam got in on the driver's side, fastened his safety belt and started the engine.

Jeannie knew that he would never be able to touch her again without wondering if she was experiencing his emotions, feeling what he felt. Friday night, the moment he realized she had gotten inside him, that she had become a part of him, he had withdrawn from her. Was he so afraid to

share himself, to open himself up to another person, even
someone who cared for him?

Jeannie sat silent and unmoving, aware that Sam opposed this short trip down Beach Boulevard to the small
Congregational church where she'd been a member for a
dozen years. Although Julian was Catholic, his wife Miriam had been a Protestant who attended one of the oldest
congregations in Mississippi, and she had taken Jeannie to
services with her.

Sam headed the Lexus east, up Beach Boulevard, occasionally glancing at Jeannie, who seemed spellbound by the
view of the Gulf through her side window. Why did his
throat tighten and his heart pound every time he looked at
her? He'd known women more beautiful, women more vo-
luptuous. And he'd certainly known women more experienced. But he couldn't remember ever looking at a woman
and being so captivated by her loveliness, her gentleness, her
compassion.

Jeannie had secured her long brown hair in a soft bun at
the nape of her neck. Loose tendrils of silky beige curled
about her ears and forehead. The outfit she wore, a cream
shirtwaist dress with a pastel flowered scarf tied around her
neck, was as understated as her beauty, and suited her fragile facade.

Every time Sam glanced her way, she was tempted to look
at him, to confront him, but she didn't. Instead, she gazed
at the Gulf, at the murky water and the barrier islands she
could barely see in the distance. One huge gambling casino
after another—a reproduction of a pirate ship, an old riverboat—lined the coast, and rows of motels flanked Beach
Boulevard. The beach was empty, except for the gulls.
Jeannie knew that if she rolled down her window she would
be able to smell the fishy scent so prevalent along the Gulf
shore.

Within a few minutes, Sam caught a glimpse of the small
Congregational church in the distance, a white cross positioned prominently above the arched upstairs windows. He
turned the Lexus onto the narrow street beside the wooden
church, breathing a sigh of relief when he saw only four cars

in the parking area and only a woman and a child outside the building.

Not one relevant detail of Jeannie Alverson's life had escaped being printed in the newspapers or broadcast on the television and radio. Everyone in Biloxi, Gulfport, Pass Christian and Ocean Springs knew where Jeannie went to church. Hell, the whole state of Mississippi probably knew. Luckily, no one would be expecting her to arrive at church for early-morning prayers, since this was not her normal routine.

Sam parked the Lexus, rounded the car and helped Jeannie to her feet. With his arm securely planted around Jeannie's waist, he led her up the sidewalk.

Suddenly, the little boy who had been standing beside his mother at the front of the church fell to his knees at Jeannie's feet. She stopped dead still and stared down at the dark-haired child. A thin woman with huge brown eyes stepped forward and lifted the child to his feet.

"Please, Jeannie, help my little boy. I came early, wanting to be first in line to see you. Matthew is only six years old, and he lives with unbearable pain. Touch him and take away his pain." Tears streamed down the woman's pale face and dripped off her nose and chin. "He's such a little thing. It isn't right that he suffers so much."

Sam nudged Jeannie, urging her to move on, not to stop, but she leaned against him and whispered. "She didn't ask me to heal him. All she asked was that I take away his pain. I can do that much for the child."

"No, Jeannie, don't." The bitter, metallic taste of fear coated Sam's tongue. If she took away the child's pain, didn't that mean she would have to endure it?

"What's wrong with Matthew?" Jeannie asked.

"He has a severe form of arthritis that causes him great pain. He's been suffering all night. When I heard on TV that you always attend Sunday services here, I knew what I had to do. I've been here over an hour, waiting, knowing in my heart you'd come today and that you'd help my child."

Jeannie looked at Matthew. Such a pretty little boy, but his eyes told the story of his suffering. "Bring Matthew inside the church with me."

The woman grabbed Jeannie's hand and kissed it. "Thank you." New tears filled her eyes. "God bless you." She lifted her child into her arms.

"Jeannie?" Sam questioned her, yet he knew he couldn't stop her doing what her heart dictated.

"The minister's study is down the hall to the left. When we're inside the vestibule, it'll be the first door," she told him.

Jeannie made certain the woman and her son entered the building first, and then she followed, Sam helping her maneuver the short row of steps. Once inside, Jeannie went directly to the minister, who stood at the doorway to the sanctuary. When she whispered her request, he simply nodded his agreement and glanced forlornly at Jeannie, then smiled at the tormented woman and her sick child.

Once inside the study, Jeannie sat in a sturdy wooden chair directly in front of a bookshelf-lined wall.

"Please, close the door, Sam."

He didn't want anything to do with this. If he couldn't prevent what was going to happen—and he knew couldn't— he'd prefer to step outside and wait.

"You don't have to stay, if you'd rather not," Jeannie said.

Oh, he'd rather not, all right, but he would. Hell would freeze over before he'd leave her alone at a time like this. He closed the door, then blocked the entrance with his massive body. Crossing his arms over his chest, he stood there, a silent sentinel, feeling powerless against Jeannie's determination.

"Bring Matthew to me." Jeannie held open her arms.

The mother placed her child in Jeannie's lap and knelt at her feet. Jeannie encompassed Matthew's skinny little body with her arms. She closed her eyes. Matthew squirmed.

"Don't be afraid, sweetheart. All I'm going to do is hold you, and very soon the pain will go away and you won't hurt for a while."

The wide-eyed mother wiped the tears from her eyes. Jeannie sighed. A soft brightness surrounded her; a sweet, flowing current rippled through her body. The first minute twinges of discomfort ebbed and flowed, coming and going, then returning to stay. Jeannie gasped. Sam flinched. Matthew sobbed.

The minister's opening prayer floated down the hallway from the sanctuary, the words muted by the closed door of the study. Acting as a receptacle, Jeannie allowed Matthew's pain to slowly drain from his body. She was still aware of her surroundings, of the child's mother trembling at her feet, of Sam staring at a spot somewhere over her head, refusing to watch the performance of her task.

Sam gritted his teeth. He focused his vision on the certificates on the wall behind the minister's desk. Matthew breathed so deeply that the sound drew Sam's attention. The boy appeared relaxed, almost asleep, as he lay in Jeannie's arms. All the color had drained from Jeannie's face, leaving her normally rosy cheeks pale. Sam looked away, taking note of every picture on the walls, scanning the bookshelves, tracing the stripes in the wallpaper, searching for stains on the carpet.

Jeannie groaned, low and soft in her throat, the sound gaining Sam's instant attention. She had released her hold on Matthew. Her arms lay at her sides, her hands gripping the edge of the chair. Her body shivered, once, twice, and then she opened her mouth, leaned her head back and sucked in gulps of air. As she continued drawing in deep breaths, she began to moan quietly.

She was experiencing physical pain. Matthew's pain. And there was absolutely nothing Sam could do to help her. Sweat broke out on Sam's forehead. Moisture coated the palms of his big hands.

Time ceased, standing still for the four people in the minister's study. When Matthew slipped out of Jeannie's lap and into his mother's open arms, Sam didn't know for sure whether minutes or hours had passed. The torment he'd felt at watching Jeannie suffer seemed to have lasted for hours, but when he looked at his Rolex, he realized that less than fifteen minutes had gone by.

When Matthew's mother tried to thank Jeannie, she did not receive a response. Jeannie appeared to be unconscious.

"It doesn't hurt, Mommy," Matthew said, smiling broadly. "I don't hurt at all." The boy pulled free of his mother and walked around the room. "And I can walk, and it still doesn't hurt." Matthew raced around the room in a circle. Grabbing the child by the shoulder, Sam halted his jubilant running.

"Please, take Matthew and go," Sam said. "Jeannie's done all she can for him. She needs her rest now."

"Thank her again for me," the woman said. "Even if the relief lasts only a few hours. Tell her for me."

"I'll tell her."

Sam held open the door for Matthew and his mother. Once out in the hallway, Matthew stopped, turned around and waved at Sam. Sam waved back at the child.

"Mommy said the angel at this church would take away my pain, and she did."

Closing the door, shutting out the world and all its problems, Sam leaned his shoulders and head back against the stained wood surface and closed his eyes for one brief moment. Then he looked at Jeannie, who was lying slumped in the chair, tears sparkling in her dark eyelashes like diamonds on sable. He walked over, bent down on one knee and pried her clenched fists away from the chair's edge.

"Jeannie?"

She moaned. Her eyelids flickered. Sam brought her hands to his lips, opened her palms and anointed them with kisses. Jeannie moaned again.

"Sam." His name was a mere whisper on her lips.

"What can I do to help you? Just tell me, and I'll do it." He had no idea what she needed from him, but he wanted to do something, anything, to help her.

"Hold—hold me."

He enveloped her in his arms, stroking her tense back, trapping her arms between their bodies. She swayed into him, brushing her face over the side of his face, resting her cheek against his. Feeling the dampness on his cheek, Sam looked down and saw that Jeannie was crying.

"Don't cry. Please, don't cry." He lifted her into his arms, not sure it was the right thing to do, but unable to stop himself.

Jeannie tried to lift her arm to his neck, but she didn't have the strength. Sam sat down on the small love seat in the far corner, bringing Jeannie down into his lap. He lifted her arm and placed it around his neck. She laid her head on his shoulder.

"How long will this last? Isn't there anything I can do?" Frustration on an incomparable level clawed at his guts.

"Not long. Just a little while." She opened her eyes, those warm, compassionate brown eyes, and looked at Sam.

The bottom dropped out of his stomach. "Rest, Jeannie. Rest."

"Take care of me, Sam." She closed her eyes and went limp in his arms.

"Jeannie? Jeannie?" He shook her gently. She didn't move. He shook her again. "Jeannie!"

He realized then that she was unconscious. Shudders racked his body. He pulled her close, burying his face against her neck.

They sat there for endless minutes, Sam wishing more than ever that he'd asked J.T. to come to Biloxi to guard Jeannie instead of coming himself. He was prepared to act as her bodyguard, but he wasn't suited to playing nursemaid. And he sure as hell hadn't expected to have to watch her perform one of her miracle healings. Seeing her suffer had ripped him apart. He'd known from the beginning that this assignment would be more than a simple business arrangement, but he hadn't counted on just how personal it would become. What man in his right mind would want to become involved with a woman who possessed Jeannie's miraculous abilities? He sure as hell didn't.

Jeannie awoke, weak and pale. "Sam?"

"Are you all right? You scared the hell out of me when you passed out that way."

"We've missed most of the church service, I'm afraid." She touched his face with her fingertips. He flinched. So sensitive—her strong, fearless warrior. "Take me home, Sam. I'll be all right. You musn't worry so. When I was a child, I took all the pain from at least half a dozen people each night."

"Your childhood was a living hell, wasn't it?" Sam had never thought about what it must have been like for her, going from town to town, from one revival meeting to the next, always expected to perform her miracles.

"I suffered every day of my life. I remember feeling very little except pain."

"Other people's pain."

She nodded. "I'm fine, Sam. Really I am."

"You didn't have to take away Matthew's pain."

"Yes, I did." She caressed his cheek. "How could I look at him and not want to help him?" Jeannie sighed. "His mother understood that I couldn't heal him. She knows his pain will return."

Jeannie tried to stand. Sam picked up her cane and handed it to her. Bracing the tip of the walking stick on the floor, Jeannie lifted herself to her feet. Sam stood up beside her. The moment Jeannie took her first step, her knees gave way. Crying out, she grabbed for Sam. He swooped her up in his arms.

"I can't walk," she said. "I suppose it's because I felt all Matthew's arthritic pain in my legs, and they're already weak."

Sam carried Jeannie outside, hoping he could take her away before any reporters or curiosity seekers arrived. Only the minister and three church members remained inside the building, and outside one lone reporter and his photographer waited. Tory Gaines watched from afar, then started to approach them. Sam glared at the man.

"You come near her, Gaines, and you're a dead man." Sam didn't pause.

Tory Gaines stopped where he stood, not moving a muscle as he watched Sam carry Jeannie to her Lexus.

Traffic wasn't terribly heavy, so Sam drove them home in record time, while Jeannie closed her eyes and rested. Neither of them said a word. He carried her into the house and up the stairs to her bedroom, not once inquiring what she wanted. Easing her down onto her bed, he removed her beige heels, then sat beside her.

"Don't look so worried," she said. "I told you I'm fine."

"You may be, but I'm not." Leaning over her, he positioned his hands at either side of her shoulders. "Guarding you has turned out to be a lot more than I bargained for. How could I protect you from what happened today? I had to stand there and watch you suffer and know there wasn't a damned thing I could do about it! How do you think that made me feel?"

"Helpless?" She twined her arms around his neck.

"I don't ever want to see you suffer like that again. Not for anyone, but especially never again for me. Do you understand what I'm saying?"

"Yes, Sam, I understand."

She understood only too well, but she doubted he did. For the first time, Sam truly accepted the fact that she had taken away his pain the day she saved his life. He hadn't wanted to believe she was a true empath, that her psychic talents were strong enough not only to probe inside his mind, but to actually experience his emotions and share his feelings. Friday night's events, coupled with those at the church today, had forced him to admit the truth. This was a beginning, Jeannie realized, but only a beginning. Sam was not the kind of man who would ever surrender easily. He knew she wanted to help him, but he wasn't ready to accept her help. If she pushed him too hard and too fast, he would balk. As it was, he would fight her every inch of the way. If she was ever to reach his soul and save him, she would have to start by using whatever means were available.

Jeannie smiled. She accepted the inevitable. She was falling in love with Sam Dundee, but she knew he might never love her, might never willingly take what she had to offer him. Was she brave enough to accept him on his terms, share a purely physical relationship, when she so desperately needed more?

Pulling him down to her, she lifted her lips to meet his. She nibbled at his bottom lip, and sighed when he groaned.

"I've never wanted anyone else. You're the first and only man I've ever desired," she told him.

"Don't say things like that to me. I'm having a hard enough time as it is, keeping my hands off you."

"I make you feel helpless. I make you feel afraid. And those aren't emotions you're familiar with, are they, Sam Dundee?" She gave him a quick kiss. He groaned again. "I can get inside you, feel what you feel, experience your pleasure, as well as my own." She licked a circle over his lips.

"Maybe you *are* a witch," he said. "God knows you've bewitched me."

He took her lips completely, with a tender savagery that sent pinpricks of pleasure through her body. He wanted her with a quiet desperation, knowing she wasn't ready to make love, realizing that he needed to progress slowly, allowing both of them to become accustomed to their unique ability to unite on an emotional level.

Deepening the kiss, exploring her mouth with his tongue, encouraging her to reciprocate, Sam unbuttoned her dress. Slipping his hands inside, he caressed her shoulders, easing her dress apart. He ran a loving hand over her collarbone. Clutching his shoulders, she thrust her hips off the bed and rubbed herself against him. He nuzzled her neck, then kissed the swell of each breast rising over the lace cups of her bra. His big hands spanned her waist.

"Sam, I—I'm aching. I need… You need… We want…"

He unsnapped the front closure of her bra, peeled it off her high, round breasts and lowered his mouth to cover one beaded nipple. Jeannie cried out from the pleasure, the sheer sensual delight.

The ache grew more and more intense. The throbbing sensation pulsing through her robbed her of her breath. She gasped for air. Trembling, his own breathing ragged, Sam kissed her on the forehead and sat up, making sure he didn't touch her again.

She caught her breath. "Sam?"

"It was almost too much, wasn't it?" He stood up beside the bed. "You're going to be the death of me, Jeannie Alverson." Sam smiled. "I'm not used to waiting for what I want, but in your case, I have no choice."

"Do you think the wait will be worth it?"

Sam walked over to the door, opened it and paused. "Get some rest. I'll check on you later, and carry you down for lunch whenever you're hungry."

"Thank you for taking care of me."

"That's what I'm here for," he said, and closed the door behind him as he walked out into the hall.

He couldn't stay there, looking at her, wanting her, needing her, when she wasn't physically or emotionally strong enough to make love. She was worried that once they'd made love, he'd think the experience hadn't been worth the wait. Didn't she know, couldn't she sense, that just kissing her turned him inside out?

Oh, she knew, all right. She felt his fear, sensed his helplessness. And she'd said she understood. Did she? Did she really know that the thought of making love to her scared the hell out of him?

Chapter 7

Jeannie walked slowly over to where Sam stood looking through the long, narrow windows in the kitchen. Outside, the morning sunshine brightened the small garden and patio, which were surrounded by a privacy fence. She laid her hand on his back; he tensed immediately at her touch and stepped away from her.

Although he guarded her day and night, Sam had kept his distance—an emotional distance. Something had happened to him Sunday, something he didn't like in the least. Jeannie had indeed gotten inside him, had become a part of him. And he hated it!

Seeing her suffer Matthew's pain had hurt him deeply, reaching inside to touch a part of him that he hadn't even known existed. A part of him he didn't want to exist. Then, after they returned home and he kissed her again and caressed her intimately, he'd been forced to admit the truth to himself, the truth Jeannie already knew. She did make him feel helpless and afraid. Not only was Sam unaccustomed to those emotions, he hated them. Except for a few regrettable lapses, Sam was always in control, of himself and those around him. And although he had experienced fear on a few rare occasions, no woman had ever evoked that emotion within him. But then, he'd never known a woman like Jeannie Alverson.

"I feel I must do everything possible to defuse this situation before it gets any worse." Jeannie stood behind Sam, staring at his broad shoulders, her hand itching to touch his back again.

"You've already talked to him once, and all it did was incite him to condemn you as a witch." Sam opened the back door. "Do you honestly think talking to him again will change his mind?"

"It might," Jeannie said. "Besides, I can't see where it can do any harm."

Cursing under his breath, Sam stepped out onto the back porch, leaving Jeannie standing in the open doorway. She had asked Reverend Religious-Fanatic Reeves for a little private tête-à-tête today, in the hope she could convince him she wasn't evil. A lot of damned good it would do! From the preliminary reports Sam had received on Reeves, the man didn't know the meaning of the word *compromise.* He was completely unwavering in his narrow-minded beliefs, which were his own warped interpretation of the Bible.

Jeannie followed Sam outside onto the patio. "I've already issued the invitation. He'll be here soon."

"He's already here," Sam said. "In spirit, if not in the flesh. Just listen, and you'll hear Reeves's own brand of evil at work."

Listening, she heard a soft breeze waltzing through the huge live oaks that spanned the width of the Howell property in the backyard. She heard the chirping of birds, the hum of traffic, the muted song of the Gulf waters. And she heard the sound of marching feet on the pavement out front, and the combined voices of the Righteous Light brethren in a familiar chant. "Witch, witch... Witch, witch..."

Pinpricks of dread chilled her. For the past three days, ever since the newspapers had printed the story about her "Sunday miracle" in the Monday morning newspaper, Reeves's followers had picketed her house. Twice the police had been called to disperse the crowd, but each time the reverend's disciples had returned in larger numbers.

From her bedroom window this morning, Jeannie had counted over twenty men and women, of various ages and races, carrying signs and spouting condemnation of her as they trooped up and down the sidewalk in front of her home. It had been at that precise moment that she decided to offer an olive branch to Maynard Reeves. He had accepted her invitation quite readily, almost as if he'd been expecting her to telephone him.

Sam opposed the meeting, and she understood his reservations, especially since the police lab's report plainly stated the blood on Jeannie's gift Bible and bookmark had been human. Reeves posed a real threat to her. She hoped that by meeting with him she could change his mind about her, remove the threat or, at the very least, lessen the man's hatred of her.

"I don't want you to be upset with me." Jeannie wished Sam would look at her, but he kept his back to her. "I know I should have discussed my decision with you before I called Reverend Reeves and invited him over here this morning."

"Yeah, you should have discussed it with me. I would have told you the idea was insane, just like so many of your other ideas have been."

Jeannie leaned on her cane. Although she had recovered from Sunday, she was still weaker than normal. "I don't think it's insane to want to reach a peaceful settlement with—"

"With a man who isn't going to compromise, a man who truly believes that if you aren't on his side, then you're against him, and if you're against him, you're against God." Sam turned quickly, his steely blue-gray eyes focusing directly on Jeannie's face. "My gut instincts tell me to keep you as far away from him as possible."

"If this meeting fails, I promise to stay away from Reeves, to never contact him again." She took a tentative step in Sam's direction, never breaking eye contact as she held out one hand, using the other to steady her cane. "Tell me you aren't really angry with me, and that we have a deal."

Sam glared at her. Dammit! A sweet, loving angel shouldn't have such a wide stubborn streak in her. He'd never had half as much trouble controlling wilder, more worldly, self-centered women. But the only thing other women could give or take away from him had been sex. If sex was all there was between Jeannie and him, he wouldn't feel so uneasy. But things weren't that simple.

He looked at her hand. Don't touch her, he told himself. Every time he touched her, he wanted her, and she knew it. And every time he touched her, it gave her an excuse to try to get inside his head.

Clenching and unclenching his hands repeatedly, Sam grunted. "After today, you stay out of harm's way. No more public appearances, no more invitations to the enemy. Do we have an agreement?"

"If I can't persuade Reverend Reeves to stop his persecution of me, then yes, no more public appearances." Jeannie sucked in air between her clenched teeth, then bit down on her bottom lip. "Except—"

"No exceptions!"

"Just one," she said. "I'm already obligated for tomorrow night. It's a private affair. Practically everyone there will be an old family acquaintance, many of them members of Julian's Fleur-de-lis Society."

"What are you talking about? What private affair? And what on earth is this Fleur-de-lis society?"

"The owner of the *Royale Belle* Casino has offered the riverboat for a charity night this Friday. All the proceeds from the invited guests' gambling losses will go directly to the Howell School."

While Sam listened to her explanation, Jeannie moved closer to him, taking one cautious step at a time. Her protector could be a bear at times, ferocious and growling. She'd learned to approach him slowly, gentling him gradually.

"There will be a dinner, followed by dancing and gambling." Jeannie stood beside Sam, only inches separating their bodies. "I'm the cochairman of this function. I have to be there." She raised her face, looking at him with her most pleading expression. "The Fleur-de-lis Society consists of descendants of the old French families who settled Biloxi. Julian's grandmothers were from two of the most prestigious families in this area."

"I see." A person's lineage had never impressed Sam. What the hell difference did it make who your great-great-grandfather had been? If you weren't in line for the throne of England, he couldn't see how your ancestry had any bearing on your life.

"After tomorrow night, I'll follow your rules and regulations, whether or not I agree with them." Jeannie lifted her hand, intending to caress Sam's stern face. He grabbed her hand in midair, manacling her wrist.

A current of awareness passed between them. Sam's stomach tightened; Jeannie shivered.

"Can't you control it?" Tugging on her slender wrist, he pulled her close, her breasts grazing his chest. "Can't you turn it off, keep it from happening?"

"It isn't just me, you know," she said. "It's you, too. It's both of us. That's what makes it so powerful. You're beginning to experience tiny little sparks of what I'm feeling."

He dropped her wrist, as if touching her flesh had burned him. He backed away from her. "I don't know what you're talking about."

"Yes, you do."

Ollie opened the back door, stuck out her head and called Jeannie's name. She turned to face the housekeeper. Sam moved in behind her, his big body forming a shadow of protection.

"That awful Maynard Reeves is at the front door. Says he's been invited." Ollie twisted her thin lips into a disapproving frown.

"Please show Reverend Reeves into the front parlor and offer him refreshments," Jeannie said.

"I'd like to offer him a cup of tea laced with arsenic," Ollie said.

Sam chuckled. Whipping her head around, Jeannie glared at him. "Nothing can be accomplished unless we treat Reverend Reeves as a welcome guest," she said.

"I'll go invite the black-hearted devil into the parlor." Grumbling to herself, Ollie slammed the back door.

Sam gripped Jeannie's shoulder. "I'm going to stay with you every minute that man is in this house."

"But, Sam, you'll intimidate Reverend Reeves and put him on guard. If the two of us are alone, he might be more at ease and willing to accept—"

"I hope I do intimidate Reeves. I hope I intimidate the hell out of him. I want him to know that the only way he's ever going to be able to hurt you is by going through me."

Jeannie felt it again, that wild, primeval, possessive need inside Sam, that powerful protective instinct that claimed his soul whenever any thoughts of her came to his mind. And the strange thing was, she realized, Sam had absolutely no control over the way he felt, and that made him hate his feelings and fight against them all the more.

Knowing Sam would never agree to leave her alone with Maynard Reeves, she complied with his demand. "All right, Sam. I understand. You'll stay in the room with us. But, please, let me do all the talking."

"We'll see," Sam said.

When Sam and Jeannie walked into the hallway leading to the front parlor, they saw Ollie, hands on her hips, standing at the open front door, shaking her head. Then they heard Reeves's singsong, pulpitarian voice as he addressed the crowd. The man stood on the front veranda, facing his entranced followers, who stood at rapt attention on the sidewalk. Maynard Reeves had cultivated a pure, clean-cut look with his neat, well-tailored black suit and white shirt, his short sandy hair, and the silver cross he wore around his neck.

"I give you my solemn vow that I will be on guard during my exchange with the devil's daughter," Reeves shouted, his voice deep and clear. "And I will report back to you, my faithful brethren, on whether or not I was able to win back her soul from the evil one."

"Report back to the press, you mean, you scalawag preacher," Ollie mumbled, loud enough for Sam and Jeannie to hear her.

"You don't need to witness this spectacle." Sam tugged on Jeannie's arm. "Wait for him in the parlor. I'll personally escort the good reverend to you."

"Now, Sam, this is supposed to be a friendly meeting."

"Yeah, sure. You can't get much friendlier than soul-saving, can you?"

"Don't be sacrilegious."

"I'm not the one making a mockery of everything holy."

Jeannie nodded in agreement, admitting Sam was right. "I'll wait in the parlor."

Reeves continued his unholy message of hate. Sam laid his big hand on Reeves's shoulder; the man shuddered, then froze on the spot, halting his speech in midsentence.

"Ms. Alverson is waiting to see you," Sam said.

"I shall be with you momentarily, sir. I will not be summoned before I'm prepared. I need a moment of prayer before facing the powers of darkness."

Dropping his hand from Reeves's shoulder, Sam lowered his voice to a deadly whisper. "You're going to need more than a prayer if you keep Ms. Alverson waiting one more minute to continue this sideshow of yours."

Raising his arms in the air dramatically, Reeves closed his eyes. "Pray for me, brothers and sisters. Pray for me."

When Reeves turned around, Sam stepped aside to allow him entrance into the foyer. The moment the two men entered the house, Ollie closed and locked the front door behind them.

"She's waiting for us in the front parlor." Sam nodded the direction. "The doors to the left."

Reeves hesitated outside the double panel doors, but didn't turn to face Sam. "Waiting for *us?*" he asked. "She led me to believe this would be a private meeting between the two of us."

"It will be." Sam slid open the panel doors. "I'm simply here to guard an angel while she tries to make peace with the devil."

Reeves gasped. His boyishly handsome face turned crimson beneath its dusting of freckles as he turned toward Sam. "How dare you!"

Sam looked at Jeannie's adversary; the man trembled. "Please, go right on in, Reverend. She's waiting for you."

Reeves obeyed instantly, entering the front parlor with the same caution he might have used in entering a den of lions. Before approaching Jeannie, who sat in a tapestry-upholstered rosewood chair, Reeves watched Sam Dundee take a protective stance across the room. Sam crossed his arms over his chest. Reeves glanced at Jeannie.

"Won't you please sit down, Reverend Reeves?" Jeannie glided her arm through the air, gesturing for her guest to sit across from her on the red velvet settee.

Reeves sat uneasily, perching on the edge of the Victorian sofa. "Little good will come of this meeting if I feel threatened." He dared a quick glance in Sam's direction.

Jeannie laughed. "You can't possibly be referring to Mr. Dundee."

Reeves jumped to his feet, obviously unnerved by her reaction. "I most certainly am. I came here in good faith, expecting a private audience with you."

"I have no secrets from Mr. Dundee. You see, he is my protector. His job is to make sure no harm comes to me. He isn't a threat to anyone, unless—"

"Yes, yes, I quite understand." Reeves sat down again, slowly, focusing his attention on Jeannie's smiling face. "When you called and asked to see me, I hoped that you'd changed your mind about joining my ministry. It isn't too late. All I have to do is go outside—" leaning toward Jeannie, Reeves lowered his voice "—and tell the Righteous Light brethren and the media that I fought the devil for your soul and won."

The urge to giggle would have overcome Jeannie if she hadn't been aware of the threat behind the reverend's offer. "But you haven't fought the devil for my soul, because my soul is my own, and my powers are not derived from any evil source."

"If you do not use your powers in his name, doing his work, then Satan controls you. There is much good you could do. You and I together could form a strong force to combat this sinful world."

Jeannie noticed the wild, glazed stare in Reeves's eyes, an almost otherworldly glimmer. Ripples of suspicion jangled her nerve endings.

In so many ways, Maynard Reeves reminded her of her stepfather, a man who had exploited her, never caring that his fanatical needs had condemned her to a living hell. She hated remembering those endless days and nights of pain from which she'd had no escape. Only in God's own good time and in his way had she been set free. She would never willingly be used to further an unscrupulous minister's career.

"I spent my childhood as the main attraction of my step-father's ministry."

"And you would be the crown jewel in mine!" Reeves rose from the settee, lifting his arms as if to beseech heaven. "There is nothing that we couldn't do—together!"

Jeannie knew there was only one way to discover the truth, to prove or disprove her suspicions. But how would Sam react? His interference could prove disastrous. She had to make him understand that he was not to interrupt her probe, not even if she appeared to be in danger.

She called out to Sam silently. He didn't try to block her entrance into his mind, because he hadn't been expecting it. She glanced across the room at him; he gave her a quizzical look. Why wouldn't he open his mind and allow her to connect with him? If only he would admit that a telepathic link existed between them, it would be so easy.

I'm going to connect with Reverend Reeves, Jeannie told Sam telepathically, hoping he would open his mind to her.

Sam clenched his teeth. A muscle in his jaw twitched. He uncrossed his arms, lowered them to his sides, and knotted his hands into tight fists. He wouldn't listen to her. He had to shut her out once again.

Jeannie lifted her cane, braced the tip on the floor and rose from her chair. "Reverend Reeves, you understand all about possessing special powers, don't you?"

Spreading his arms in a circular motion as he brought them downward, Reeves stepped back, his legs bumping into the edge of the settee. "I know that there are powers from the devil and powers from God, and that those from the devil must be destroyed and those from God must be cultivated and used in his service."

Seemingly spellbound, Reeves watched her walk slowly toward him. He didn't so much as flinch when she reached out and touched him.

Jeannie held his hand with a strong but gentle clasp. Within seconds, she sensed a subdued energy pulsating weakly inside him. Gradually the sensations grew stronger, and the transference began in earnest. Fear. Pain. Anger. So much anger.

Sam moved inward from the far wall, stopping a few feet behind Reeves. She could not relay a telepathic message to Sam as long as she was connected to Reeves, and she dared not break the tenuous bond she had just formed.

Closing her eyes, Jeannie blocked out the world around her and concentrated on Maynard Reeves's emotions, on the haunted thoughts and painful memories swirling around in his mind. She sensed him trying to pull away, trying to break their link. But he was powerless against Jeannie's determination.

Sensing Maynard's fear, Jeannie connected to the memories he was recalling. *Don't whip me again. Please, Mama, don't. I promise I'll never do it again. I'll be good.*

She felt the pain, the child's pain that had twisted and festered and rotted within Maynard Reeves.

She saw the blood dripping from welts on the little boy's buttocks. *No, Daddy. I'm sorry. I don't want the mean old devil inside me. I'll make him go away. I'll never use his evil powers again.*

Anger. He would rid the world of Satan's magic, the way his parents had beaten it out of him. But a residue of that power remained inside him. Nothing he did could make it go away. But no one knew. No one must ever know that, sometimes, he used the power. And sometimes he prayed for more.

Jeannie swayed on her feet as she slowly, patiently, drew the fear and pain and anger from Maynard Reeves's alter ego, a frightened and badly abused little boy. The pain was no longer physical, but a deep psychological hurt that tormented Reeves. Poor, poor little boy. Swaying unsteadily, Jeannie gripped her cane, then drew in deep, gasping breaths. Tears welled up in her eyes. Through the mist of her pain—sad, pitiful little Maynard's pain—she heard Sam moving closer. Not yet, she tried to tell him. Almost. Please wait. But she knew he hadn't heard her.

Sam grabbed Reeves by the back of his neck, jerking him away from Jeannie, tossing him down on the floor. Reeves cried out, covering his head, as if to protect himself from an expected blow.

Jeannie could no longer brace her weak legs with the aid of her cane. Her knees buckled, but before she slumped to the floor, Sam lifted her into his arms. She felt the strength that held her safely in its embrace, and knew nothing could harm her. The pain would pass, but it would take time to make its way through her mind, through her body, through her heart, before shattering into nothingness within her soul.

Reeves rose from the floor into a crouch, looking wild-eyed and frightened, like a cornered animal. "My God! My God! Her power is strong, so strong. I could feel her draining my very soul out of me."

"You're out of your mind!" Sam didn't even look down at Reeves as he walked out of the parlor with Jeannie in his arms.

"Only a witch could possess such powers." Reeves stood, his legs trembling, his hands shaking. "Only Satan's child."

Sam ignored the man, his only thoughts of Jeannie's comfort and safety. "Ollie! Ollie!" He stopped at the foot of the stairs when Ollie Tyner came bustling down the hallway.

"What's wrong?" Seeing Jeannie in Sam's arms, Ollie gave Reeves a condemning stare. "What's he done to her?"

"Show Reverend Reeves to the door, Ollie," Sam said.

"Gladly." Flinging open the front door, Ollie planted her hand on her hip and waited for Reeves to depart.

"Thou shalt not suffer a witch to live!" Reeves shouted as he entered the foyer, his face suffused with color, his eyes glazed over with a rage born of realization.

"Get out of here!" Sam tilted his head just a fraction, just enough to glare at Reeves, giving the other man the full impact of his killer stare.

Standing in the open doorway leading to the porch, Reeves pointed an accusatory finger at Sam. "You protect the devil's daughter. When God destroys her, he will smite you down, also."

Ollie slammed the door on Reverend Reeves, hitting him squarely in the rear end. Swiping the palms of her hands together, she smiled. "Good riddance to bad rubbish."

"Activate the alarm system," Sam said. "We don't want any snakes trying to crawl back into the house. I'm taking Jeannie to her room."

"I'll bring her up some tea in a bit." Ollie shook her head sadly. "When she comes out of it, she'll be thirsty."

Sam nodded his agreement, then carried Jeannie upstairs and laid her on her bed. She clung to him, refusing to release her hold around his neck. Sitting down on the bed, with his back braced against the headboard, he lifted her onto his lap. She cuddled against him.

"Sam?" Her voice was weak, breathless.

"I'm here."

"Reeves . . . Reeves is . . ." She didn't have the strength to speak.

"Hush. It's all right. He's gone, and I'll never let him get close enough to touch you. Not ever again." Sam held her close, wishing that he could somehow absorb the aftershocks of pain hitting her now.

She lay quietly, her breathing gradually returning to normal as the color reappeared in her face. Sam stroked her back, soothing her, longing to give her his strength.

She opened her eyes and looked up at him. "I'm all right. Don't worry so."

"Don't talk. Just rest." He caressed her face with his fingertips, each touch filled with deep concern.

"Reeves was psychic as a child," she said.

"What?"

"His powers are very limited, but they do still exist."

"You tapped into those powers? Is that what happened?"

"Partly." Lifting her head off Sam's shoulder, she stared him directly in the eye. "Only his parents knew about his abilities, and they beat him severely anytime he used them. They—"

"Shh...shh... You're overexerting yourself." He placed his right index finger over her lips.

Jeannie covered his hand with hers and pulled it away from her face. "His parents thought little Maynard had received his psychic powers from the devil. They abused him unmercifully. There is so much pain and anger and fear inside him. I had just tapped into those emotions and had begun to drain them when you broke our connection."

"I'm sorry, but I can't waste my time worrying about what happened to Reeves when he was a child, what psychological damage his parents caused that turned him into a lunatic."

Jeannie squeezed Sam's hand. "He sees me as a threat, now more so than before. I know his secret. I know that he believes, despite all that he's done and everything his parents did, that the devil still occasionally works through him."

"What are you not telling me?" Sam lifted her hand to his lips.

"He was willing to join forces with me, had I been agreeable. He knows that I know he was willing to sell his soul to the devil in order to share my power." Jeannie took a deep, cleansing breath, releasing all the residue of Reeves's emotions. "He cannot allow me to live. He sees me as an evil threat, a seducer with the devil's own power."

Sam buried his lips in Jeannie's open palm, then grabbed her into his arms, holding her with fierce protectiveness. "I'll never let him near you again. Whatever it takes, I'll keep you safe."

"Yes, Sam. I know you'll guard me with your life."

"Damn right about that!"

Chapter 8

Stepping aboard the *Royal Belle* was like entering another world. Nineteenth-century charm and lavish elegance combined with the glitter and excitement of Las Vegas. The gambling casino, docked just off the Biloxi shore, was a security problem. Public access gave anyone the opportunity to come and go as they pleased. A quick and unobserved getaway would be simple—drive out of the parking lot and onto Beach Boulevard or escape by private boat. It would be easy to get lost in the horde of tourists who flooded the area from daylight to dark.

Three decks high, gaming on two levels and a restaurant-lounge on the third, the floating palace was ideal for a society charity function. Although two levels had been secured for the private affair, the bottom level of the riverboat remained open to the public, which meant it was possible for an uninvited guest to slip by security.

When Sam had been unable to dissuade Jeannie from attending this black-tie affair, he'd asked Rufus Painter to the Howell home for a private meeting. Painter agreed with Sam's opinion of Maynard Reeves as a fanatic, with the potential to become violent, but since the man stayed just within the law, Painter's hands were tied. Sam understood the officer's limitations. Before the police could do anything about Reeves, they needed some sort of proof that the man had broken the law.

Sam had stayed on the right side of the law all his life. He'd done a stint in the marines before college, and then joined the Drug Enforcement Administration. And since starting his own private security agency, he had, for the most part, adhered to government rules and regulations.

But to keep Jeannie Alverson safe, he was willing to do anything, and if that meant breaking a few rules, Sam wasn't about to lose any sleep over it. Yeah, he and Painter understood each other. They both had jobs to do; they were just bound by slightly different codes of conduct.

Yesterday, he'd had J.T. send down a couple of Dundee Private Security's newest recruits. He'd told J.T. the two-day stint would give the men some experience in the field and allow him to evaluate their performance. He knew J.T. didn't buy the excuse, but he was too good a friend to ask questions, even after Sam told him the agency would cover the cost.

Gabriel Hawk, a former CIA agent, and Morgan Kane, once a navy SEAL, hardly needed any field experience. Sam had evaluated their records thoroughly before bringing them into the business to replace two of his best men. Ashe McLaughlin wouldn't be returning. He had married his childhood best friend and decided to move back home and begin a new life. And Simon Roarke, who'd been severely wounded in the line of duty, needed several months to recover.

Upon their arrival from the airport yesterday morning, Sam had left Hawk at the Howell home to guard Jeannie while he and Kane checked out the *Royal Belle*.

Even with his own men assisting the private security provided by the *Royal Belle,* Sam felt uneasy. He had halfway expected to find a troop of Righteous Light brethren picketing the casino, but to his great relief, there hadn't been a sign of Reeves or his followers. Sam wasn't so sure that was a good sign. He'd much rather have these people out in the open than sneaking around in dark corners.

* * *

Constantly vigilant, Sam repeatedly scanned the room, which was filled with the Mississippi Gulf's elite, along with visitors from Mobile and New Orleans. Many of the people who belonged to Julian Howell's social circle, though cordial and nauseatingly polite to Jeannie, had watched her every move for the past hour during dinner. What the hell were they expecting? That she'd sprout wings and fly? Or cast a spell over the whole room? Unfortunately, there had been one dear old lady who, despite her breeding and sophistication, had been unable to refrain from requesting that Jeannie heal her spastic colon.

Julian rose from his chair, held out his hand to Marta McCorkle and asked her to dance. The warmth of her smile softened the age lines around her eyes and mouth, making her appear years younger than sixty.

Sam noticed the way Jeannie watched the couples on the dance floor and couldn't help wondering if she had ever danced.

"Would you like to go downstairs and play the slot machines?" Sam asked.

"Not yet," she said. "I haven't finished my dessert." Lifting her spoon, she dipped into the chocolate mousse.

Sam concentrated on Jeannie's mouth. Full. Soft. A warm peach color. And so inviting. She ate the spoonful of mousse, then unconsciously licked her bottom lip. Sam swallowed, thinking of how her tongue had felt, mating with his, sampling his taste.

His gaze moved over her face, across her nose and her delicately tinted cheeks to her expressive brown eyes. When she smiled at him, her eyes smiled, too. Her pale eyes were almost identical in color to her beige-streaked ash brown hair.

Sam tried to return her smile, but somehow he had never perfected the art of smiling. Without opening his mouth, he curved his lips slightly. His niece Elizabeth had told him he needed to smile more, that he most certainly needed to laugh occasionally. And sometimes, with Elizabeth, he had.

"Everything's just perfect, isn't it?" Jeannie reached across the table, laying her hand flat, her palm open, gesturing for him to respond. "The weather is wonderful, not too hot, even for August. The casino is lovely, and everyone is having a good time."

Julian and Marta had kept a steady stream of conversation going during dinner, but Jeannie had been very quiet. He had noticed she wasn't prone to idle chitchat and that suited him fine. What didn't suit him was the way she kept getting inside his head. He had felt her probing a couple of times and had blocked her entrance. They were alone at the table now. If she had something to say to him, she could use the normal means of communication.

"Are you having a good time?" he asked, glancing at her hand, wanting to cover it with his. But if he touched her, she would connect with him. She would feel what he felt. And he'd be powerless to stop her.

"I'm pleased that we've had such a good turnout. If this function brings in a lot of money for the Howell School, Mr. VanDevere, the CEO of the company that owns the *Royal Belle,* has agreed to make it an annual affair."

Sam followed Jeannie's gaze to the dance floor, to Marta in Julian's arms. The older couple were gliding smoothly in a slow two-step.

Sam glanced down at Jeannie's hand again. She curled her fingers, relaxed them, curled them, relaxed them, signaling him to touch her. "How long have Julian and Marta been dating?"

"For several years. They've known each other since they were children. Julian and Miriam were close friends with Marta and her husband, who died a year after Miriam."

"Julian told me before we left the house that he wouldn't be coming home until morning." Sam watched her face for a reaction. "He said that you'd know where to reach him."

"He and Marta have been lovers for about a year now." Jeannie's smile widened. A sigh of humming laughter vibrated from her throat. "You aren't surprised, are you?"

"No. Besides, it's none of my business." He wished she'd take her hand away; the temptation to accept her invitation overpowered his common sense.

He laid his hand in hers. She grasped it gently. He repeated the gesture. Sam stared directly into her compelling brown eyes and knew he'd have a hell of a time denying this woman anything. Just as a tingle of awareness passed between Jeannie and Sam, Hawk tapped him on the shoulder.

Sam released Jeannie's hand, scooted back his chair and stood. He stepped away from the table, making sure Jeannie couldn't overhear his conversation. ''What's wrong?''

''Maynard Reeves just arrived with a lady named Danette Suddath.'' Hawk inclined his head to the left.

Sam scanned the area to their left, catching a glimpse of Reeves's sandy hair, gleaming in the muted lounge light. Swearing under his breath, he grabbed Hawk by the arm. ''Why the hell did the guards let him in here?''

''The lady has an invitation, and he's her guest,'' Hawk said. ''Kane is making a phone call to check on this Suddath woman, but she acts like she belongs here. She's spoken to several people, calling them by their first names.''

''Reeves is a strong antigambling advocate.'' Sam repeatedly clenched and unclenched his hands. ''I wonder how he'll justify socializing in this den of iniquity.''

''I'll keep tabs on Reeves,'' Hawk assured Sam. ''And as soon as Kane gets any information on the woman, I'll let you know.''

''I don't want Reeves here, but there seems to be nothing we can do at the moment.''

Turning around in her seat, Jeannie called out to Sam. ''Is something wrong? Is there some problem I should know about?''

''Make sure he doesn't come anywhere near her,'' Sam told Hawk. ''Stop him before I have to.''

Hawk nodded, then made his way across the room, heading directly to the lounge area. Sam held out his hand to Jeannie. Staring up at him, she gave him a quizzical look.

''No problems,'' he lied, and wondered how long it would take her to realize the truth. ''Hawk was just checking in with me.'' Sam wiggled his fingers. ''Come on, Jeannie, dance with me.''

He saw the warm, glowing light in her eyes die. Dammit! Had she already seen through his lie? Was she aware of Reeves's presence?

"I—I don't dance," she said.

"What?"

"I don't dance, because of my legs." She bowed her head deliberately, to avoid looking at Sam. "You know I can't walk without my cane. I can't dance. I'd only make a spectacle of myself if I tried."

"Have you ever tried?"

"Once, when I was a teenager. Miriam tried to teach me, but we soon realized it was hopeless. I'm not able to move without bracing myself with my cane."

Sam lifted her walking stick and handed it to her. "How about a stroll around the deck instead?"

Raising her head, she nodded agreement, a flicker of a smile forming on her lips. She stood, supporting herself with her cane, and took Sam's hand. He slipped his arm around her waist and led her away from the lounge area and out onto the open deck of the riverboat.

It was not quite eight-thirty, and the sun had just set. The summer twilight spread gold across the sky, gilding the clouds, as the aureate Gulf waters rhythmically bathed the tawny shore. The evening breeze, pleasant and soothing, caressed Jeannie's hair; several loose tendrils blew across her cheeks.

They walked the length of the deck, reaching a secluded corner. The music from the live band echoed on the wind and water. Sam slowed their walk, then halted. Jeannie glanced up at him.

"Are you going to tell me why you rushed me outside so quickly?" she asked, sensing the tension in Sam's big body, knowing from merely touching him that he was concerned about something.

Tightening his hold around her waist, he turned her to face him. He lifted her left hand, placing it on his shoulder. "Hold on tight," he said, then took her cane out of her hand. Gasping loudly, she grabbed his other shoulder with her right hand. He hung her cane on the deck rail.

"What are you doing?"

"We're going to dance. I'll support you securely in my arms. Trust me. You can dance. You can dance with me."

"Sam, no, I—"

"No one can see us. We're all alone out here."

"I can't. I—"

"Kick off your shoes, then lift your left foot and put it on top of mine," he told her.

"What?"

"Don't ask questions. Just do as I say."

She obeyed his command, stepping out of her shoes and placing her left foot on top of his. "I don't see how my stepping on your feet is going to—"

"Haven't you ever seen little girls dancing with their fathers?"

"You can't mean . . ."

"Put your right foot on mine. We're going to dance."

"I'm not a little girl. I'm a grown woman. And I'm not light as a feather."

"I'm a big man, with big feet," he said. "And you're a small woman, with small feet. You'll feel as light as a feather to me."

Slowly, reluctantly, she lifted her right foot and placed it atop his. The moment the deed was completed, Sam moved, cautiously, without any sense of rhythm at first, allowing Jeannie a few moments to adjust to the new and unusual sensation of someone else actually walking for her. And that was all Sam did for a while, simply walked her backward and forward. With her arms draped around his neck, her body pressed intimately against his, she gradually relinquished all control to Sam. Her trust in him was that great.

"See how easy it is when you do what I tell you to do?"

She jerked her head up, glaring at him, but when he smiled, she smiled, too, unable to resist the magnetism of his smile. No wonder he didn't do it often, or so completely. His smile was devastating.

"You like being right, don't you?" Laying her head on his chest, she cuddled closer, and was pleased when she heard his indrawn breath.

"Yeah, I like being right." With one hand still bracing her back, he eased his other hand downward, from her waist to the curve of her buttocks.

The romantic strains of "I Love How You Love Me" floated on the night air, strings and brass blending into a sweet harmony. Sam moved his big body to the soft, slow melody, encompassing Jeannie in his embrace as he carried her across the deck, her small feet welded atop his much larger ones. Their bodies swayed in perfect unison, in tune with each other and the flow of the music.

She closed her eyes, absorbing the beauty of the moment, allowing herself to enjoy the pleasure of dancing and the joy of being in Sam Dundee's strong arms. She had never known anything like this incredible sensation. Dancing. Dancing in Sam's arms. Gliding across the floor as if she had wings on her feet.

Opening her eyes, she glanced over Sam's shoulder and saw the pale form of the moon, the darkening sky and the first glimmer of a twinkling star. She tilted her head.

Sam looked down at her. She smiled at him. Lowering his head, he rubbed his cheek against hers.

"Thank you," she said, then closed her eyes again, sighing, wishing this moment could last forever. Sam had given her this gift. Dancing in the moonlight.

She could not imagine any woman not wanting to be in Sam Dundee's arms. He was so incredibly handsome, so big and powerful. So absolutely debonair in his black tux and unadorned white shirt. In the pale moonlight, his blond hair had turned to burnished flaxen silk, and his eyes had warmed to a smoldering slate blue.

As he waltzed her around the deck, Jeannie sensed the hazy glow she often felt just before connecting with another person's emotions. Then she felt the tiny electrical currents of awareness that came when she began picking up signals from within the other person. She could block these feelings if she tried hard enough, if she ended the physical contact. But this was Sam, unguarded and receptive. How could she not take the opportunity to share what he was feeling?

Jeannie. Sweet Jeannie. She was the very embodiment of femininity, of a woman's loving, nurturing nature. Her generous heart exposed her to the pain of others, and her healing touch absorbed that pain. How unfair life was, that a woman this gentle and kind had the ability to suffer the most excruciating pain for others, even healing them on a temporary basis, and yet was unable to ease her own pain, either physical or emotional.

Sam ran his hand over her buttocks, savoring the feel of the light peach silk covering her body. Pressing her against him, into his arousal, he kissed the top of her head. She sighed.

He wanted to take her mouth, to lift her in his arms and carry her away, to bury himself deep within her body. And he wanted her to know exactly how he felt. Slowing his movements, he danced her back against the wooden surface of the outer wall. She made no protest, verbally or telepathically. Indeed, she welcomed him, clinging to him, sending him a silent message of acceptance.

Lifting her off his feet, anchoring her between his hard body and the wall, supporting her with his arms, Sam circled her lips with the tip of his tongue. Her moist lips opened, issuing him an invitation. On the verge of losing his reason, he kissed her. She returned the kiss, enticing him with her body and her mind. He read her clearly, and knew she understood precisely what he wanted from her.

Her kisses were pure sweet fire, burning him in their intensity. Throwing caution to the wind, he devoured her, thrusting his tongue into her mouth, gripping her buttocks, straining against her. She clung to him, joining fully in the savagery of his kiss, returning full measure the heat of his passion.

He knew that she felt what he felt, wanted what he wanted. And in a sudden, blinding flash of realization, Sam sensed her physical yearning and her emotional desires. My God, it wasn't possible! He couldn't have actually tapped into her feelings.

The pleasure for both of them intensified, building higher and higher as they kissed and touched, their bodies undulating to the sensuous beat of primeval mating. He wanted to rip her clothes off her body and take her, here, now, with no thought of the consequences.

He had to stop, or there would be no turning back. He ended the kiss, his breathing ragged, his face and hands damp with sweat. Jeannie pressed her face against his shoulder.

"Oh, Sam . . . Sam . . ."

He eased her slowly to her feet, slipped his arm around her and held her close. He could feel the rapid beat of her heart. When she tried to comfort him by taking some of his throbbing need into her own body, he stopped her, knowing she ached with the same painful desire that racked him from head to toe.

"I can handle it," he said. "I may not be as strong as you are, angel, but I'll survive until—" he cupped the back of her head in his big hand "—until you take away this sweet ache when we make love."

"Tonight," she whispered, not knowing where his desire ended and hers began.

"Tonight," he agreed, kissing her again, but ending the kiss quickly. "Come on, Jeannie, dance with me again."

"Oh, yes, Sam, I'd like that. I'd like that very much."

With her arms draped around his neck and her feet atop his, Jeannie surrendered herself to the sensual pleasure of dancing with Sam. He glided her across the deck, the soft evening breeze caressing their bodies as the twilight shadows surrounded them.

Glancing over Jeannie's shoulder, Sam saw Hawk standing in the doorway. Hawk nodded, then returned inside the restaurant. Quickly Sam checked his watch. They'd been on deck nearly an hour; it was time for Hawk to report in. Was Reeves still aboard the *Royal Belle?* Sam wondered, still trying to figure out why the reverend had made an appearance tonight. There was something not quite right about Reeves showing up at this charity function.

Feeling the sudden jolt of unease that hit him in the stomach, Jeannie looked at him, willing him to explain. He walked her to the deck's rail, removed her cane and placed it in her hand. Bending on one knee, he lifted her foot and slipped on her shoe, then repeated the process with her other foot.

He started walking them around the deck, but she halted, and he had little choice but to stop. Trying to block his emotions so that she couldn't pick up on them, Sam refused to look at her.

"What's the problem?" she asked. "What do you not want me to know?"

"There's no problem. I've got everything under control. Enjoy the evening, and don't worry." There was no need for her to know that Maynard Reeves was on board the *Royal Belle*. Hawk and Kane would follow orders and keep the man away from Jeannie.

She knew Sam wasn't going to tell her what was bothering him. She appreciated his wanting to protect her from any unpleasantness, but at the same time, she resented his treating her as if she were made of spun glass, some fragile, easily broken doll. With an unexpected flash of clarity, she heard the words *fragile angel,* and knew she'd read Sam's thoughts, without his knowledge.

He brushed the side of her face with the back of his hand, caressing her tenderly. "How long do you have to stay at this function in order to be socially correct?"

"I need to make an appearance in the gaming room." There was no point in pressing him about whatever was bothering him. Sooner or later, even if he chose not to share it with her, she would sense it. "We can play the slot machines or try the blackjack table. It doesn't matter, as long as I lose some money to set an example for the other guests."

"I suppose knowing their losses are going to a worthy cause will make losing a little easier."

Leading her inside to the restaurant level, Sam glanced toward the lounge. No sight of Maynard Reeves or Hawk, but Kane was headed in Sam's direction.

"I need to speak to Kane," Sam said. "Would you mind waiting back at the table for a few minutes?"

"All right." She patted him on the arm. "It's only a couple of yards away. I can walk over there without your help."

Acting as if he hadn't heard her, Sam escorted her to their table and seated her, then turned around and met his agent. Pulling Kane aside, making sure Jeannie couldn't overhear their conversation, Sam placed his hand on the other man's shoulder.

"Where's Reeves?"

"Hawk followed him and his lady friend downstairs into the gaming room," Kane said.

"Did you get any information on the woman?"

"She's an invited guest, a widow whose husband left her millions."

"Any idea what her connection is to Reeves?" Sam was aware of how charming Reeves might be to a lonely widow with plenty of money in the bank and the right social connections.

"She's a new convert to his Righteous Light Church." Kane hesitated, drew in a deep breath and looked Sam straight in the eye. "She has a daughter who's a student at the Howell School."

"Damn!"

"I've got a bad feeling about this, Sam. After your briefing on the situation, my instincts tell me Reeves has some sick reason for being here tonight."

"Yeah, my instincts tell me the same thing. But he hasn't tried to approach Jeannie. He hasn't even made a scene by preaching against the sins of gambling, when I know for a fact that he's given the casino owners hell for the past few years."

"There's something going on we don't know about."

"Go down and tell Hawk not to let Reeves out of his sight. I'll have to bring Jeannie downstairs. Even if I can't keep her from seeing him, I can make sure he doesn't come near her."

Nodding his agreement, Kane headed straight for the exit. Sam walked over to Jeannie, helped her to her feet and escorted her to the elevator.

They entered the elaborately decorated gaming room, which was crowded with the cream of Mississippi Gulf society. Sam spotted Hawk's black ponytail, then saw Maynard Reeves and his date standing a few feet to the agent's right, with colas in their hands, observing the gamblers.

Jeannie followed Sam's line of vision. Her muscles tensed, freezing her to the spot, the moment she saw Maynard Reeves. "That's what you didn't want me to know, isn't it?"

"He's not going to bother you. I promise." Sam squeezed her hand.

"How did he—? I don't believe it," she said. "He's with Danette Suddath. Her daughter Missy is a student at the Howell School. I've known Danette socially for years."

"She's a new convert to the Righteous Light Church," Sam told her.

"He's taking advantage of her." Jeannie gripped her cane fiercely. "She's lonely and insecure, and trying to raise a Down's syndrome child alone. There's no telling what sort of lies that snake has told her."

"Danette Suddath isn't my concern," Sam said. "It's not that he's used her to get into this private party tonight that worries me, but why he's here."

"I can find out." She took a step away from Sam.

He held her back. "No!" He hissed the word between clenched teeth.

"Tell me that you don't feel the danger. It's all around us. There's something terribly wrong, and you know it as well as I do."

"Don't try to play mind games with Reeves," Sam said. "If anyone's powers come from the devil, I'd say his do."

"His psychic powers are limited, and very weak. I'm far stronger than he is." She noticed the skeptical frown on Sam's face. "Comparatively speaking, Reverend Reeves is a little squall and I'm a full-fledged hurricane."

"Well, Ms. Hurricane, you aren't going to—"

"I can do it from across the room, from where I'm standing now, but it would be easier if I were close enough to touch him. I can sense feelings and emotions without touching, but the sensations are usually very faint, too weak for me to completely connect with the person."

"No." He didn't give a damn about her ability to sense Reeves's emotions, and thus discern the reason he'd suckered some poor woman into bringing him here tonight. He wasn't going to let Jeannie anywhere near that lunatic.

She wouldn't argue with Sam now, Jeannie decided. She'd bide her time and figure out some way of getting closer to Maynard Reeves.

"Let's join Julian and Marta at the craps table." Jeannie waved at her foster father, who smiled and returned her wave.

Sam watched while Jeannie won a thousand dollars at craps, then methodically lost two thousand. While he kept a close eye on her, he occasionally sought out Hawk, knowing Reeves would be within spitting distance. The good reverend and his date circled the gaming room slowly, Reeves smiling and laughing and flirting with the widow.

"I think we'll call it a night," Julian said, bending to kiss Jeannie on the cheek. "It's nearly eleven. Time for a man my age to be going to bed."

"See you tomorrow." Jeannie waved goodbye as the older couple left.

Ten minutes later, Sam escorted Jeannie to the ladies' room. Waiting outside impatiently, he noticed Hawk following Reeves and his date, who were coming in Sam's direction. His muscles tightened. His nerves came to full alert. When Reeves was within three feet of him, Sam stepped forward, but the other man ignored him, turning in the opposite direction, heading toward the doors leading out on deck. At that precise moment, Jeannie ventured out of the rest room. Sam stepped in front of her.

She walked around Sam and reached out, just grazing Reeve's sleeve before Sam grabbed her hand. Reeves jerked around, his gaze focusing on Jeannie as a wide smile spread across his face.

"Good evening, Jeannie," Reeves said. "What more appropriate place to find Satan's daughter than in one of his houses of sin?"

"Reeves, I'm warning you..." Sam said.

Reeves glanced behind him to where Hawk stood, then laughed aloud. "A host of fallen angels guarding the master's offspring. How appropriate."

"Danette, what are you doing with Maynard Reeves?" Jeannie asked.

Danette Suddath gasped, apparently startled by Jeannie's question. "Don't speak to me, you witch. Reverend Reeves has warned us all about your evil powers. If you ever return to the Howell School, I'll withdraw Missy immediately."

"Danette, how can you believe—" Jeannie reached out her hand "—this man's lies? You've known me for years."

Danette lifted her hand as if she intended to touch Jeannie, but Reeves slapped Danette's hand away, and when he did, Jeannie grasped his hand, threading her fingers through his. For a split second, he froze, fear etched on his face.

She sensed his anger and his hatred. Such cruel, ugly hatred. And a thirst for retribution.

Tonight they will die. All of these sinners will reap what they've sown. And the witch will burn with them. The flames will wipe them from the face of the earth and cleanse us of their evil.

Reeves jerked his hand away at the same moment Sam grabbed Jeannie. Hawk closed in, gripping the reverend by the shoulder. Reeves pulled out of Hawk's grasp. He whispered something to Danette Suddath, and the two of them rushed out the door.

"Let them go," Sam said.

"No!" Jeannie cried. "Stop Maynard Reeves!"

Sensing her need for him, Sam turned just as she swayed toward him and dropped her cane to the floor. He caught her in his arms. "Jeannie?"

Gripping the lapels of his tuxedo, she gazed up at Sam. He recognized the fear in her eyes. "What's wrong? You picked up something from his emotions when you touched him, didn't you?"

Jeannie gasped for air, the hatred and anger she had tapped into when she connected with Maynard Reeves still swirling around inside her. "Get everyone out... Get them off... now... Something's wrong. He—he's going to destroy this riverboat, and everyone on board."

Chapter 9

Sam lifted Jeannie into his arms, then turned to Hawk. "Contact Kane immediately. The two of you work with security to evacuate the casino."

"What the hell do I tell the security chief?" Hawk asked.

"Tell him—" Sam said.

"Fire. Flames. Destruction." Jeannie spoke the words as if reciting a chant.

"A bomb?" Hawk asked.

"Yeah." Sam nodded. "That would be my guess."

Hawk removed his small cellular phone from his jacket, speaking to Kane as he walked to the elevator with Sam and Jeannie. Redialing the phone, he spoke quickly, issuing orders. Returning the phone to his pocket, he held the elevator door.

"Kane's on his way to look for Reeves, and I've alerted the casino's security chief to the situation. I'll start evacuating this level as soon as I have a couple of men up here to help me keep everyone in line. Once this thing gets under way, more than one person is bound to panic."

"Sam?" Jeannie's voice was a little stronger, but she could barely open her eyes.

"I'm getting you out of here now," he said.

"Tell them ... Hurry. Soon, I think. Soon."

Hawk looked at Sam, who nodded. Hawk stepped back, the elevator door closed, and Sam drew Jeannie closer to his body as she cuddled against him. When they reached the bottom level of the *Royal Belle,* Sam noticed the security guards in a huddle. Hawk and Kane weren't wasting any time. Good. If Jeannie's instincts were correct, and he had no doubt they were, disaster could strike at any moment. If Reeves intended destroying the gambling casino's patrons en masse, Jeannie included, the most likely means would be a bomb, or several bombs, strategically placed.

Sam carried Jeannie out on deck, down the wide gangplank that connected the *Royal Belle* to the dock, and onto shore.

"There's Marta and Julian," Sam said. "They're in the parking lot. Julian sees us."

"Take me to him, please. I'll—I'll have to explain what's happening."

Before they reached Marta's Mercedes, Julian was hurrying toward them, his eyes wide and questioning. "What's wrong?"

"Reeves ..." Jeannie said. "I think he placed bombs on the riverboat."

"My God!" Julian touched Jeannie's cheek, his hand trembling, then looked at Sam. "You must get her away from here. And the casino must be evacuated."

"An evacuation is in the works as we speak." Sam lowered Jeannie to her feet, holding her close, bracing her against his body. "As soon as Kane apprehends Maynard Reeves, I'll send him with you and Marta to take Jeannie home."

"Sam?" Jeannie covered his hand with hers. He glanced at her and understood, without words, what she was asking.

"It could be dangerous if you stay here," he said.

"I can't leave. Not until everyone is safely onshore."

"If there is a bomb..." God, he hated the very thought of it. "Even if everyone gets out safely, once the bomb explodes, there's going to be a mad rush. You have no idea what the scene of a bombing looks like. And if people are hurt, you're going to want to help them. I can't let you do that. Can you understand? I won't let you suffer anyone else's pain.''

"I have to wait. I can't leave." Not when you're staying, she wanted to say, but didn't.

Tilting his head back, Sam stared up at the starry night sky. Closing his eyes, he took several deep breaths. He couldn't allow her to stay and wait for the worst to happen. Enduring pain of that magnitude could kill her. Even if she was willing to take the chance, he wasn't.

Sam saw Morgan Kane searching the parking lot for him. Lifting his hand, Sam motioned to his agent. He didn't have Reeves with him. What had he done with the man?

Kane rushed over to Sam. "Reeves got away. He and his date were getting into her BMW by the time I found them. I tried to stop them, but the woman nearly ran me down. By the time I got to my car, they were lost in traffic on the boulevard.''

"Damn! The police can't touch him without some evidence." Sam balled his right hand into a fist, wishing he could smash Reeves's pretty face. If he could have gotten hold of Reeves and questioned him before the police arrived, he might have been able to get the truth out of the bastard. "Look, Kane, make sure Jeannie gets home safe and sound. I'm going back in to help with the evacuation."

Jeannie lifted Sam's tight fist into her hand. "I'm not leaving. Not until everyone on board is safe and you can take me home yourself."

"Now is not the time to argue with me."

"Go do what you have to do, and take Mr. Kane with you. I'll be safe here with Julian and Marta."

"I don't think—"

"Give Julian your gun." Jeannie squeezed Sam's hand. "He knows how to use it. Don't you, Julian?"

"Give me the gun, and you two men go get those people off the riverboat," Julian said. "Maynard Reeves is nowhere around. I think I can protect Jeannie for the time being."

Music from the *Royal Belle* drifted in the air. The Gulf waters lapped at the sides of the big riverboat.

"Look!" Marta said. "People are crossing the gang-plank by the dozens. The decks are filled with people."

Sam removed his Ruger from his holster and handed it to Julian. "If we're lucky, this will be a false alarm." He lifted Jeannie up onto the hood of Marta's Mercedes. "I wish to hell you'd go home, where I know you'd be safe."

She tugged on his sleeve, drawing him down toward her, then kissed his cheek. "Be careful."

Jeannie sat there watching Sam and Kane go back aboard the *Royal Belle*. Dear God, what if the bombs exploded while Sam was aboard? What if he died? No, no, no. She couldn't allow herself to think that way. She had to stay calm and prepare herself to help the injured.

"Julian, do you have your medical bag with you?" Jeannie asked.

"No," he said. "I was thinking the same thing. If there is an explosion, I'll be needed, won't I?"

As streams of people exited the casino, some running, some walking slowly, with dazed looks on their faces, a few women in tears, the loud wail of sirens could be heard in the distance. Within minutes, three police cars pulled up, each one blocking a gangplank entrance to the riverboat. Sam recognized Lieutenant Painter's bulky form and shock of silver hair.

The policemen, aided by the *Royal Belle*'s security force, kept order as best they could. Only a few people panicked, creating a disruptive scene that slowed the mass exodus from the riverboat.

"There's so much fear in the atmosphere," Jeannie said. "All those people are afraid they're going to die before they reach safety." She sensed impending doom. Closing her eyes, she said a silent prayer, asking for the strength to do all she could to help those who needed her. And she asked for Sam's safety.

People rushed into the parking area. Cars roared to life. Within minutes, a huge traffic jam existed, and a sleek black Jaguar collided with a Ford pickup truck.

Boom! Boom! The thundering roar of an explosion rent the night air. Jeannie screamed. Marta grabbed her hand as the three of them gazed at the *Royal Belle*. Fire shot straight up, lighting the darkness, streaking the sky with flames. The force of the explosion tossed the people on the gangplank forward. Most of them landed flat on their faces on the ground. A few were flung into the water. Terrified screams mingled with the sizzle of the fires and the echo of the bomb blasts.

Boom! Boom! Another explosion? Two bombs? Maybe more. This shouldn't be happening; it wouldn't be, if Maynard Reeves was not so determined to kill her.

Where was Sam? Please, dear God, let him be all right.

"Do you see Sam anywhere?" Jeannie asked.

"No," Julian said. "But you mustn't worry, my dear. Mr. Dundee can take care of himself."

Two ambulances arrived in quick succession. Lieutenant Painter issued orders in his gruff, commanding voice. Medics quickly attended to the injured, while two policemen tried to control the traffic.

Jeannie saw Morgan Kane in the middle of the panicked crowd, an unconscious woman in his arms. He handed her to a medic and returned to the forefront, immersing himself in the madness. Then she noticed a soaking-wet Hawk dragging himself out of the Gulf waters and onto shore.

"He's hurt," Jeannie said, straining forward, but unable to walk. "Please. I must do something. I can't just stand here and watch. Maynard Reeves did this because of me."

"This isn't your fault," Julian said. "You mustn't feel guilty."

"Please, Julian, I have to find Sam. I have to know he's all right. And I can help Mr. Hawk, and all these other people."

"You aren't going anywhere. Do you hear me? You aren't to try to search for Mr. Dundee. He'll make his way to you. And don't go trying to help these people. There will be too many injuries. You'll endanger your own life if you try to save them." Julian handed Marta Sam's Ruger. "I want you and Marta to wait inside the car. I'll go see what I can do to help."

"I should be helping, too." Jeannie looked at Julian with the wide-eyed innocence of a child, her voice pleading, her expression beseeching. "I will feel guilty if I don't try to help these people. Please, Julian. I'll only help those who are seriously injured, those in the most pain."

"Think what it would do to you," he said. "There are too many injured people for you to help them all."

"But if I don't try to help them, my mental torment will hurt me far worse."

"It would be too dangerous. You will stay in the car until Mr. Dundee comes for you."

Julian and Marta assisted Jeannie into the Mercedes, and then Julian rushed off, speaking to the ambulance attendants and medics.

Once Julian was out of sight, Jeannie turned to Marta. "I have to find Sam. Please, Marta. See if you can find him. If you speak to Mr. Hawk or Mr. Kane, maybe they can help you find Sam."

"I can't leave you here alone." Marta shook her head. "Don't ask me to go against Julian's wishes."

"I'll lock the door," Jeannie said. "You can leave Sam's gun with me. Please, Marta. I'm very worried about Sam. If something weren't terribly wrong, he would have come back by now."

"I don't know. Julian will be very upset with me."

Sam swam to shore, dragging an elderly gentleman, one of over a dozen people he'd fished out of the water since the second explosion had hit. Hauling the unconscious man to shore, Sam called out for a passing medic, then saw Dr. Howell, down on one knee, giving a hysterical young woman an injection.

If Howell was helping the victims, who was guarding Jeannie? Lifting the wounded man in his arms, Sam carried him to where Dr. Howell and the medics had set up a makeshift emergency room in the parking lot while they waited for more ambulances to make return trips from the local hospitals.

Sam laid the man on the ground, then clasped Dr. Howell's shoulder. "Where's Jeannie?"

Julian gasped, then smiled when he saw Sam. "Thank God you're all right. Jeannie is beside herself with worry."

"Where is she?"

"She and Marta are in the car. Locked in. And Marta has your Ruger." Julian grabbed Sam's wrist. "She's bound and determined to help these people. I know Jeannie. If it's possible, she'll find a way."

"What would it do to her to try to help this many people?"

"It could kill her," Julian said.

Sam's chest tightened with fear. The sickening taste of panic rose in his throat. "I'll make sure she doesn't do anything stupid."

A weak smile faded from Julian's lips. He nodded. Sam made his way across the parking lot, stepping around people lying on the ground and speaking to the policemen he passed. He scanned the area, wondering where Kane and Hawk might be, hoping they were both all right.

Lieutenant Painter stopped Sam, questioning him about Maynard Reeves and how Jeannie had known there were bombs set to explode aboard the *Royal Belle*. Sam gave the lieutenant all the information he had, knowing it wouldn't be enough to arrest Reeves.

"I'll haul him in for questioning," Painter said. "But unless we can find some solid evidence to link him to this bombing, then he'll get off scot-free."

"Then you'd better find some sort of evidence, and soon," Sam said. "Otherwise—"

"Don't step over the line, Dundee. You're one of the good guys, remember?"

"Yeah, sure." Sam checked his watch. The damn thing was still running, even though the crystal was broken. Nearly two hours had passed since all hell had broken loose. Most of the parking lot had been cleared, and half a dozen ambulances had taken the injured to hospitals in Biloxi and surrounding towns. Several dozen people remained, waiting for returning ambulances.

Sam spotted Morgan Kane standing near the one remaining ambulance. As he drew near Kane's side, Sam looked inside the ambulance, and for one split second his heart stopped. Jeannie sat beside a badly burned dark-haired woman, holding her hand, absorbing her pain.

"What the hell's going on?" Sam gripped Kane's shoulder. "How did she get here?"

"Ms. Alverson sent Ms. McCorkle to look for you, and when she couldn't find you, she told me Ms. Alverson wanted to see me."

"You took Jeannie out of the car? You brought her here?" Sam's facial muscles tensed. He glared at Kane. "Do you have any idea what you've done?"

"She said she wanted to help these people, and she told me it would be all right with you as long as I was with her." Kane reached inside his jacket, pulled out Sam's Ruger and handed it to him. "She gave me this. It's yours, isn't it?"

Sam stuck the gun in his holster. "How many people has she helped?"

"How many?"

"Yeah, how many?"

"Ten, maybe twelve."

Sam cursed, the words strong and expressive.

"Hey, I don't know what the hell she's been doing," Kane said, "but every person she touched seemed to get better instantly."

"Didn't you happen to notice that she's been suffering more and more every time she *helped* another person?" Sam knew exactly what she'd been doing. She'd gone from person to person, alleviating their pain, absorbing enough of their suffering to reduce their chances of dying. Just thinking about what she'd put herself through tormented Sam.

"Where's Marta McCorkle?"

"She stayed with Ms. Alverson until a few minutes ago, then she left to look for Dr. Howell," Kane said. "Look, Sam, I'm sorry if by doing what Ms. Alverson asked I put her in some sort of danger. I haven't left her side for a second."

"Forget it," Sam said. "The damage's done. Besides, I know how persuasive Jeannie can be."

Releasing his hold on Kane, Sam stepped up into the ambulance. Jeannie was too deep into her healing trance to see him. Her colorless face was streaked with tears—the tears of others. He jerked her away from the burned woman. Jeannie groaned, then opened her eyes and stared at him.

"Sam, no. Please, just this one more. She's in so much pain." Jeannie tried to lift her hand to clutch Sam's sleeve. Her hand wouldn't cooperate. She let it fall to her side.

"You're in pain," he told her, pulling her out of the ambulance and lifting her into his arms. "You're so weak you can't even lift your hand. I'm taking you home. Now."

"But I can't—"

"We're not discussing it."

Standing just outside the open doors of the ambulance, Sam motioned to Kane. "After you and Hawk make your statements to the police and get a once-over in ER, fly back to Atlanta and take a few days off."

Jeannie squirmed in Sam's arms. "I don't want to leave. These people are suffering... because of me, because... Maynard Reeves wanted... to kill me."

Not only was Sam not going to allow Jeannie to do any more healing tonight, but once he took her home, he had no intention of allowing her out in public again. Somehow he'd persuade her to leave town. If Reeves was determined to see the "witch" burn, Jeannie wouldn't be safe anywhere Reeves could find her.

Ignoring Jeannie's pleas, Sam spoke to Kane again. "Phone J.T. and tell him to call in as many favors as need be, but I want something found on Reeves that can give the police reason to force him to stay away from Jeannie." Sam knew that, somewhere out there, someone knew something about Reeves's past dealings. A thirty-two-year-old zealot with obvious mental problems was bound to have screwed up, at least once, in the past.

Jeannie took a deep breath. "Sam Dundee!" Her voice trembled. "If you don't let me help these people, I'll... I'll never forgive... you. Don't you see? It's my... fault."

He felt her exhaustion in every cell of his body, his nerve endings alert to her weakness. And he knew she was exerting her last ounce of strength to fight him.

"Lift your hand and touch my face," Sam told her. "Let's see if you have the strength to do more than you've already done."

She tried, but her hand would not cooperate. Tears welled up in her eyes. "Damn you, Sam. Damn...you." With that said, her energy expended, she closed her eyes and fell asleep.

Holding her close, Sam carried her away from the death and destruction that surrounded them.

Sam opened the French doors that led out onto the up-stairs balcony. Dawn light coated the eastern horizon, to the left of the Howell home. Overhead, a pink glow coated the charcoal sky. A warm, pleasant breeze blew in off the gulf. Sam looked across the road at the deserted beach and, just beyond, the pale gray water.

Turning his head, he glanced into the bedroom, checking once again on Jeannie. She had thrown off the sheet and light blanket, leaving her body, from the waist up, exposed to the early-morning air. She had slept fitfully the past few hours, occasionally moaning in her sleep. But she seemed peaceful for the moment, her face serene, her breathing evenly paced.

Beautiful beyond compare, Sam thought. With her waist-length hair spread out over her pillow and across her shoulder, she lay there in the floor-length cream silk gown Ollie had put on her early yesterday morning, when Sam brought her home from the *Royal Belle* disaster. She had been asleep more than twenty-four hours. When Julian rushed home yesterday, he had assured Sam that it was perfectly normal for Jeannie to require extended periods of rest after using her extraordinary skills, especially to the extent she'd used them after the casino bombing.

Sam had left Jeannie's side only long enough to shower and change clothes. Ollie had remained with her, bathing her and slipping her into a gown. Sam hadn't eaten all day yesterday, until Ollie brought him his dinner on a tray. She'd threatened his life if he didn't eat every bite of the hearty meal.

Julian had spent the past twenty hours at the hospital. Although officially retired, he was needed, because of the sheer number of patients brought in from the *Royal Belle*.

Last night, Sam had slept at Jeannie's side, holding her in his arms whenever she cried—and she'd cried often—never once waking. He had wondered how long it would take her to recover from the ordeal she'd experienced. What could it possibly be like to endure that much pain and anguish?

If he could have stopped her, he would have. When he should have been taking care of her, he'd been busy saving other people's lives—just as, in her own way, Jeannie had been.

Sam looked back at the vastness of the ocean, the endless water and sky. In a few hours, traffic would begin to move, the beach would slowly fill, the all-nighters would leave the casinos and the early-morning crowds would arrive. And the local and state authorities would continue to sift through the remains of the *Royal Belle* for evidence. They'd keep questioning employees and patrons alike, hoping someone could shed some light on whoever had planted the bombs.

Awaking with a start, Jeannie sat straight up in bed, her mouth forming a silent cry. She glanced down at her body, then at her bed and around the room. Someone had removed her clothes, slipped on her gown and put her to bed. Sam? She smiled. Sam and Ollie.

A soft breeze surrounded her, chilling her bare arms. She hugged herself, took in a deep breath and blinked her eyes several times. The room lay in semidarkness, the only light coming from the windows, the faint, rosy illumination of daybreak.

She saw Sam standing on the balcony, his broad shoulders slightly drooped. He's tired, she thought, and worried. He wore dark slacks, slightly wrinkled. Had he slept beside her during the night? She had a vague memory of being held in his arms, a faded recollection of his wiping away her tears.

Usually the epitome of the well-dressed gentleman, Sam looked a bit disheveled in his wrinkled slacks, the tails of his pale blue shirt hanging around his hips, his hair windblown.

She searched the room, looking for a walking cane. Her favorite, a gift from Miriam, had probably burned inside the *Royal Belle*. Jeannie shuddered at the memory, the sound of the explosions echoing in her ears as well as the cries of wounded people. So many people in pain.

She wanted to go to Sam, to tell him that she was all right and that she forgave him for being so bossy and high-handed. She'd been so tired, so completely drained, that she hadn't been rational. Sam had done the right thing in forcing her to leave the disaster area.

Moving to the side of the bed, Jeannie slid her legs off the edge. She had no idea how she looked. She couldn't see a mirror from where she sat. Threading her fingers through her hair, she combed it to each side, allowing the mass to fall down her back. She lifted the twisted bodice of her gown to properly cover her breasts and smoothed out the wrinkles over her stomach and legs.

"Sam." Her voice sounded weak and very faint, even to her own ears.

He turned quickly. The moment he saw her, his lips curved into that seldom-used but devastating smile. "Jeannie." With a few giant steps, he was at her side, kneeling, slipping his arms around her.

She cradled his head in her lap and caressed his head, her fingers brushing over the stubble of his cheeks. He hadn't shaved, she realized. Since when? How long had she been asleep?

"This isn't the morning after the casino bombing, is it?" she asked.

Lifting his head, he looked up into her eyes, wanting nothing more than to protect her from the world, from all the ugliness, from a truth he could not change. "You've been asleep over twenty-four hours. Do you remember fainting in the back of the ambulance?"

"Yes, sort of. I remember telling you I'd never forgive you if you made me leave."

"I did what I thought was best for you. I brought you home." Sam rose to his feet, then sat down beside her on the bed. "Ollie undressed you and washed you and put you in your gown while I took a shower and changed clothes."

"You've stayed with me all this time, haven't you? You even slept with me last night."

"How do you know all that?"

"I sensed your presence." She leaned against him; he put his arm around her waist.

"How do you feel?" He kissed her forehead.

"Tired. But I'm all right."

"You did too much."

"It was a horrible disaster. So many injured people." She clutched Sam's hand. "Did anyone die?"

Sam took a deep breath. "Two of the casino's security men didn't make it off the riverboat. They were caught in the bottom-deck explosion. Only those two. There are about a dozen in critical condition, but, luckily, we had evacuated almost the entire casino when the bombs exploded."

"Have the police arrested Maynard Reeves?"

"They have no evidence against Reeves."

"But I know he's responsible." She bit her fingers into Sam's arm, tugging on his sleeve. "I sensed all those horrible emotions inside him. He couldn't block what he was feeling."

"I know, Jeannie. I know." Sam tried to soothe her, stroking her back with one hand while he cupped her chin in the other. "But they can't arrest Reeves just because you say you sensed his guilt."

She pulled away from Sam, covering her face with her hands as she bowed her head. She sat there for several minutes, then tossed back her head, squared her shoulders and turned to Sam. "I need some fresh air. Find me a cane, please. And walk out on the balcony with me."

"I can carry you outside." He stood, but before he could lift her, she threw up her hand to stop him.

"I want to walk." She nodded toward the huge, ornately carved wardrobe. "Look in the wardrobe. There should be two or three canes in there."

Sam obeyed her command without hesitation. He'd learned that sometimes it was easier not to fight Jeannie, especially when she was damned and determined to have her own way. He retrieved a black metal walking stick, with a gold tip and a fancy flower design engraved on the handle.

Handing her the cane, he watched while she positioned the tip on the floor and lifted herself to her feet. He walked behind her, not touching her, and followed her out onto the balcony. The downstairs veranda and the upstairs balcony surrounded the three-story antebellum-style house on all four sides.

"I never tire of looking at the ocean," she said. "This is a beautiful view, but nothing to compare with the view from the veranda of my house on Le Bijou Bleu."

Mention of the island where Sam had washed ashore six years ago brought back painful memories to him. Memories he had tried to erase from his mind.

"We should go to your island," Sam said. "There, I might be able to keep you safe."

She shivered from the chill of the early-morning breeze as it tickled her bare arms and shoulders. "Maynard Reeves wants to kill me, and he doesn't seem to care how many people he has to destroy to do it."

Sam wrapped his arms around her. "Julian told me that only a handful of people even know about Le Bijou Bleu, that when your parents bought the island they used it as a retreat and kept its location a secret."

"Julian's right. Other than Julian and I, and of course Manton, only our lawyer and Marta even know about the island. I've used the place as my personal retreat all these years. When Miriam was dying, we visited Le Bijou Bleu several times. The trip always seemed to revitalize her."

"You'd take her to the island and suffer her pain for her, wouldn't you?" Sam hugged Jeannie fiercely. "You'd take her away so that Julian wouldn't have to see the two of you in pain."

"I loved Miriam like a mother." Jeannie sighed. "She was far more a mother to me than my own ever was."

"Are you willing to go to Le Bijou Bleu and stay as long as it takes to free yourself from Reeves?" Sam asked.

"What if he won't give up? What if he waits us out? You have a life of your own, Sam. I can't expect you to move to Le Bijou Bleu and live with me indefinitely."

"We're digging into Reeves's past. Somewhere there has to be some information that will help us put a stop to him. Otherwise . . ."

She gripped Sam's forearms where they crisscrossed her waist. "Otherwise what?"

"Otherwise we'll have to find another way to get rid of the man."

"I can't help but believe that God will punish him. He has committed so much evil in God's name. What greater sin could there be?"

"I'll make arrangements for us to leave Biloxi immediately. The sooner I can get you out of Reeves's grasp, the better."

"I can't leave yet," Jeannie said. "Not until..." She hesitated, turning her head and looking up at him. She wondered how he would react when she told him what she wanted.

"Not until what?"

"I want to stay a few more days, go to the hospitals and try to help the people who were injured in the bombing."

"No! Absolutely not!"

"Hear me out. Please."

Releasing Jeannie, Sam walked around her and over to the balcony's edge. With his back turned to her, he gripped the top of the banister. "You damn near killed yourself night before last, and you expect me to allow you to—"

"You do not *allow* me to do anything," Jeannie said. "Night before last, you were right. I had exhausted my energy. I wouldn't have been able to be of help to anyone. But I'm rested now. I need to help the people who are suffering because of me."

"You're being irrational, you know." He wished he could shake some sense into her compassionate little head. "You are not responsible for what happened to those people. Maynard Reeves is."

"And he bombed the riverboat because I was on board!"

"Dammit, Jeannie, what am I going to do with you?"

She walked over to the balcony's edge and laid her hand over his. "Night before last, you were going to bring me home and make love to me."

Every nerve in his body screamed. Neither of them spoke for endless moments. With her hand resting atop his, Sam and Jeannie watched the sun rise over Biloxi.

Jeannie had never wanted anything as much as she wanted Sam Dundee to be a part of her life forever, but she knew how impossible the dream was. Would any woman ever capture Sam Dundee's heart? Did a woman exist who was strong enough to be his equal?

Sam had never wanted anything as much as he wanted to protect Jeannie Alverson—from Reeves's insanity, from suffering the pain of others, and even from him. The desire he felt for this gentle, loving woman was so strong it could destroy her. He couldn't let that happen.

"It's all right, you know." She stroked his hand. "I want you, too."

"Jeannie?" His muscles tensed; his heartbeat accelerated.

"If there had been no explosions aboard the *Royal Belle*, you and I would have become lovers yesterday morning, when we got back here to the house," she said.

"You don't know that for sure."

"Yes, I do. And so do you. I haven't forgotten what happened out on deck when we danced. I remember exactly how we both felt, what we both wanted."

"Don't remind me."

He turned around and looked at her. Dear God, what was he going to do about Jeannie Alverson? She was driving him insane. He couldn't remember ever wanting a woman so badly or ever being so scared. Once her life was no longer in danger, he would return to Atlanta. He'd be safe there, far away from Jeannie.

She wanted too much from him. She wanted things that weren't in him to give. She thought he was a far better man than he actually was. She thought he was worth saving, worth suffering for, worth the pain of delving into his tormented soul. He'd never been a coward, never backed down from any challenge, but Jeannie was something else all together. What man was equal to the challenge of being Jeannie's mate, of understanding her enough to allow her to be the woman she was—an empath with a blessed talent? What man was strong enough to spend the rest of his life watching her suffer other people's pain.

"Sam?"

"Two things have been driving me crazy while you slept. I was worried sick that you'd suffered too much pain, that you might have permanently harmed yourself. And all the while I was worrying, I hated myself for wanting you so desperately, for thinking what might have been if—"

"Once we're on Le Bijou Bleu, we'll have all our days and nights to make love."

Sam swallowed hard. "When you're no longer in danger, I'm going back to Atlanta."

Jeannie sighed. "Yes, I know. I understand."

"Okay, then. I see no reason to delay our departure. We'll sail for your island today."

"I'll go with you to Le Bijou Bleu day after tomorrow, when I've had a chance to put things in order around here and do what I feel is right and necessary."

Dammit, he knew what she was planning to do. "I won't allow you to put yourself in any more danger."

"Everything is going to be all right," she said, only half believing her own words. "Somehow we'll find a way to make it right."

She slipped her arms around him, kissing him with a strength and passion that startled him. Within seconds, Sam had taken charge of the kiss, the power of his feelings ripping him apart inside. He needed to make love to Jeannie, and soon, or he was going to lose his mind. He'd never known desire so strong, passion so all-consuming, need so powerful. And somehow he knew Jeannie felt the same way, that even though sexual desire was a new experience for her, the desperation of her need matched his own.

But he would have to wait until she was fully recovered from the ordeal following the bombing of the *Royal Belle*. When they made love for the first time, Jeannie would need all her strength. When they made love, she would experience sexual fulfillment—both his and hers.

Chapter 10

Tapping the china rim with her fingernails, Jeannie stared into the teacup she held with both hands. She lifted the cup to her lips, took a sip of the warm, sweet liquid, then held the cup in front of her. Was she forgetting anything? She would go over her checklist again before she and Sam left in the morning. He had wanted to go to Le Bijou Bleu today, but she had insisted on waiting for tomorrow. That would give her enough time to get things in order around the house and make sure that, between Ollie and Marta, Julian would be taken care of properly. He insisted he could take care of himself, but Julian was one of those men who had always had a woman to handle life's daily annoyances.

And Jeannie really had wanted to visit the hospitals to see those injured in the explosion aboard the *Royal Belle*. But upon further discussion, she and Sam had compromised. She wouldn't go to the hospitals if he agreed to stay in Biloxi one more day so that she could put things in order before their departure. After all, what difference could one day make?

"There's no point in your worrying about things over which you have little or no control." Laying the medical journal he'd been reading in his lap, Julian looked at Jeannie. "What happened aboard the *Royal Belle* was an atrocity, but it could have been much worse. If you hadn't sensed that monster Reeves's emotions, everyone aboard the riverboat might have died. You did all you could to prevent the disaster and to ease the suffering of those who were injured."

"Sam has told me the same thing, but I can't forget that if Reeves wasn't so determined to destroy me, he probably wouldn't have had bombs placed aboard the boat."

"You don't know that for sure. The man has been preaching against gambling ever since it was legalized and the casinos went into business along the Gulf."

"But he's never blown up one of the casinos before," Jeannie said. "He's never done anything violent, until now."

Sam Dundee entered the room, a sheaf of papers in his hand. "The man is totally irrational when it comes to you."

Jeannie's heart skipped a beat. Just the sound of his voice excited her, and one look into those steely gray eyes aroused her. She'd never known what it was like to want a man, to long for the feel of his hand in hers, the touch of his lips, the pleasure of his strong embrace.

"Reeves believes I'm a witch, possessed with powers from Satan." She set her teacup in its saucer on the mahogany table beside her chair. "I know he isn't going to leave me alone. He wants to destroy me." She shivered; the feel of Reeves's evil lingered inside her like a tiny sprinkling of ashes from a fire which had long since died.

"Reeves's obsession with destroying you is why it's imperative you leave Biloxi." Standing, Julian glanced down at the medical journal that had fallen from his lap. Grumbling under his breath, he reached down, picked up the magazine and laid it in the chair. "All the preparations have been made. I telephoned the Broadwater Marina. Your boat will be ready for your departure in the morning. And you've contacted Manton to let him know when to expect you and Mr. Dundee."

Jeannie nodded agreement. "I've packed a few things to take with me, but I keep so many things at the house there, I won't need much." She glanced across the room at Sam, who was standing by the windows, seemingly absorbed in reading the stapled sheets of paper in his hand. "And I've sent Ollie out to buy Sam a bathing suit and some shorts and stuff. The man brought nothing but business suits. Can you imagine? He came to Biloxi without a bathing suit."

Sam grunted, glanced up from his reading and gave Jeannie one of his half smiles. Already she'd learned that that was the usual extent of his smile, an upward curve of his lips that didn't show any teeth.

"I came to Biloxi to work," he said. "Not to play."

"What are you so interested in?" Jeannie looked at the papers in his hand.

"J.T. faxed me more information on Reeves." Sam walked over to where Jeannie sat and handed her the report. "There's only one new piece of information that might interest the police. Reeves is a known religious fanatic whose followers have been jailed time and again, but Reeves himself has a spotless record. He seems to always be on the fringes of anything his church does that's illegal. It's obvious someone else always does his dirty work and takes all the risks."

Julian placed his bony hand on Sam's shoulder. "What piece of information is suspicious?"

"It seems that when Reeves was sixteen, both of his parents died in a house fire. The fire inspector said it was out-and-out arson, but they never found the arsonists, never prosecuted anyone."

"Where was Reeves when his parents' house burned?" Julian asked.

"He had spent the night with a friend, a boy named Wayland Krenshaw. Krenshaw is a deacon in Reeves's Righteous Light Church, and the two are fast friends to this day."

Jeannie read through the report quickly, then handed it back to Sam. "The police suspected young Maynard Reeves, but they had no proof, and he had an alibi."

"Why would the police suspect Reeves?" Julian glanced from Jeannie to Sam.

"Two weeks before the fire, a next-door neighbor had heard Reeves threaten his father, telling him that if he ever

beat him again, he'd kill him," Sam said. "And the elder
Reeves, a hellfire-and-brimstone preacher, told his son that
the evil powers inside him would eventually destroy him.
Then Reeves's father knocked him to the ground."

"My guess is that his father caught young Maynard using his psychic abilities," Jeannie said. "Obviously the man
didn't realize that his son probably had little control over
those abilities."

"And there are no other suspicious incidents in Reeves's
past?" Julian pointed to the report in Sam's hand.

"There are countless suspicious incidents." Sam shook
the sheaf of papers. "But that was the only time Reeves was
directly linked to the happening. Our good reverend possibly has been behind numerous fires, bombings and even a
couple of shootings, but there's no proof to link him to any
of the incidents. And not once has one of his followers accused Reeves of any wrongdoing, even if it meant serving
prison time themselves."

"Are you saying that this Righteous Light Church has
members who are in prison because of—" Julian's dark eyes
narrowed to mere slits. He slammed his hand down on the
mahogany table beside Jeannie's chair, sending her empty
teacup crashing to the floor.

Jeannie lifted herself, bracing herself with her cane. She
grabbed Julian's arm. "You musn't get upset like this. It
isn't good for your heart."

"Why can't the police do something to stop Reeves? It's
obvious he's no man of God. If anyone is a child of the
devil, he is!" Julian's swarthy olive complexion flushed with
crimson. He knotted his hands into fists. "If I wasn't such
an old man, I'd—"

"Calm yourself." Jeannie slipped her arm around her
foster father's waist. "Sam is taking me away to Le Bijou
Bleu in the morning. You, Ollie and Marta will be the only
people who'll known where we are. Reeves doesn't know
about my island, and the few people who know aren't about
to tell him."

"I agree that the safest place for you is Le Bijou Bleu, but
you can't hide out there for the rest of your life." Julian
hugged Jeannie to his side. "If only the police could arrest

the man. My God, he's threatened your life more than once."

"Technically, he hasn't," Jeannie said. "There is no law that prevents him from calling me names, and we have no proof that he sent me the Bible with the blood-spotted marker, or that he was responsible for the bombing of the *Royal Belle*."

Julian rubbed Jeannie's arm, then patted her tenderly on the shoulder. "If there's no other way to keep you safe, we'll leave Biloxi. We can go anywhere in the world. I'd do anything to protect you."

Jeannie hugged Julian. "I know you would, but I'm hoping that if I leave Biloxi for a few weeks, the media coverage on me will die down and perhaps Reeves will return to New Orleans and find some other poor soul to persecute."

When Sam grunted, Jeannie and Julian looked at him. Sam turned, picked up the report, folded it in half and stuffed it into his coat pocket. "In going to Le Bijou Bleu, we're taking Jeannie temporarily out of harm's way and buying us some time. If we can't legally nail Reeves's hide to the wall, then I'll have to find another way to handle him."

"What do you mean?" Jeannie asked, but really didn't want to know.

"There's no point in discussing alternatives until the present plan fails," Sam said.

"What present plan?" Julian asked.

"I've called in some favors." Sam tried not to look at Jeannie, who watched him closely. "I was a government agent for ten years. I know a lot of people. I have men on my payroll who are former CIA, former Green Berets and navy SEALS. My partner, J. T. Blackwood, left the Secret Service after he lost an eye and nearly died."

"What does who you know have to do with this plan to stop Maynard Reeves from...from killing me?" Jeannie willed Sam to face her, knowing he couldn't lie to her if he looked her in the eye.

Sensing her need for the complete truth, Sam made eye contact with Jeannie. "Since the bombing of the *Royal Belle*, the feds are involved. I've asked for and been prom-

ised one of their best men to head up the investigation. Dane
Carmichael should be arriving today. He'll work directly
with Lieutenant Painter. If there's any way to prove a connection between Reeves and the explosions aboard the *Royal
Belle,* they'll find it. We just need to keep Jeannie out of
harm's way until Reeves is behind bars. Painter and Carmichael are coming by to question us later this evening.''

"Let's pray this plan works," Jeannie said. "I don't know
if I could live with the alternative."

She tried to disguise her feelings, but they showed plainly
on her face.

Knowing her so well, and caring for her so deeply, Julian
could read her like a book. "We'll hope and pray Reeves will
be found out and the police discover the proof they need to
put him away." Gripping Jeannie by the shoulder, Julian
stared at Sam. "But if it comes to—" Julian cleared his
throat. "You'll do what must be done, what I'd do if I
could. Her life is in your hands, my boy. I trust you to keep
her safe."

"There's nothing I wouldn't do to protect her."

Sam couldn't sleep. If he hadn't been forced into a compromise with Jeannie, allowing her one extra day in Biloxi,
he'd have taken her away today. Sam glanced at the bedside
clock. Nearly midnight. They'd be out of the house before
seven and on the gulf before eight.

Their talk with Lieutenant Painter and Dane Carmichael
had lasted over an hour, with Jeannie reconstructing the
events of three nights ago, aboard the *Royal Belle,* and explaining again and again why she knew Reeves had been
behind the bombing.

Maybe, if they were lucky, Reeves had made a mistake, or
perhaps someone in his organization would talk. Sam didn't
know how long he'd have to keep Jeannie on Le Bijou Bleu,
how long he'd have to act as her bodyguard, but he'd already asked J.T. to take control of Dundee Private Security. Sam hadn't had to tell J.T. that this case had become
very personal. He'd just known. And J.T. was too astute to
ask questions. Sam appreciated his friend and partner's
keen perception. How the hell could he ever explain his

feelings about Jeannie to someone else, when he didn't truly understand them himself?

Le Bijou Bleu. The Blue Jewel. Out there somewhere in the gulf. Sam drew back the curtains at the window and looked up at the star-filled sky. Tomorrow night they would be together on Jeannie's island retreat. Alone. Except for Manton. Sam had only the vaguest memory of the huge man. Dark skin. Bald head. How would Manton feel about Jeannie bringing Sam to the island? Would Manton instinctively know what was happening between Jeannie and Sam? Would he approve or disapprove?

Sam had no idea where Le Bijou Bleu was located. When he was tossed into the ocean six years ago, his body had washed ashore on Jeannie's uncharted island. Sam had checked and double-checked to make sure there was no way Reeves could discover the location of the island. Although Ollie and Marta knew about the island, as did the family lawyer, only Manton, Julian and Jeannie knew its exact location.

Years ago, the only means of communication had been a shortwave radio. With generators providing electricity to the house, Jeannie had provided Manton with a computer and fax-modem and had installed a telephone. One of the first things Jeannie had done after waking from her twenty-four hour rest, was to fax Manton, something she did almost every day.

"He'll be worried if more than a couple of days pass without hearing from me," she'd said.

So like Jeannie, caring about others, worrying about the people in her life, loving wholeheartedly, giving freely, taking on suffering that was not hers.

Sam didn't pretend to understand the depth of Jeannie's goodness, but the purity of her soul made him question his right to desire her. Of all the men in the world, why would she want him to be her first lover? She knew he could promise her nothing permanent, that he could offer her a physical relationship and nothing more. Why didn't she wait for some gentle, kind man whose soul would be in tune with hers? Why would she want a man who wasn't even sure he possessed a soul?

Sam heard the distant beeping sound and couldn't quite identify what it was was or where it was coming from. When he went out into the hall, he heard it more distinctly, a repetitive alert coming from somewhere downstairs.

Jeannie cried out his name. The beeping continued. Sam listened carefully. A smoke detector!

"Sam!" she cried again.

"I'll check it out," he said, knowing she could hear the alarm, too. "It could be nothing. I'll be right back."

He flew down the stairs, followed the warning signal into the smoky corridor leading to the kitchen and flung open the door. Growling at the sight before him, he swore loudly. Flames engulfed the kitchen, the curtains burning in seconds as he watched. Smoke filled the room.

Ollie touched Sam on the shoulder. He jerked around to face her. "Get out of the house. Fast. I'll send Julian and bring Jeannie down."

"Can't I help?" Ollie asked.

"Don't argue. No time. Get out!"

Sam slammed shut the door, raced back upstairs, calling Jeannie's name. Julian, wearing pajamas and a silk robe came out into the hall. "What's wrong? Is that the smoke detector?"

Ignoring Julian, Sam rushed into his bedroom, retrieved his cellular phone from his jacket, went back into the hall and tossed the phone to Julian.

"Go downstairs and out the front door quickly. I've sent Ollie out. Dial 911. Get the fire department here before this old house burns to the ground."

"Jeannie?" Julian hesitated, but then he saw the look in Sam Dundee's eyes and, clutching the phone in his trembling hand, hurried downstairs.

Jeannie sat upright in bed, the lamp on the nightstand illuminating her frightened face. "The smoke alarm went off downstairs. Is there a fire?"

Sam lifted her into his arms. "The whole kitchen's on fire."

She had known somehow that the alarm hadn't gone off by accident, that it signaled a true danger. The moment she heard it, she'd called out to Sam, telepathically at first, but he hadn't responded.

She saw the panic in his eyes and realized how afraid he was for her. She held out her arms, waiting for him to rescue her. Nothing could ever truly harm her as long as she had Sam.

Although his mind functioned and he'd thought out every move in a reasonable fashion, one overriding emotion dictated Sam's actions—his concern for Jeannie. He had to get her to safety!

Jeannie clung to him as he rushed out of her room, dashing down the stairs, taking them two at a time. Billows of black smoke met them in the foyer. Fire licked at the walls. Jeannie closed her eyes against the destruction, coughing when the smoke filled her nostrils and crept into her throat. Ahead of them, the front door stood wide open. Sam didn't hesitate; he ran outside, down the steps and into the front yard, where Julian and Ollie stood huddled together.

"The fire department is on the way." Julian touched Jeannie's face and smiled. "Maybe they'll make it here in time to save the old place."

Jeannie knew how much Julian loved the house his grandfather had built, the home where he'd grown up, the house where he'd brought Miriam as a bride. To lose this magnificent old mansion would be like losing a part of himself.

"Could the fire have been an accident?" Jeannie asked Sam, her voice a whisper against his ear. "Or do you think Maynard Reeves—?" She swallowed, her emotions momentarily choking her.

"My gut instincts are shouting Reeves's name," Sam said. "We won't know for sure whether or not this was an accident until the fire inspector hands in his report."

Jeannie felt Sam's frustration, his fear for her and his savage anger at Reeves. She could hear his heartbeat, loud and strong and wild. Wild from the race away from what would have been certain death had he not carried her to safety. Wild with the desire to protect at all costs. Wild with the need to take revenge against anyone who would dare harm her.

"We're safe," she told him, and tried to draw the anger from him.

"Don't!" Tightening his hold on her, he lowered his head and nuzzled the side of her forehead. "I don't need calming or soothing. I don't want you to take away the hatred I feel. Save your strength. You'll need it later."

Sam was right. She did need her strength later. After the firemen doused the blaze and saved Julian's home from total destruction. After they stayed the night at Marta's, no one sleeping, all of them waiting to hear from the fire marshal. After they found out the house had been deliberately set afire. And after the police said they could do nothing more than question Maynard Reeves.

"He's sure to have an alibi," Lieutenant Painter had said.

Sam hadn't wanted to change their plans to leave at seven o'clock for Le Bijou Bleu, but she'd told him in no uncertain terms that she wasn't leaving the mainland until they knew more details about the fire and she saw Julian and Ollie settled.

She hadn't expected the fire marshal to detect the cause of the fire so quickly. The arsonist had done nothing to conceal his handiwork. And she certainly hadn't expected Marta to find Julian a temporary home that same morning.

Sam pulled Jeannie's Lexus up in the driveway behind Marta's Mercedes. The house, a small Victorian cottage between Long Beach and Gulfport, belonged to Marta's recently divorced son, who'd asked his mother to see about renting the place until he decided whether or not things would work out with his new job in Mobile.

Unlocking the front door, Marta stepped back and waited for everyone to enter. "All their furniture is still here. Joel hasn't touched a thing since Patsy Ruth left him."

The house wasn't half the size of Julian's home in Biloxi, but it was charming and homey and certainly large enough to accommodate Julian and Ollie for a few months until the restoration of their fire-damaged house was completed.

"I think the place is lovely," Jeannie said. "We're fortunate you hadn't already found a renter."

"The place is Julian's as long as he needs it." Marta turned to Jeannie. "We'll get everything set up today. A new computer and fax machine for Julian. Luckily, we hadn't had the power turned off or the telephone disconnected. Joel left for his new job in Mobile only last week."

"Yes, dear, you must contact me as soon as you arrive at Le Bijou Bleu and let me know all is well." Julian kissed Jeannie on the cheek, then offered his hand to Sam. "Take care of her. Her value cannot be assessed."

"I know that she's priceless." Sam shook Julian's hand, and the two men exchanged stares, one man pleading, the other promising.

"Get her beyond Maynard Reeves's grasp." Ollie placed her hand on her hip. "If I ever see that scripture-quoting weasel again, I'll boil him in oil."

"You musn't delay any longer." Holding Jeannie's hand, Julian lifted it and placed it over his heart. "There's no telling what the man is capable of doing."

"But what about you, Julian?" Jeannie couldn't bear the thought of her foster father being in danger because of her. "What if Reeves tries to harm you."

"I'm not his target, my dear, you are."

"But he's crazy, isn't he? That means he's unpredictable." Jeannie sighed. "Why don't you come to Le Bijou Bleu with us?"

"I'm not in any danger." Julian glanced at Sam, then shifted his attention back to Jeannie. "I'm needed here. I still consult at the hospital, you know, as well as being on the board. And since you can't continue your work at the Howell School, I'll keep an eye on Marta and the teachers for you." Looking over Jeannie's shoulder, he smiled at Marta, who nodded her head in amused agreement. "Besides, I'll have to be around to oversee the work on our home. I want everything rebuilt as close to the original as possible."

"We'll stay in daily contact," Jeannie said. "If you need me—"

"Take her away, now," Julian told Sam. "Before we're both in tears."

"I don't anticipate any problems for you," Sam said. "But if there is, let me know. I'll get Hawk or Kane back down here as quickly as possible."

Sam forcibly turned Jeannie, draped his arm around her shoulders and walked her outside to the car. When they reached the Lexus, she looked back, saw Julian in the doorway and waved goodbye.

Sam drove down highway 90, straight to the Broadwater Marina, where Jeannie's small cruiser awaited them. He had been anxious to get Jeannie out of Biloxi and away from Reeves before last night, but now, after the fire, he knew the only way to completely protect her was to keep her on Le Bijou Bleu until Reeves no longer posed a threat. And that meant until the authorities arrested him—or until Sam was forced to settle the matter himself.

Chapter 11

They arrived at Le Bijou Bleu late in the afternoon, just as the August sun began its descent into the western sky. A warm, humid wind surrounded them as they disembarked. Two smaller craft were anchored snugly a few feet away from the cruiser. All three rested in their slips. An enormous brown-skinned man, his bald head glistening in the sunshine, stood on the pier.

Sam swept Jeannie up into his arms, lifting her off the boat, then turning to face Manton. Remembering only bits and pieces of his hours on this island six years ago, Sam wasn't sure what to expect from the man who had helped Jeannie save his life. What he saw was a seven-foot giant, his huge, muscular arms crossed over his wide chest and his green eyes focused on Jeannie.

When Sam took a step forward, she tugged on his sleeve. "Put me down and give me my cane. I want you to meet Manton again, and then, after we've settled in and I've let Julian know we arrived safely, I want to show you my island."

Sam obeyed her request, wondering all the while if Manton would have tried to break him in half if he dared disagree with her.

Jeannie walked steadily toward Manton, who didn't move a muscle until she stood directly in front of him. A wide smile spread across his face, softening his hard features and putting a sparkle in his eyes. Opening her arms, Jeannie squealed with laughter when the gentle giant lifted her off her feet and into a bear hug.

Standing to the side, Sam watched the loving exchange and saw an affection between Jeannie and Manton similar to that between her and Julian Howell. Though several years younger than the doctor, Manton was twice Jeannie's age and seemed to consider himself another substitute father.

When Manton set her back on her feet, Jeannie clutched her cane and turned her head. Smiling at Sam, she motioned him forward. "Sam, come meet the man who saved your life six years ago."

The two men sized each other up, taking a full inventory. Sam extended his hand; Manton saw Jeannie's happy smile and accepted Sam's handshake. Despite his size and obvious strength, Manton did not grip Sam's hand with any undue force. His handshake was firm, quick and nonaggressive.

Looking directly at Manton, Sam said, "I owe Jeannie and you my life. Thank you."

Manton nodded toward Jeannie, moving his hands rapidly, signing to her, then looked back at Sam.

"He's too modest to accept any thanks. He claims that all he did was help me get you to the hospital."

"That saved my life," Sam told him.

Manton grinned, signed again and waited for Jeannie to translate.

"He says that all the thanks he needs is for you to keep me safe."

"I'll do whatever it takes to protect her," Sam said.

Instinctively Sam knew that Manton understood his meaning without further words and knew, too, that this second substitute father was concerned about his and Jeannie's relationship.

He noticed that Jeannie and Manton seemed to be conversing, though Jeannie didn't speak and Manton didn't sign. They're talking telepathically, Sam thought, and wondered what they were saying.

Manton nodded, walked away and boarded the cruiser. Jeannie turned to Sam.

"He's getting our luggage." She held out her hand, motioning Sam to her. "Manton usually carries me from the dock to the house. It's an uphill climb from here. See the steps over there?"

Sam took note of the curving set of rock steps that led up from the beach to the hill above. From where he stood, he couldn't see the house.

"What were you saying to him a few minutes ago?" Sam asked. "I know you were communicating with him."

"I told him to go ahead and get the luggage, that you would carry me up to the house."

An undeniable pleasure spread from the pit of Sam's stomach to his whole body. The sensation was ridiculous, he told himself, but he could not argue against the truth. Jeannie looked to him for care and protection. Not to Julian Howell, and not to Manton. Not any longer. The girl had become a woman, gently but firmly choosing Sam, instead of either surrogate father, to be her protector.

Sam lifted Jeannie into his arms, as he had done so many times recently, but this time the ritual was fraught with deep meaning. And they both knew it. Carrying her to the house was a symbolic giving of herself, a placing of herself into Sam's hands—not only to keep safe, but to possess, to pleasure, to love.

Sam had no idea the walk from the dock to the house would take so long. No wonder Manton had always carried Jeannie. Once at the top of the rock steps, Sam drew in his breath, an appreciative sigh escaping his lips. Green grass spread out as far as the eye could see. Live oaks climbed toward heaven, while some of the limbs curled downward and grew back into the earth. Spanish moss hung heavily on the trees, dripping almost to the ground here and there. Palm trees swayed in the summer wind. In the distance, blue sky and water met.

Sam couldn't remember anything about Le Bijou Bleu except the beach. He had no memory of the docks.

"Six years ago, I didn't wash up near the pier, did I?" he asked.

"No, I found your body on the other side of the island. Manton carried you to the boat."

"When they tossed me overboard, I didn't think I had a prayer." Sam caressed the top of her head with his chin, then turned his head sideways and rested his cheek against her hair.

"You have to put the past behind you," Jeannie said. "It can't be changed."

Halting his steps momentarily, Sam closed his eyes. With the hot sun and warm wind on his face, he allowed Jeannie entrance into his thoughts. The moment they connected, his eyes flew open and he gripped her fiercely. It would be so easy to let her take away the painful memories, at least for a while. He wanted to forget, but how could he allow her to experience the guilt for him?

"No," he said, mentally and emotionally withdrawing from her. "Don't. I can handle it."

"All right. If that's what you want. But sooner or later, you're going to have to deal with the pain you've buried deep inside you." She touched his cheek. He flinched. "If you share it with me, I can help you put the past to rest."

The sound of Manton climbing the rock steps reminded Sam that he and Jeannie were not completely alone. "Where's the house?" Sam asked.

"Look straight ahead. You can see the roof through that grove of trees."

With Manton at his side, Sam carried Jeannie across the wide, seemingly endless stretch of verdant ground leading to the house. The two-story raised French cottage had been built on the top of a rise, giving the occupants a view of the ocean from all sides.

A menagerie of animals greeted their arrival. A half-dozen cats of various sizes, colors and ages were curled around the banisters, their curious eyes staring at Sam. Four panting mixed-breed dogs, tails wagging playfully, rounded the side of the house.

Jeannie spoke to the animals, calling each by name. They purred and woofed in unison, welcoming their mistress.

Manton hurried ahead of them, rushing up the steps and onto the huge veranda to open the front doors. The rooms were large and airy, with floor-to-ceiling windows and double French doors leading to the veranda. The windows had been opened, and the warm breeze fluttered the lace curtains as it filled the rooms.

Jeannie reminded Sam to set her on her feet when they entered the front parlor, a spacious room with clean white walls, Victorian sofa and chairs upholstered in cream damask, and a baby grand piano in the corner.

He slid her slowly down the length of his body, allowing the intimate contact to linger. Wrapping her arms around his neck, she gazed up at him dreamily. He wanted to kiss her. She closed her eyes, waiting for his kiss.

Manton paused in the doorway long enough to make eye contact with Sam, then proceeded to carry the luggage down the hall to the bedrooms. Jeannie cleared her throat. Sam grinned.

"Is he going to be watching us the whole time we're here?" Sam asked.

Opening her eyes, Jeannie frowned. "Manton will be here all the time, but he won't be watching us. We'll feel his presence, because he is a part of this island. As much a part of it as the earth and the trees, the flowers, the birds, the animals."

"I think I'll have a difficult time considering him just part of the scenery." Sam kissed the tip of her nose, and chuckled when she wrinkled her nose and frowned at him. "Where does Manton sleep?"

A tentative smile began spreading across her face. "He has rooms downstairs on the lower level." Her smile widened. "Our rooms are on the main level, just down the hall."

Lowering his head, his breath mingling with hers, he brushed a light kiss over her lips. "Are we going to need separate rooms?"

She drew in a quick breath, then released it on a deep sigh. "No." That one word said it all. The acceptance of the inevitable. The promise of ecstasy. The knowledge that no power on earth could keep them apart.

But as surely as Jeannie knew that Sam Dundee was destined to become her lover, she knew that he would never be free to love her as long as his past possessed his soul. Every time she touched him, she sensed his unease and uncertainty. He wanted her with a fierce and desperate hunger, but he was afraid of her, of her special talents—and he felt unworthy.

How could she ever make him understand that she was as afraid as he was? The power of Sam's primitive nature, his savage strength, his iron will, all just barely concealed beneath his sophisticated surface, made her doubt she could ever possess him, truly possess him, heart and soul.

Not only did the vast differences in their basic natures stand between them, but so did Sam's guilt-ridden conscience and Jeannie's endangered existence. No matter how they might long to be together, Jeannie knew she had no choice but to accept the likelihood that she and Sam had no future together.

Jeannie shuddered at the realization.

"What's wrong?" he asked when he felt her tremble.

"We're safe for now, aren't we? Here on my island, no one can harm us. We can be happy for a while."

His kiss combined the elements of passion and protectiveness and sent ripples of excitement through her, while at the same time, it soothed her concerns. Pulling away from Jeannie, Sam looked into her eyes. Warm, compassionate brown eyes that had haunted his dreams six long years.

"Yes, we're safe," Sam said. "You're safe here on your island, and I'm going to make sure nothing goes wrong. The authorities back on the mainland will monitor Reeves. They'll know where he is at all times. Besides, he has no idea where we are."

"Then we can truly relax here on Le Bijou Bleu, and spend our days and nights—"

"Making love."

His next kiss sent shivers of desire rocketing through Jeannie's body, hardening her nipples, flushing her face, moistening her femininity.

Sam sensed her arousal and knew she had tapped into his, increasing her own passion. She gripped his shoulder with one hand. While standing on tiptoe, she dropped her cane onto the hardwood floor and caressed his neck with her fingertips. He lifted her off her feet, cupping her hips as she threaded her fingers through his hair and sighed deep in her throat as he deepened the kiss.

Manton knocked softly on the doorpost, announcing his presence. Slowly, reluctantly, Sam eased Jeannie back down on her feet, ending the kiss gradually. Holding on to his forearms, she stepped back, separating their bodies. Clasping Jeannie about the waist with one hand, Sam bent over and picked up her cane.

Manton glanced at Sam, giving him a brief but thorough inspection, then looked at Jeannie. Smiling, she nodded, then laughed aloud. Sam had no idea what they were saying to each other.

Jeannie wondered how long it would take Sam to realize that Manton approved of him, that he was actually encouraging Jeannie to explore her feelings for Sam.

I think a romantic dinner on the veranda would be appropriate, Jeannie told Manton telepathically.

Leave everything to me, Manton responded in the same nonverbal manner, his green eyes sparkling with delight. *He has returned to you, as I knew he would. Now, little one, you must claim him. Once you do, he will be yours forever.*

The danger hasn't ended for me, or for Sam, Jeannie said. *I don't know how much time we'll have here on the island together, but however long we have, I want to make that time special.*

I understand. Manton nodded.

Sam shook Jeannie's arm gently. "What's going on here?"

Turning her radiant smile on Sam, Jeannie hugged up to his side. "We were just planning dinner for tonight." She tugged on his hand. "Come on, let's change clothes before I give you a tour of the house and then the island."

"Change clothes?"

She looked him over from head to toe. "You don't plan on wearing a suit while we're here, do you? After all, Ollie went to a lot of trouble this morning, washing your new casual clothes before she repacked them."

"What should I wear?" He followed her out of the parlor, nodding cordially to Manton as he passed him in the doorway.

"Put on some shorts and a T-shirt. And sandals."

Jeannie led him down the hallway, stopping in front of an open door. "This is my room." She pointed to the next room down, directly beside hers. "And that's your room. To come to my room, all you have to do is walk out on the veranda. Every room in the house has access to the veranda."

He jerked her into his arms. Gasping, she gripped her cane, but did not resist him. "Why don't you come to my room with me?" he asked, with a playful leer.

"Go change clothes, and I'll meet you in your room." Pulling away from him, she gave him a shove in the right direction.

Turning around, not waiting to see if he obeyed her request, Jeannie slipped into her room and closed the door behind her. Sam waited for a couple of minutes, then walked to his room. Inside, he found a sunny space of beige-and-yellow warmth. The center point of the room was an old walnut tester bed without a canopy. Black-and-white ticking material had been fashioned into a coverlet and into pillows that mixed with beige-and-yellow down pillows. Sam's clothes bag lay across the foot of the bed; his carryall rested on the seat of a large overstuffed chair.

Shorts, T-shirt and sandals. Jeannie wanted their time together to be a vacation, not an escape from danger. He intended to give her what she wanted. An interlude from the real world.

In the next room, Jeannie sat down on her bed, a huge white oak four-poster with a fancy black ironwork canopy. Hooking her cane over the bottom post, she lay down and breathed in the fresh salt air blowing in off the ocean. She looked around her room, loving every precious inch that she had decorated as a teenager. The heart of pine floors and planked ceilings gave this old house a country charm. While examining the room, she saw, lying on the floral chintz chaise longue, the clothes Manton had laid out for her. Her pale pink-and-lavender-striped sundress. Strapless, with a hem that fell to midcalf. A romantic dress. Beside the dress lay a wide-brimmed straw hat.

Hugging herself, Jeannie laughed.

Manton served their dinner on the veranda. White linen tablecloth and napkins. Polished silver and glistening crystal. After placing their dessert of fruit with a light cream sauce before them, he lit the candles that flanked the small bouquet on the table, then excused himself. The sun hung like a ball of fire in the western horizon, its heat singeing the sky with radiant splashes of purple, magenta and golden orange.

The balmy ocean breeze surrounded Sam and Jeannie, gently flickering the candle flames. They lifted their wineglasses in a toast.

"To heaven here on earth," Sam said. "Thanks to you, my very own angel."

Her eyes glazed with tears. Happy tears. Accepting his toast, she sipped the wine.

"What do you think of Le Bijou Bleu?" She set her glass on the table.

"I see where it got its name. Blue sky and blue water everywhere. I suppose whoever christened this island considered it his own personal blue jewel."

"And now it's my blue jewel," she said. "*Our* blue jewel," she amended.

"I never thought I'd return to this island. The few memories I have of this place are bittersweet. I wanted to forget what happened before and after I was shot."

"I realized how difficult it was for you to come and see me six years ago, when you got out of the hospital." She looked down at the fresh tropical fruit resting in the crystal bowl. "You came only because you felt you owed your life to me."

"I did owe you my life," he said, watching her pick nervously at the linen tablecloth. "When I left Biloxi, I buried the past deep inside me." He tapped his chest with his fist.

"You didn't want to live." Jeannie lifted her eyes, meeting his gaze directly. "You felt you had no right to live."

"I don't want to talk about the past. Not now."

Casting her gaze downward, she hesitated. He was afraid of the complete truth. If he was ever going to heal, he would have to face a guilt too heavy for him to bear alone.

The sweet, melodic strands of a piano solo drifted in the air, like celestial background music. Sam cocked his head to one side, listening. He could have sworn the music wasn't taped, that someone was playing the baby grand in the front parlor. He glanced at Jeannie, his eyes questioning her.

"Manton plays beautifully, don't you think?"

"Manton? But how is it possible for him to play? He's deaf, isn't he?"

"Totally, irreversibly deaf. But he has the talent of a genius."

"I don't understand how—"

"He feels the music." Reaching across the table, Jeannie clasped Sam's hand in hers. "He's played since childhood. A natural talent, one even he doesn't understand. The piece he's playing is his own creation. I believe his talent is truly a gift from God."

"He can't hear what he plays. He can't—"

"It defies explanation. Yes, I know. But so does my empathic ability." She looked into Sam's eyes and told him what she wanted. "There is magic on Le Bijou Bleu. It drew Manton here first, and then me. And now..." She did not allow herself to even think about what she knew in her heart, what Sam was not yet ready to accept.

He sensed her need to be in his arms, to move to Manton's mystical music—a twilight solo so utterly beautiful that Sam knew, without question, that the composition had been created for Jeannie.

Julian Howell's Jeannie. Manton's Jeannie. But, above all else, Sam Dundee's Jeannie. For she belonged to him now, and in ways she could never belong to another. This night would seal her fate. She would become his completely.

But not forever. Their affair here on Le Bijou Bleu would be days and nights out of time. He had no right to want or expect more. Jeannie was an ethereal creature, truly pure of heart, never meant to belong to a man whose hands were stained with blood. But he could not deny himself the chance to become her lover, to capture, if for only a brief while, the magic and wonder of possessing an angel.

Sam stood, rounded the table, pulled out Jeannie's chair and lifted her. Shivering with desire and anticipation, she kicked off her white sandals and allowed Sam to lift the soles of her small, delicate feet atop his big feet.

She wanted to dance the way they had the night on the riverboat. But here on the veranda of her home there would be no interruptions, nothing to intrude on the enchantment. They would be free to follow their hearts, to seek the fulfillment their bodies desired. Tonight was theirs.

Sam waltzed her around the veranda. Her skirt flowed in the breeze. They didn't speak aloud, but they communicated their feelings, exchanged their thoughts and shared their mutual desire.

Sam had opened his mind to her, no longer blocking her entrance into his privacy. Jeannie wondered if he had any idea that he had taken the first step in the healing process that could lead to his salvation. Only if he could trust her enough to share his guilt and pain could she help him face his demons and learn to forgive himself.

Did she have the strength and courage to be the woman Sam needed? Could she ever reach that golden core of goodness inside Sam and help him become the man he was meant to be?

The music swirled inside Jeannie's head as she gave herself over to the rhythm and surrendered completely to Sam, trusting him without hesitation. In his arms she took flight, experiencing once again the freedom she would never know without his support.

When Manton stopped playing and quiet descended, Sam led Jeannie back to the table. She retrieved her cane before they left the veranda for a moonlight stroll on the beach behind the cottage.

The new moon glimmered in the black sky, almost translucent in its pale beauty. A scattering of distant stars winked at them. The ocean waves spread their moon-kissed white foam across the beach, then, recalling the tide, washed away their tracks in the sand. Sam supported Jeannie with his arm around her waist as they stood on the beach, the water licking at their legs.

When Jeannie tired, her slow gait hampered by the sand, Sam lifted her in his arms and carried her to the top of the knoll that overlooked the beach where she'd found his nearly lifeless body six years ago. Placing her on the ground, he sat beside her and pulled her close. She laid her head on his shoulder.

Words were unnecessary. Each knew what the other thought and felt. Sam could not deny how he felt about Jeannie, how desperately he wanted her, how much a part of him she had become.

They sat on the knoll, their damp legs entwined, holding hands and listening to the ocean's gentle rumble as they looked at the night sky.

Then Sam turned to her, cupped her face with both hands and whispered her name aloud. She sighed. A lone teardrop fell from her eye onto his hand.

"It's all right, angel," he said. "This will be a totally new experience for both of us. I have no idea what will happen. The first time for most women is—"

She covered his lips with her index finger. "I'm not like most women. And you, Sam Dundee, are most definitely not like most men."

"I don't want to hurt you." He kissed her tenderly.

"The pain of wanting you without having you is far worse than any pain I'll feel. It will be a pain I'll soon forget in the pleasure that will follow." Curling her arms around his neck, she returned his kiss as their combined emotions began flowing inside her. "Sam?"

He rubbed his hand up and down the side of her thigh, bunching the cotton material of her full skirt, lifting it higher and higher with each upward motion. They fell back onto the ground. Lowering his head, Sam kissed the tops of her swollen breasts rounding above the strapless bodice of her sundress. He palmed her feminine mound through the silk of her panties. She arched up to meet his touch.

Sam leaned over her, his mouth and hands exploring the woman who lay beneath him. Jeannie. Sweet, beautiful, innocent Jeannie.

She moaned into his mouth when he kissed her again. Clinging to him, whimpering her need, stroking her body against his, she incited him to deepen the kiss. He ripped away the material covering her breasts, then slid his hand inside her panties and delved into her moist, welcoming heat.

Overwhelming desire claimed her. Desire so all-consuming she thought she would die from its intensity. Her desire. And Sam's desire.

Releasing her mouth, he breathed deeply. "Not here. Not on the hard ground, exposed like this. Not our first time."

"Then take me home, Sam. Take me home and make me yours."

With his heartbeat wild, his desire at fever pitch, he lifted her into his arms and carried her to the house. He opened the French doors leading from the veranda into her bedroom, walked into the moonlit sanctuary and laid her down on the pure white bed.

Chapter 12

Moonlight suffused the room, coating the walls with pale luminance, casting a yellow-white glow over the floor and furniture, surrounding Jeannie like a body halo of purity. The summer breeze swept inside through the open windows and French doors, encompassing them in a warm cocoon. The ocean's undulatory melody drifted in on the night air.

Jeannie sat up in the middle of the bed and removed her sundress. Wearing only a pair of pink silk panties, her breasts thrusting forward as she braced the palms of her hands on each side of her hips, she smiled and called his name.

"Sam..."

She was a siren now, an enticing vixen with a woman's needs. And yet she was still an angel, so pure and innocent and compassionate.

Jeannie lay back on the bed, her heartbeat drumming in her ears, as she reached up, inviting Sam into her arms. She burned with a need she had never known before Sam Dundee entered her secure world. He had changed everything. After she saved his life, nothing had ever been the same again. And now that he had returned, possessed with a need to protect her, to care for her, their fate was sealed.

Since the night she had suffered agony for him, they had been partially united, their souls connected by a thin, invisible cord. With each passing day they were together, they became closer, their feelings for each other growing stronger. Tonight they would become one. There could be no going back, only forward, straight ahead into the bonding of their souls.

Sam could remember nothing in his life he'd ever wanted more than he wanted Jeannie. His Jeannie. His sweet, beautiful angel.

With arms uplifted, her face kissed with moonlight, she waited for him. He wanted to rip off his clothes and thrust into her with wild abandon. But Jeannie was no ordinary woman. What was happening between them was special, unique. Something to be experienced fully, savored lovingly. He could not rush their lovemaking. For her, this would be the first time. And it would be a first for him, too. Making love to a woman who could feel his every emotion, who could experience his desire and his pleasure. The very thought of what lay ahead scared him as much as it excited him.

Sam unbuttoned his short-sleeved cotton shirt, slid it off his shoulders and tossed it onto the floor at the foot of Jeannie's bed. The way she looked at him—her eyes caressing him, her lips tasting him, her hands tormenting him without once touching him—stirred his blood and hardened his body.

Thick, cascading strands of her silky brown hair covered one bare breast, leaving the other an uncovered temptation. Her breasts rose and fell as she breathed. Her lips parted on an indrawn sigh.

He sensed her longing, her need a viable force, strong enough to sweep them both over the edge of conscious action. He had to remain in control for just a while longer, until he was certain he wouldn't hurt her, wouldn't destroy her with the power of his desire.

Unzipping his navy blue shorts, Sam didn't take his eyes off Jeannie. He trembled, wanting her, needing her. Lured by her femininity, lost to her seductive charms, he surrendered to the desire he could no longer control.

Sliding his shorts down to his ankles, he kicked them aside. He stood before her, all power and masculine muscle, in a pair of navy blue briefs, his sex straining against the silk fabric. Perspiration moistened his hands and forehead; dots of sweat broke out across his upper lip. A white-hot need seared him to the bone.

Jeannie wanted to touch him, to run her hands over every inch of his body, caress every bulging muscle, kiss his tiny, pebble-hard nipples, thread her fingers through the thatch of thick brown hair on his chest. If only he would come to her, allow her to touch him.

Her magnificently beautiful, elegant savage.

Sam eased down on the bed, placing his knees on either side of her feet. Crawling slowly up her body, bracing himself with his hands so that the contact was whisper light, he covered her body with his. She touched him hesitantly at first, sweeping her hands across his shoulders. He shuddered; she trembled.

And then exactly what she had been waiting for happened. The connection. The blending. Gradually, with just faint glimmers of awareness, Jeannie felt Sam's hunger and knew that it more than equaled hers. He was a virile man, experienced in the ways of the world, and yet he was uncertain. He was afraid his desire would be too much for her to handle, that it would be too powerful for her fragile innocence.

He needed her reassurance. She had to do more than issue an invitation; she would have to be the persuader, seducing him beyond the point of no return.

Arching her body, lifting herself closer to Sam, she kissed his chest, then drew a damp circle around first one and then his other nipple. He sucked in a deep, excruciating breath.

She felt the first crack in his iron control. She kissed his shoulder. He eased his body lower, his chest brushing her breasts. She gasped when her breasts tightened, almost painfully, and sent a signal straight to her core.

Slipping her arms around his waist, she buried her face in his shoulder. Her tongue drew spiraling circles from his shoulder, up his neck and to his ear. She squirmed beneath him, well aware of what her movements were doing to him.

He was holding back, trying to be patient. And it was killing him!

Didn't he know, she wondered, that she felt every painful throb of his sex, every pulsating ache? Had he no idea that the longer he postponed their lovemaking, the more painfully aroused she would become?

She kissed his cheek. The pulse in his neck twitched. She covered his mouth, licking like a kitten lapping cream until he opened to her insistent little tongue, taking her inside as he followed her lead. Intensifying the kiss, Sam devoured her as he gripped her hips, lifting her up and against his arousal. She cried out, the sound trapped in his mouth, as shudders of intense pleasure skyrocketed through her.

Continuing the kiss, he divested her of her pink panties and eased his hand between her legs, parting her thighs. With an equal amount of urgency, she tugged on his briefs, pulling them down and over his firm, rounded buttocks, pausing to stroke him lovingly. Using her foot, she slid his briefs to his ankles and off onto the floor.

With each touch, each kiss, each urgent moan, the link between them grew stronger, until Sam, too, faintly sensed Jeannie's feelings. Knowing she wanted him as much as he wanted her only added fuel to the blazing flame of his passion.

He touched her nipple, already beaded and throbbing. She swallowed a moan. He placed his mouth on her, suckling her breast. She wrapped herself around him, her soft little cries a plea for release.

"Please, don't wait any longer," she whispered as he suckled her other breast. "Oh, Sam, put an end to our pain."

Too soon! Too soon! his mind told him. *Now!* his body urged. *She feels what you feel,* his heart told him.

"I need to protect you," he said.

"I need no protection from you, Sam."

And then he sensed her probing, seeking entrance inside his mind. He allowed her to come in, and when their minds joined, each realized the searing-hot fire and uncontrollable force of their combined madness. Knowing he would hurt her, if only briefly, Sam tried to be gentle, lifting her hips, entering her by slow degrees.

He was so big; she was so small.

He was a savage brute; she was a gentle angel.

No! she cried out silently. *I'm as savage as you are and you are as gentle as I am. Take me, Sam. Please take me now!*

Sam responded by thrusting to the hilt, giving her all of himself. She groaned, accepting the quick, hot pain. He stopped, his breathing ragged, sweat dripping from his body onto hers.

Heaven help him, but he'd felt her pain. How was that possible? It wasn't.

The pain subsided. She knew he'd felt it, too, but had dismissed it as impossible.

Jeannie moved, lifting up, wrapping her legs around Sam's hips, urging him to resume. Pleasure rippled through him as the pressure built. Pulling partly out of her, he hesitated only a second before plunging deeply again and starting the primeval mating dance.

His iron control cracked in a dozen places, weakening his defenses, making him more vulnerable, open to her possession. The agony intensified, the pressure inside them close to exploding. Jeannie clung to him, whispering his name in gasping little chants. Sam moaned dark, desperate, erotic words to her.

Release hit them simultaneously, or so Jeannie thought, but she soon realized that the fulfillment she felt was Sam's. Wild, hot, savage. He emptied his seed into her, shudders of pleasure jerking his big body. The sensations rocketed through her, and she cried out, trembling with the aftershocks.

Agony turned to ecstasy. But before she fell from the heights of rapture, she gripped his hips, lifting herself up against him, stroking her body against his frantically. Strong, forceful spasms clutched her sex, then threw her headlong into the heaven of carnal fulfillment. She clung to him as wave after wave of joyous release washed over her.

Sam held her, aware of her completion, and fully aware that in some way, though faint and subdued, he shared her release.

Easing off her and onto his side, he drew her into his arms and kissed her forehead. They lay there in the aftermath of a loving so profound neither of them could find the words to express how they felt. When their ragged breathing settled to normal, Sam got out of bed, lifted Jeannie in his arms and smothered her with passionate kisses. She clung to him, knowing that she was now Sam Dundee's woman in every sense of the word. She had never felt closer to anyone in her life.

Sam carried her across the bedroom, kicked open the bathroom door and stepped into the shower. When he turned the faucets, a spray of cold water hit their naked bodies. Jeannie squealed. Sam held her with one hand while adjusting the water temperature. The shower poured over them with refreshing warmth. He picked up a bar of white soap, smelled its sweet perfume, then grinned.

"If I use this stuff, I'll smell like you," he said.

"You already do."

He laughed. She loved the sound of his laughter. So hearty. So genuine. She had to make sure he laughed more.

"And you smell like me." Lowering his head, he licked her breasts, from one nipple to the other. "And you taste like me."

He lathered her body slowly, taking special care to be gentle as he cleaned away the residue of her innocence. He braced her against the ceramic wall, washing her thoroughly.

Lowering himself to his knees, he held her hip with one hand while he spread her legs farther apart. She gripped his shoulders. Her body clenched, released, then repeated the process. While the warm water cascaded down Jeannie's body and onto Sam's back, he sought her feminine core and began a sensual assault that left her breathless and pleading. His mouth covered her, his tongue driving her crazy with its strong, sensuous attack.

She swelled and tightened, then turned to liquid fire. She cried out; he groaned, the sound rumbling from deep in his chest. She splintered into a million pieces of indescribable pleasure; his sex hardened painfully when fragments of her fulfillment sizzled through his body. Tiny sparks of white-hot ecstasy claimed him as surely as they had Jeannie.

During the moments of downward-spiraling release, Jeannie squeezed Sam's shoulders, urging him to stand. He stood slowly, sliding himself up and against her. She circled him with her hand. He gritted his teeth, trying not to cry out, and covered her hand with his, instructing her movements. Once. Twice. Three times. He thrust his tongue inside her mouth at the precise moment he erupted into completion. He threw back his head as a deep, guttural cry escaped from his lips, torn from his body with the force of his release. Experiencing to an infinite degree the explosion of Sam's sensations and emotions, Jeannie wrapped her arms around his waist. They clung to each other, weak and exhausted, as the water washed over them. Finally, Sam reached out and shut off the water.

Covering Jeannie in a huge white towel, he dried her with the patience of a parent tending to a child. She reciprocated, drying him, delighting in his playful growl when she stroked him intimately.

Naked, clean and sated, they gazed longingly into each other's eyes. At that precise moment, words were redundant. He kissed her gently; she returned the kiss. Lifting her in his arms, he carried her back to her bed, stripped away the soiled coverlet and jerked the floral blanket up into the air. He flung the blanket over his shoulder, half of it covering Jeannie. She peeked out from beneath the blanket as he carried her outside, onto the veranda. He kissed her on the nose. She giggled.

Sam covered a huge wicker rocker with the floral blanket, then sat down, Jeannie in his lap. She cuddled in his arms, their naked bodies warm against each other. They sat in the wicker rocker on the veranda, man and woman, lovers for the first time, and the bonding that had begun on the beach six years ago grew stronger. They both felt what was happening. She acknowledged it in her heart; he fought the truth, unable to relinquish complete control.

For endless moments, time having become meaningless, they absorbed the beauty of the night, the moon and stars, the soft, balmy breeze, the ocean's song.

Hours later, Jeannie awoke in his arms and lifted her head, seeking his mouth, initiating a kiss that quickly turned passionate. Turning her body, she rose over him, straddling him, bracing her knees on each side of him. "Make love to me again, Sam." She nuzzled his ear with her nose.

"It's too soon. You're sore, and I don't want to hurt you again." He stroked her hip.

"I'm not that sore," she told him. "I ache with the wanting, and I know you do, too."

Gripping her buttocks, he lifted her as he stood and carried her across the porch, resting her on the top of the wide banister. She kept her arms locked around his neck as he positioned himself, bending his knees, pulling her forward. The joining was swift and complete. Jeannie gasped; Sam moaned. Clutching her hips in his big hands, he guided her back and forth, lifting her completely off the banister. She wrapped her legs around him, clinging to him as the hard, hot plunges stroked her to an unbearable pleasure. She spiraled out of control, crying out her completion. Sam shook from the sensations he experienced, then fell headlong into oblivion with one final, forceful lunge. While he trembled, she quivered, and he held her in his arms, her legs and arms wrapped around him, their mouths locked in a passionate kiss. And the intimate bonding of their hearts and souls continued, binding them together, strengthening their ability to share every feeling.

From inside the house, they heard the soft, sweet strains of piano music. Jeannie's song. Manton knew. And he was paying tribute to their love.

Jeannie kicked the sand with her bare toes. Sam rubbed suntan lotion on her delicate skin, coating her back and arms thoroughly, then starting on her legs. Beautiful, silky legs. But physically weak, unable to fully support her slender weight. He kissed her inner thigh. She ruffled his thick blond hair.

Sam looked up at her and smiled. "I promise you, my childhood was boring and meaningless. I don't know why you want to hear about it."

"Because I picture you as this serious little boy who went around with a frown on his face." Jeannie giggled when he tickled her foot. "Come on, tell me. This is called getting to know each other. You go first."

Sam completed his suntan detail, recapped the bottle and tossed it on the blanket beside the picnic hamper. "My father was a career soldier, so I didn't see much of him, even before he died. After our mother's death, James and I lived with an aunt and uncle, and I stayed on with them when James joined the marines. Aunt Harriet and Uncle Pete are both gone now."

"Were you a happy child?" Jeannie rummaged around inside the picnic basket, retrieved a bottle of wine and two clear plastic glasses. She handed the wine to Sam.

He opened the bottle, filled their glasses, then reached around Jeannie to place the wine back in the hamper. "I guess I enjoyed my childhood as much as any kid does, but I never had a lot of friends. I was a bit of a loner." Jeannie handed Sam a glass of wine. "I idolized my father. So did James. I thought my dad was a real hero. I wanted to be just like him."

"I never knew my real father." Jeannie placed cheese, apples and wheat crackers on a plastic plate. "My mother got pregnant when she was sixteen. She was only twenty-two when she married Randy Foley." Jeannie shook her head from side to side, making her long ponytail bounce from shoulder blade to shoulder blade. "Julian and Manton have both been like fathers to me."

"Yeah, well, when our old man died, James became my substitute father. I followed him into the marines as soon as I turned eighteen. And when he got married, James's wife told me that their home would always be mine. Sandra was a special lady."

Jeannie clasped Sam's hand. "It's all right to still feel sad about their dying so young."

"Elizabeth was only twelve. She really needed her parents, but she was lucky. She had a great-aunt who understood what it meant to be psychic. Legally, I was Elizabeth's guardian, but her great-aunt Margaret was the one who raised her.''

"You love Elizabeth dearly, don't you?"

Sam brought Jeannie's hand to his lips, kissed the open palm and laid it over his heart. "She's the only person I had in my life to love." He gazed down into the wine, sighed, then took a sip. "But she's a grown woman now, married and a mother. Every time I look at her little boy—"

"You want a child of your own, don't you, Sam?" She sensed the need in him, tapping into his emotions simply by touching him. Big, macho, hard-edged soldier, government agent and bodyguard, Sam Dundee had a central core of goodness, a wellspring of pure golden love just waiting to be lavished on a child.

He jerked away from her, spilling his wine. Standing, he faced the sun, then shaded his eyes with his big hand. She watched him, his broad shoulders moving slightly when he breathed.

"I'm sorry," she said. "I couldn't help picking up on what you were feeling. I didn't mean to intrude on something that's obviously painful for you."

She knew! Dear God, she knew. She had gotten that deep inside him.

Sam willed himself not to think about what had happened six years ago, about what had happened to the child who might have been his. "Your childhood was pretty rotten, wasn't it?" he asked her, deliberately changing the subject. "Until you went to live with Julian and Miriam Howell."

"You can't imagine." Jeannie sipped the wine slowly. "From when I was six and Mama married Randy Foley, until I was thirteen and they died in the car crash that crippled me, I lived in pain every day of my life. Except..."

Sam sat down again on the quilt beside Jeannie, cupped her chin in his hand and tilted her face upward. She stared into his eyes. "Except when you came to Le Bijou Bleu for vacations."

"This island was my heaven. And Manton was my guardian angel. He was the first person I communicated with telepathically. I never told Mama and Randy. It would have been one more thing they would have tried to exploit. And I didn't try to develop the talent. It never happened again until Miriam became sick and . . ." Tears gathered in Jeannie's eyes; she bit her bottom lip. "I loved her so dearly."

"Cancer can be a horrible way to die," Sam said.

"She suffered unbearably near the end." Jeannie swallowed her tears as the memories of Miriam's final days flooded her memory.

"And you shared that suffering. You made it bearable." He pulled her into his arms, stroking her back, resting his head atop hers, his cheek brushing her hair. "It must have been terrible for you."

"Yes and no. It would have been worse for me if I hadn't been able to absorb some of her pain, to take away the suffering for just a few hours, to give her a little relief. There came a time when the drugs didn't help."

"She was very fortunate to have you." Sam kissed the side of Jeannie's face.

She slipped her arms around his waist, touching his naked skin beneath his loose cotton shirt. "I was fortunate to have her for a mother for so many years. She was an extraordinary woman. Beautiful. Brilliant. Compassionate. I would have done anything for her."

"And you did." He soothed her with his hands, caressing her tenderly.

"Can't you understand?" She looked at him, asking him to put himself in her place. "If you saw someone you loved in excruciating pain, wouldn't you want to make the pain go away? Wouldn't you, if you could, suffer that pain for them?"

Sam kissed her. Hot. Fierce. Demanding. Yes, he understood what it meant to care so deeply for someone, to be willing to die for that person if necessary. When he released her mouth, she gasped for air.

"Sam?" She'd felt it, that tiny kernel of emotion called love. It was there, buried so deep within Sam that he wasn't even consciously aware it existed. All these years, there had been no one to keep love alive in Sam, no one except Elizabeth.

But Sam had never been deeply in love, had never bonded with a woman. Not until— But their bonding was incomplete, despite a week of making love and sharing private thoughts and feelings. He wouldn't allow himself to love her. The risk was too great. And as much as he wanted a child—even if he denied that great desire—he had not made love to Jeannie again, after that first night, without using protection.

And just who was he protecting, she wondered, her or himself?

Sam peeled off his shirt, dropped it on the quilt and nodded toward the ocean. "How about a swim before we eat lunch?"

Jeannie held up her arms to him. He lifted her, carried her across the beach, and together they dived into the water. Within minutes, his dark mood lightened and the sadness left her eyes. They frolicked in the Gulf like two playful children. Later they sat in the shade of a huge old live oak with branches that drooped to the ground and had taken root. They ate the cheese and fruit, drank the wine and made slow, sweet love.

With each passing day, with each shared intimacy, Sam and Jeannie's joining became stronger. If Sam could ever bring himself to love her, truly love her, they would become one. Every beat of his heart, hers. Every breath she took, his. Her thoughts, her emotions, her feelings, would belong to him, and his to her. How deep the bonding would go, even Jeannie did not know.

Chapter 13

Jeannie cuddled in Sam's arms. The late-afternoon sun was behind them, the ocean breeze soft and warm on their bare skin. With an occasional backward sweep of his foot, Sam kept the wooden porch swing in slow but continuous motion as he held Jeannie close. Caressing her shoulder with one hand, he rested his cheek against the side of her head. Her fresh, clean smell surrounded him. Turning her head just a fraction, she glanced up at him and smiled. Bringing his mouth down on hers, he kissed her with the wonderful sweetness of familiarity. In the twenty days they'd spent on Le Bijou Bleu, Sam had allowed himself to drown in the pleasure of loving Jeannie, of being at her side night and day, of discovering the incredible sensations of having his lover experience his every emotion, just as he was beginning to experience hers.

They hadn't spoken about what was happening to him, the fact that he was becoming more and more attuned to Jeannie's thoughts and feelings with each passing day. Although Sam didn't scoff at the idea of psychic powers, having been exposed to Elizabeth's psychic talents for so many years, he'd never experienced any himself. Until now, with Jeannie. Although whatever was happening to him was on a limited basis, he had to admit that he could communicate with Jeannie telepathically, to a certain extent. And each time they made love, the sensation of feeling what she felt grew stronger and stronger. He couldn't imagine what it was like for her, experiencing his fulfillment and her own.

Manton's piano music drifted through the open French doors. Every afternoon, without fail, the gentle giant of a man played his sentimental compositions.

"Listen," Jeannie said. "That's something new. He's never played it before."

The tune seeped into Sam's mind, and for some odd reason, its sweet, vibrant melody resurrected long-buried memories. That night six years ago, a three-piece band had played on the riverboat nightclub owned by Louis Herriot, a man the DEA wanted badly enough to place Sam and new agent Brock Holmes in a dangerous undercover operation. And everything had gone exactly as planned, until Connie Bell inadvertently walked into the middle of things as the sting was coming down.

"Sam?" Jeannie touched his face.

He jumped, then stared at her, suddenly aware of where his thoughts were leading him. "I'm all right."

"No, you're not." She caressed his cheek.

Closing his eyes, loving the feel of her, he covered her hand. "There's no point in talking about what happened. It's over and done with, and I'll have to live with the consequences the rest of my life. All the talking in the world won't change anything."

"Talking might help you deal with the grief and the guilt." She sensed his resistance, his fear, his guilt. Several times she had been right on the verge of telling him she was aware of the terrible pain eating away at his soul, but he'd sealed himself off from her, and she had respected his privacy.

"Don't you know you can share anything with me and I'll understand? If you'll only let me, I can ease your suffering."

Releasing his hold on her, he moved away, then stood, keeping his back to her. He thrust his hands into the front pockets of the cutoff jeans he wore. "Like you did the day you saved my life?"

She shivered with the force of his anger as it spiraled inside her. Reaching for her cane that rested against the wall, she slid to the edge of the swing. "Yes, like I did the day I found you on the beach. You felt guilty for two people's deaths. You didn't think you deserved to live."

"Yeah." Sam walked down the veranda, stopping several feet away from her. "I thought I was dying, and when I came to and saw you, I thought you were an angel." He emitted a grunting laugh. "Ironic, isn't it? As it turned out, that's exactly what you were."

"You can't spend the rest of your life blaming yourself, hating yourself, letting that guilt destroy your ability to live and love." Positioning her cane, Jeannie stood and took several steps toward Sam. She laid her hand on his back. He flinched.

"Don't do this," he said. "I don't want you to suffer for me. I don't want you to know what it feels like."

"Please trust me, Sam." She slipped her arms around his waist, holding tight when he started to withdraw from her. "You must know how much you mean to me. You're the one person in this world I most want to help."

His unrelenting guilt hit her with shattering force. She clung to Sam, resting her head on his back. Dear God, the pain inside him was unbearable. Dark, bitter rage simmered in his soul. Damned forever. Oh, her poor Sam. A lesser man would never know such guilt.

"Stop it!" He realized what had happened, what he had allowed to happen. Dammit, he wasn't going to let her absorb any more of the tormenting grief from which he could never escape. His grief and guilt were his punishment, not hers. She was innocent, so very innocent.

"Talk to me about what happened. Let it go. Give it to me and let me share your burden. Allow me to help you." While she held him with the fierceness of that abiding protective devotion, she gave those very feelings over to him, allowing him to experience the great depth of her emotions.

"I don't want your help!" Jerking out of her embrace, he stalked off the veranda and across the wide expanse of lush green lawn.

Jeannie stood on the veranda and watched him walk away. Tears filled her eyes, ran down her cheeks, trickled off her nose and over her lips. She couldn't force him to come to her, expose his heart's deepest emotions and bare his soul. But neither could she let him suffer alone, as he had done for the past six years. If he would not allow her to take away his guilt and grief for a few hours, she could still be at his side, supporting him while he grieved anew.

She took one step down from the veranda, then heard Manton call to her. Turning around, she saw him standing behind her.

Did you like the new composition I played for you and Sam today? he asked telepathically.

It was lovely, but—

It made Sam very sad, didn't it?

Yes. It made him think of something he would like to forget.

I wrote the song for your child, Jeannie. For your and Sam Dundee's child.

Jeannie stared directly into Manton's piercing green eyes. Several days ago, she had made the first connection with the new life growing inside her. If she had not been so overwhelmed with all the new feelings she'd experienced the first time she and Sam made love, she would have known immediately that she had conceived his child.

"I knew I couldn't keep the child a secret from you," she said her lips moving silently.

You should not keep her a secret from her father, either.

Jeannie laid her hand tenderly over her flat stomach. Sam's child. The most precious gift God could have given her. She had been given so much. Dare she ask for Sam's salvation from guilt and grief? Dare she ask that he be freed from the past so that he could open his heart and love her? Perhaps she had been blessed with more than enough. Perhaps what she and Sam had already been given was all heaven would allow.

I can't tell Sam now. It's too soon. He has to deal with his old grief first.

Then go to him, Manton said. *He will never be able to come to terms with what is destroying him without your help.*

Jeannie embraced Manton, her heart filled with love for him. He was the dearest of men, his soul so pure that it was on its final journey to completion.

She walked down the steps and into the yard. She knew where Sam had gone. Back to the beach where he had washed ashore six years ago.

She found him looking out at the ocean, his body statue-hard, the wind whipping his hair into his eyes, his face etched with tense lines of agony.

When she approached him, she didn't touch him, but he sensed her presence. Turning around, he looked at her with dead eyes, eyes of pure gray steel. She took a tentative step forward; he didn't move. Another step. And another.

He watched her, his gaze fixed to hers. She stood directly in front of him, one hand holding her walking stick, the other clutching the side of her peach gauze skirt. A muscle in his neck throbbed. His lips parted. He sucked in a deep breath.

Tearstains marred her face. The hand with which she held the cane trembled, the movement barely discernible. She looked at him with eyes of love and understanding and compassion. His big shoulders slumped ever so slightly. His eyes softened from steel to blue-gray.

He was losing this battle, and he knew it. He might be twice Jeannie's size, his body far more powerful, but inside that fragile body, within that enormous heart of hers, lived a strength for which Sam was no match.

A fine glaze of moisture covered his eyes. He blinked away the evidence of emotion, but he could not turn away from Jeannie. He pulled her into his arms. She went willingly, gladly, dropping her cane onto the sandy beach. She wrapped him in the warmth of her embrace, petting his back with gentle up-and-down strokes. After six long years of running away from a truth that tormented him, Sam knew the time had come to exorcise the demon.

But, dear God, how could he endure watching her hurt for him? How could he, once again, be the recipient of her tender mercy?

"I knew better." He spoke softly, the words a mere whisper on the wind. "If I hadn't been so damned stupid!"

"You made a mistake, Sam. Everyone makes mistakes." She hugged him, absorbing his feelings.

"But not everyone's mistakes cost two people their lives." Clinging to her, he allowed her inside his mind and heart and body. He held back nothing.

Releasing her hold around his waist, she reached up and took his face in her hands. Every muscle in his body tensed. Jeannie held his face, forcing him to look directly into her eyes. "Say it. You blame yourself for Brock Holmes's death. He was a rookie agent, and you felt responsible for him. You blame yourself for the death of Connie Bell, the woman you were having an affair with, the woman who was a nightclub singer in Louie Herriot's employ. You knew better than to become personally involved with someone while you were on an assignment. If you hadn't been sleeping with her, she wouldn't have shown up at the wrong place and the wrong time and gotten shot.

"But it isn't Brock's death, or even Connie's, that you can never forgive yourself for causing. Tell me, Sam. Say it aloud. You've never done that, have you? You keep the truth hidden so deep inside you that it's festered into a rotting sore."

He glared at her, his big body shaking, his eyes dry, his face crumpling before her very eyes. "Dammit, she was pregnant!"

"I know." Jeannie slid her hands down Sam's neck and out to his shoulders, gripping them firmly. "Say it. Just this once, and you'll never have to say it again."

The pain inside him carried him to his knees, Jeannie with him. She could feel the guilt, the anguish, the gut-wrenching pain, as it began to leave him and make its way into her.

"Don't you see, the child could have been mine? I didn't have any idea she was pregnant. After I woke up in the Biloxi hospital, I found out about her being pregnant from another agent who'd been sent in to wrap up the case. Connie was two months pregnant. That baby—" he clutched Jeannie's hands, holding them between their bodies "—was probably mine."

"Say it!" Jeannie cried the tears Sam could not shed. The pain eased from him; she took it upon herself.

"It's my fault that child was never born. I'm responsible for the death of my own child!"

A heavy weight of guilt lifted from Sam. Pain and grief cleared from his heart and soul. He breathed deeply, drawing fresh air into his lungs, cleaning out the dark, dank recesses of his heart, allowing his soul a brief hint of reprieve.

At sunset, Jeannie sat in Sam's lap on the beach, cocooned in the security of his strong arms. Sam held her, never wanting to let her go.

"The grief and the guilt will always be there," she said. "You know that, don't you? But now that you've faced them, you can learn to deal with them."

"I can't change the past."

"No, but you must learn to live with it."

"I wasn't in love with Connie, and she wasn't in love with me. She'd just broken off with another guy, and I knew he was still around."

"The child could have been his or yours, and you'll never know." Jeannie took Sam's hand and laid it on her stomach, covering his hand with hers. "But the guilt is the same, because there's a good chance the child was yours."

"If I hadn't let my... I knew better. I screwed up and it cost two... three people's lives."

"The only way to atone for that mistake is to make the most of *your* life. Give all that's good and strong within you to others. Forgive yourself, and find the love buried deep inside you."

"I don't know if there's any love in me," he said.

"You love Elizabeth and her child." Jeannie leaned back, letting her head rest on his shoulder. "I know there's more love inside you, if you'll only release it. But no one else can do that for you, Sam. Not even me."

No, not even Jeannie, sweet, angelic Jeannie, could save him. Hell, he wasn't sure he wanted to be saved. He had become accustomed to his guilt and remorse. To the pain.

And the price of salvation was too high. If a man didn't care too much, he didn't put his emotions on the line. If caring for others to the extent Jeannie cared, and being willing to open himself up to his deepest emotions, was the only recourse, Sam knew he was damned. Jeannie Alverson was expecting too much from him. He could never be the man she wanted or needed.

Turning in his arms quickly, Jeannie kissed him. A tender, loving kiss. "It's all right. I'm not asking for more than you can give." She caressed his cheek, knowing in her heart that her words were a lie. She wanted Sam Dundee. All of him. His body. His heart. His mind. His very soul. And she wanted him forever. But he hadn't promised her forever. All they had was today.

The ringing telephone awoke them before dawn. Within minutes, Manton knocked softly on Jeannie's bedroom door.

"Something's wrong." Jeannie sat upright, the pastel floral sheet sliding off her naked breasts to rest at her waist. "We've received a fax from the mainland."

Sam slipped into his shorts and stepped out into the hallway. Manton handed him the faxed communication. Scanning the message quickly, Sam groaned. His stomach muscles tightened. Hell! He wished he didn't have to tell Jeannie. There would be no way to keep her on the island once she knew what had happened.

"I'll tell her." Sam looked directly at Manton so that the big man could read his lips.

Manton nodded, then signed to Sam. In the three weeks they'd been on the island, Sam had tried to learn a few basic words in sign. The best he could make out, Manton was saying he'd prepare some coffee and would bring it to them.

Jeannie pulled her pastel yellow gown over her head, lifting her body to ease the silky material down her hips. Swinging her legs off the side of the bed, she looked up at Sam when he returned with the fax message in his hand.

"It's Julian. What's happened? Did Maynard Reeves—? Oh, no, it's Julian's heart."

Sitting on the edge of the bed beside her, Sam took her hands in his. "Julian's had a heart attack. He's in intensive care. The fax is from Marta. She's with him."

"I've got to get to Biloxi." She squeezed Sam's hands. "Julian needs me. No one else can help him the way I can."

"Maynard Reeves still poses as much of a threat to you as he ever did. If you return to Biloxi, you'll be in danger."

"I know that." She bowed her head, praying silently.

"The doctors will take care of Julian. If they can't save his life, then there's nothing you can do."

She snapped her head up, glaring at Sam. "I'm going back to Biloxi. If Julian dies, I want to be there with him. And if he lives, I can help."

Sam wondered why he had even tried to reason with Jeannie. Why couldn't he just accept the fact that her compassionate heart would always win any battle against logic? For there was no logic to Jeannie's powers, no reasonable explanation. Somehow she had been blessed, or perhaps she'd been cursed, with the ability to truly bestow loving kindness on others. He, of all people, knew what it meant to be the recipient of her tender mercy.

Sam nodded. Jeannie's glare softened to a gentle stare. "I'll take care of Julian," she said. "And you will take care of me."

He kissed her on the forehead. "I'll take good care of you." Standing, he helped her to her feet and into her silk robe, then handed her a cane. "Manton's fixing coffee."

"I'm sorry our days in paradise have to come to an end," Jeannie said, looking at him lovingly.

"Anywhere I am with you is paradise. Don't you know that?"

Manton knocked on the door, then came in carrying a tray, which he placed on Jeannie's desk, an antique of white-painted wood, with a sailing ship surrounded by a circle of roses stenciled on the back. He poured Jeannie a cup, placing cream and sugar in the coffee, then handed it to her. He poured another cup and handed the black liquid to Sam.

Immediately he signed to Sam, looking to Jeannie to translate whatever wasn't immediately understood.

"He wants you to keep me safe," Jeannie said. "He senses danger for both of us. He doesn't want us to leave the island, but he understands that we must."

Jeannie patted Manton's enormous hand, then lifted it to her lips and kissed it. "We'll come back to Le Bijou Bleu as soon as Julian is well." She glanced over at Sam. "Won't we?"

Sam nodded agreement, but he wasn't sure he'd ever return to this island. Once they were back in Biloxi, he would have to deal with Maynard Reeves. After three weeks of searching for any type of evidence that would warrant Reeves's arrest, the local and federal authorities still had nothing concrete. Reeves was still a free man, waiting for Jeannie Alverson to come out of hiding.

Marta McCorkle kissed Julian's pale cheek, then thanked the young nurse who stood by his bedside. She walked out of the ICU unit and right past the man who stood with his back to her. Maynard Reeves had been told of Julian's heart attack by a Righteous Light disciple, a hospital janitor who'd been working when the medics rushed Julian into the emergency room.

Maynard had been waiting patiently for Marta McCorkle to leave the ICU. All he needed was a few moments alone with Julian Howell. For twenty days, he had tried by every method possible to discover Jeannie Alverson's whereabouts. Dundee had taken her away, was hiding her, keeping her safe. Maynard knew his only hope of finding Jeannie was to get the information from the one person who would know where she was. Julian Howell. But he hadn't been able to get anywhere near Dr. Howell, and making a psychic link with someone he couldn't touch was beyond his capabilities.

No one, except Jeannie and his old friend Wayland Krenshaw, knew he was psychic. Wayland was his right-hand man, a trusted deacon in the church they had founded together. But Jeannie was his enemy. She had refused to join his great cause, to use her talent, as he used his, in the service of the Lord.

He deeply regretted that his psychic abilities were so limited. He knew God had meant for his powers to be greater, but his stupid parents had stifled the natural growth of his powers. If only Jeannie Alverson had joined him, there would have been no limit to the heights he could have reached. Together, they could have been the most powerful force for good in the world.

But Jeannie had shown her true colors. She dared not use her powers in the Lord's service, when her real master was the devil. The woman was a witch, not a saint, as he had hoped. She and her guardian, Dundee, would annihilate him if they could. Satan had given her enormous power, power far greater than those Maynard himself had been blessed with. He had no choice but to destroy her, before she destroyed him.

"May I help you, Father?" the nurse asked.

"Yes, my child. I've come to see Julian Howell." Reeves stood tall and straight in his priest's disguise, one he knew might gain him an audience with Dr. Howell.

"Are you his priest?"

"My parish is near New Orleans," Reeves lied. "I'm a family friend who has been called in for special prayers."

"Dr. Howell's daughter hasn't arrived yet," the nurse said. "And Ms. McCorkle has gone to make a few phone calls. I really need the family's permission before I allow you to visit Dr. Howell."

"My dear child, I am here at the family's request." He lifted the white Bible he held in his hand. "They know I will be a comfort to Julian."

"Well, I don't suppose there would be anything wrong with letting you come in for a few minutes."

Maynard flashed her his most charming smile, the smile he had used often to persuade ladies to donate large sums of money to the Righteous Light Church. "I need only a few minutes."

Maynard found Julian Howell resting comfortably, his every bodily function monitored. The young nurse stayed with him, still a bit uneasy about allowing someone other than immediate family to visit an ICU patient.

Placing his hand over Julian's, Maynard closed his eyes and began mumbling something he hoped would sound like a prayer. He lowered his voice, allowing it to drift off into silence. Closing his eyes, he concentrated on Julian. Hazy, sleepy, surreal thoughts and images clouded Julian's mind. Maynard probed deeper.

Jeannie is safe, Maynard said telepathically. *Far away from Biloxi and any danger. Think about where she is and how safe she is.*

Visions of blue sky and water formed in Maynard's mind, then an island, lush and green, a big raised French cottage resting high on a hill.

Dundee had taken her to an island. But where?

When Maynard tried to delve deeper into Julian's subconscious mind, he realized Jeannie's foster father was fighting him, trying to keep him out before he acquired the much-needed information.

Julian thrashed about in the bed. The nurse rushed to his side. "I'm afraid you'll have to leave. Something's wrong. Dr. Howell is becoming quite agitated."

Maynard forced his way past the barrier in Julian's mind. Le Bijou Bleu. The distance from Biloxi and the location of the island flashed through Julian's thoughts, and then his mind closed.

"Father, please leave," the nurse repeated her request.

Opening his eyes, Maynard smiled. "Yes, of course. I'll return later, when he's awake and calm."

When Maynard opened the door to exit the ICU unit, Lieutenant Painter met him. How had that idiot found him? He'd been certain he'd ditched the policeman following him.

"Changed religious affiliations, Reverend Reeves?" Painter asked. "Or should I call you Father Reeves now?

"Reverend Reeves will do. What are you doing here, Lieutenant?"

"I was about to ask you the same question."

"Visiting the sick, of course."

"I'm sure I could hold you in jail overnight, Reverend. Impersonating a priest might not stick in court, but I could drum up some other charges to go with it so we could haul your butt in for questioning."

"The clothing I choose to wear in my role as a minster of the gospel is my business, and the fact that a young nurse mistook me for a priest is not my fault." Maynard wasn't afraid of the police. He had outsmarted them time and again. No, he didn't have anything to fear from the likes of Rufus Painter.

"What the hell is he doing here?" A deep voice roared from the doorway leading into the waiting room.

Maynard jerked around, his eyes widening with surprise. Sam Dundee. And, at his side, Jeannie Alverson. Maynard smiled. So, he would not have to go in search of the witch after all. She had returned. No doubt to cast a spell to cure her foster father.

Jeannie clung to her protector's arm. She was so sure he could guard her from the inevitable. Well, she was wrong. Sam Dundee was indeed a formidable opponent, but all Maynard needed was a little time to figure out how to bring the big man down.

"I thought y'all were watching him," Jeannie said. "How did he get in here to see Julian?"

"He's leaving right now," Painter said. "I'm driving him to the station, where he can call his lawyer before answering a few questions for us."

"This is all a waste of time," Maynard told them. "You cannot condemn an innocent man. And you have no evidence that I've committed any crime."

"Lieutenant, would you mind going with Jeannie to see Dr. Howell?" Sam asked. "Reeves is right. Taking him in would be a waste of time. Yours and his."

"How wise of you to understand," Maynard said.

"Please, Lieutenant, go with Jeannie. She's anxious to see her father."

"Sam?" Jeannie said, questioning his intentions.

"Go on. See about Julian."

Lieutenant Painter escorted a reluctant Jeannie into the private ICU cubicle, leaving Maynard alone in the waiting area with Sam.

"Watch her day and night, Dundee." Maynard laughed, the sound robust and confident. "You know not the hour or the day I will strike."

Sam grabbed Maynard by the neck, dragging his face up to his. My God, what did the man intend to do? Kill him on the spot? Maynard lifted his trembling hands, desperately trying to dislodge himself from Dundee's choking hold. Maynard gasped, then struggled for air when Sam tightened the pressure on his windpipe.

"Know this, Reeves—if any harm comes to Jeannie, you will die. And a soul as black as yours will surely rot in hell forever."

Chapter 14

Jeannie sat at Julian's bedside, his hand clasped in hers. She had stayed with him since her return to Biloxi, thirty-six hours earlier. Sam had done everything short of knocking her out and throwing her over his shoulder to get her to leave for a short rest, but she had refused. The doctors had told them Julian was out of any immediate danger, but with a heart-attack victim, nothing could be certain.

Jeannie had been given special permission to stay with Julian in ICU, but Sam had been banished to the waiting area, except for regularly scheduled visits. The past thirty-six hours had been an exercise in torture for him. Keeping guard at a distance was not Sam's style of protection.

The ICU door opened and Jeannie walked out, a wide smile on her face. "They're moving Julian to a private room. He's improving quickly. The doctors are astonished."

Sam dropped the newspaper he'd been scanning, stood and walked over to Jeannie. "They don't realize Julian's had a little extra help in his recovery." He slipped his arm around her; she leaned her body against his.

"Julian loves roses. While they're moving him, I want to order some flowers for him. Two or three dozen roses. And you can run by the house...no, not by the house, by the cottage, and pick up some pajamas and a robe for Julian, and—"

Sam kissed her into silence, then released her quickly. "I'm not going anywhere. Call Ollie and have her bring over Julian's things."

"Julian gave Ollie a much-needed vacation to visit her sister in Tupelo, while the repairs are being done on our house. Don't you remember my telling you?"

"Then have Marta pick up Julian's stuff." With his arm around her shoulders, he turned her toward the outer waiting room door. "And you can order flowers after you've eaten something. You haven't left Julian's side, except to use the bathroom and drink a few cups of coffee. You haven't eaten anything except a doughnut one of the nurses brought you." He brushed away an errant strand of hair that had come loose from her ponytail. "And as soon as you check on Julian, after he's in a private room, I'm taking you to the cottage for some rest."

"I'll eat soon. I promise. And I'll rest as soon as I'm sure Julian will be all right without me." She knew Sam was right. She needed food and rest. She was thankful Sam had been forced to remain in the waiting area. If he'd seen her faint twice, he would have taken her away from Julian, despite her protests. And if he knew about her condition—that she was carrying his child—he wouldn't allow her to give Julian the peace of mind and pain-free rest he so desperately needed.

"Dammit, Jeannie, you can't go on this way. Not eating. Not sleeping. Julian wouldn't want you to endanger your health to help him."

"The choice is mine. Not Julian's. And not yours." But there was more to consider than her own health; she had to think about her child. "Please, Sam. I'll order the flowers, then call Marta. And I'll eat something in Julian's room. You choose my menu, and I'll eat every bite. But I must stay with Julian until I'm certain he doesn't need me anymore."

How could she make Sam understand how much she owed Julian? He had been the surgeon who saved her life after the car wreck, when she was thirteen. Later, he and

Miriam had taken her into their home, helped her through years of therapy and made her the daughter they'd never had. The Howells had given Jeannie the beautiful, peaceful existence that had been hers before the truth about her past had been revealed. There was nothing she wouldn't do for Julian or for Manton, just as there had been nothing she wouldn't do for Miriam.

"You're going home tonight." His statement left no room for argument. Regardless of her protests, Sam was determined to save her from her own stubbornness.

Jeannie reached up, caressed his cheek and looked into his eyes. "When I love someone, I love them completely, with no reservations, no limitations. Like you, Sam, I haven't given my love often. I love Julian and Manton the way you love Elizabeth and her little Jimmy."

"I know how you feel," Sam said. "But understand this—I'm taking you home tonight, if I have to drag you out of this hospital kicking and screaming."

She smiled, stretched on tiptoe to drag his face down to hers, then kissed him. "See if the cafeteria is serving spaghetti. With lots of Parmesan cheese."

Sam swatted her behind. She giggled. God, how he loved the sound of her happy giggles.

Jeannie devoured the plate of spaghetti Sam had delivered from a restaurant, along with chocolate cheesecake and ice tea.

"I don't think I can eat another bite." She shoved the plate aside. "I'll save the cheesecake for later."

"You'll take it home with you," Julian told her, then looked at Sam. "You should have made her leave long before now. She's exhausted. See those dark circles under her eyes? She's done too much for me already."

"You know Jeannie. She wouldn't leave willingly," Sam said. "But she's going home tonight, willing or not."

Julian chuckled. "I'm so sorry this happened. My heart attack brought her right back to Biloxi, and put her within Maynard Reeves's grasp."

"Sam will protect me from the good reverend." Jeannie finished off the tall glass of ice tea, wiped her mouth with a paper napkin and shoved back her chair. "And as soon as the doctors say it's all right, we'll all go to Le Bijou Bleu."

Julian pointed to the television, which he'd set to the weather channel. "If that tropical depression off the coast of Africa moves in our direction, we might be in for a hurricane, or at the least a bad storm. You might be stuck here in Biloxi."

Jeannie turned her attention to the weatherman's forecast. "Or it could die out before it gets here, or move north or farther south and miss us completely."

"Nevertheless, you'll want to warn Manton to keep an eye on the weather," Julian said. "Is the storm shelter on the island in good repair?"

"Stop worrying. Everything on Le Bijou Bleu is in tip-top shape." Jeannie had been in the storm shelter only once, when she was ten and a tropical storm hit the Gulf Coast. She'd heard Julian talk about what devastation Hurricane Camille had caused back in 1969 and thanked God that Manton had survived in the storm shelter, located in the basement of the cottage.

"I don't like your being back here in Biloxi," Julian said. "It's too dangerous for you as long as Maynard Reeves walks around a free man."

"You musn't worry about me. You let Sam do that. I want you to concentrate on getting well."

"I know about Reeves's visit." Julian glanced from Jeannie to Sam. "Don't go looking for someone to blame. I overheard a conversation about the reverend passing himself off as a priest."

"I didn't want you to know," Jeannie said. "At least not until after you were fully recovered."

"I don't remember seeing him," Julian said. "I have no idea what his reason for coming to the hospital might have been."

"You were his only connection to me." Jeannie walked over and sat down in a chair beside Julian's bed. "Perhaps he thought he could threaten you into revealing where Sam had taken me."

"I can't believe the police haven't come up with something that can put that man away." Lifting himself into a sitting position, Julian clutched the bed's rails. His cheeks flushed. Beads of sweat broke out on his face. "There has to be something they can do!"

"Julian, please don't upset yourself." Jeannie grabbed his hand, instantly feeling the surge of anger shooting through him, the rise in his blood pressure, his accelerated heartbeat.

"I'll be...all...right. Don't...don't..." Julian gripped her hand when the first sharp pain struck him.

Clasping his hand tightly, Jeannie cried out as the pain entered her. She trembled from the force of his suffering.

Sam flew across the room, halting behind Jeannie's chair as he placed his big hands over her shoulders, cupping her upper arms. What the hell had happened? "Jeannie?" She didn't respond. "Dammit, don't do this. You're too weak."

Shivering, she closed her eyes and absorbed all Julian's pain, stopping the onset of another heart attack. His anger and fear trickled into her mind, leaving him at peace. Jeannie cried out; tears streamed down her face. Sam ripped Julian's hand out of Jeannie's, jerked her chair around and fell to his knees in front of her.

The anguish on her face told him all he needed to know. She was hurting, hurting badly, and all he could do was watch her suffer. If only he could give her some of his strength. If only he could absorb her pain, the way she had absorbed Julian's. He took her hands in his. She felt ice-cold. Rubbing her hands, he concentrated on mentally connecting with her. Just as he sensed the link beginning to form, a nurse rushed into Julian's room, quickly followed by an entourage prepared to administer lifesaving techniques. The moment the nurse shouted orders for Sam to move, the fragile link to Jeannie's mind shattered.

Sam pulled Jeannie up into his arms and kicked the chair aside. She lay there like a rag doll; Sam realized that she had fainted. The group of technicians hovered around Julian's bed.

"I don't understand," the nurse said. "His heart monitor showed signs of another attack."

"Machines make mistakes." Sam glanced at the nurse with cold gray eyes.

"Damnedest thing I've ever seen," a male nurse said. "Dr. Howell is fine. He's sleeping peaceful. All his vital signs are normal."

"Arrange for a private-duty nurse for Dr. Howell," Sam said. "I'm taking Ms. Alverson home. You have the number of Dr. Howell's rental house, don't you? If his condition changes, contact me."

Sam undressed Jeannie and laid her, naked and exhausted, in the bed. She had regained consciousness briefly on the drive to the cottage, but once Sam assured her that Julian was fine, she'd drifted off to sleep, unable to fight the total depletion of her strength.

Both beds in the two-bedroom cottage were doubles, neither really long enough or large enough to accommodate Sam's height and size. He'd chosen the room on the back of the house, the quieter, more secluded one, the one that would be sheltered from the morning sun. He didn't want anything disturbing Jeannie's rest.

He'd found some expensive brandy in the kitchen, obviously belonging to Julian. Sam poured himself a shot, downed it in one swallow, then put the liquor away. He didn't want anything dulling his senses, putting him at any disadvantage if he had to confront Reeves. After making a ham sandwich, he devoured it quickly and returned to the bedroom. Jeannie had thrown off the covers and lay in the middle of the bed, her small, sleek, naked body tossing back and forth.

She moaned as she squirmed about in the bed. "Sam...Sam..."

Leaning over the bed, he brushed the hair out of her face, then kissed her forehead. "I'm here, angel. I'm here."

Sighing, she turned toward him, cuddling into a ball. Sam placed his Ruger on the bedside table, then removed his clothes. His body throbbed with desire. Straightening the covers, he folded them at the foot of the bed, lay down beside Jeannie and drew her into his arms.

He didn't fall asleep until nearly dawn, awakening only when the phone rang at ten-fifteen. Jeannie moaned and cuddled closer to his back, but didn't awaken. When he reached for the telephone, his hand grasped his Ruger. He shoved it aside and picked up the receiver.

"Dundee here."

"Mr. Dundee, this is Marta McCorkle. I'm at the hospital with Julian. He's fine, but he's concerned about Jeannie."

Sam glanced at the sleeping beauty curled against him. "She's all right, but still sleeping."

"Would it be all right if I stop by to see her after I leave the hospital?" Marta asked. "I know she'll be eager for an update on Julian, and a report on the Howell School children."

"If she's awake, you can see her," Sam said. "I won't wake her. She needs her rest."

"Of course. I'll stop by sometime after noon. When she wakes, give her Julian's love. And mine."

"I'll do that." Sam hung up the phone.

Sam's stomach growled. He was hungry as a bear. He'd eaten twice in the past forty-eight hours. Easing away from Jeannie so that he wouldn't disturb her, he got out of bed, pulled the cover up to her shoulders, and picked up his wrinkled slacks. Dressing hurriedly, he went into the kitchen. Within minutes he'd set the coffee machine, put bacon on to fry and cracked six eggs into a skillet.

Jeannie found him cooking breakfast in his bare feet, wearing rumpled trousers and an unbuttoned shirt that hung open, showing the center of his broad, hairy chest.

"Are you fixing enough for two?" she asked from where she stood in the doorway.

He continued scrambling the eggs. "How long have you been standing there?" he asked, knowing precisely the moment she'd walked out of the bedroom three minutes ago.

Jeannie tightened the belt on her silk robe. "I can't imagine a more charming sight than a man busy at his domestic duties."

Sam guffawed as a wide grin spread across his face. He glanced up from his cooking, and his heart stopped for one breath-robbing moment. Jeannie stood in the doorway, her long hair falling down her back and over her left shoulder. Leaning on her cane, she put one foot in front of the other, exposing her right thigh between the open folds of her robe. Her round, full breasts pressed against the silk material, her nipples plainly outlined.

His body tightened. His heartbeat drummed in his ears. He wanted to forget breakfast, forget everything, and take Jeannie back to bed and make slow, sweet love to her all day.

"Come on in and take a seat," he said, trying to control his baser instincts. "I think I can spare a few bites for you."

She walked toward him, her gaze moving from his face over every inch of his body, returning to the bulge in his pants. "Breakfast could wait, couldn't it?" She stopped a foot away from him and smiled. "I woke up hungry." She laid her hand on his chest, then smoothed her way downward. "But not for food."

Drawing in a deep breath, Sam grabbed her hand a second before she reached her destination. "I'd like nothing better than to feed that hunger." He slid his arm around her, pulling her up against him as he lifted her hand to his lips. "But for now, you'll have to settle for scrambled eggs and bacon. Marta's on her way over here. If we hurry, we might be able to finish breakfast and catch a quick shower before she gets here.

"We could skip breakfast and go straight to the shower." Spreading apart his unbuttoned shirt, Jeannie smeared a row of tongue-moist kisses across his chest.

He cupped her buttocks, lifting her up and into his arousal. "Angel, you're being a very bad girl this morning."

"I like being bad with you, Sam."

"After you eat a good breakfast, take a shower and visit with Marta, I'll let you be as bad as you want to be." Releasing her, he grunted, then breathed deeply and gave her a gentle shove backward, keeping his hands on her arms to make sure she didn't lose her balance.

"Promise?" she asked. "I'm fine, you know. If you're worried that I'm not recovered from—"

"Stop talking, Jeannie," he said. "I'm having a hard enough time keeping myself from laying you down on the

kitchen table and taking you right here and now, without
your trying to persuade me to make love to you."

"I like knowing how much you want me. I like it even
better when you tell me."

"Yeah, well . . ." Sam seated her at the table, then turned
back to the stove, dished up the scrambled eggs and added
three strips of bacon to Jeannie's plate. "Eat up." He placed
the food on the table. "I'll get you some coffee."

They ate in silence, occasionally glancing at each other.
Jeannie smiled; Sam frowned. She took her shower first,
while he cleaned up the kitchen. He showered while she
called Julian.

Marta arrived at one o'clock on the dot, hugging Jeannie profusely, assuring her that Julian looked the picture of
health. While Marta visited, Sam took the opportunity to
survey the cottage and the surrounding yard.

"Everyone at the school misses you terribly," Marta said.
"The children ask about you continuously. They really
didn't understand exactly how you were helping them, but
they're well aware that things have changed since you've
been gone."

"As soon as this problem with Maynard Reeves is solved,
I'll return to work. I miss the children. I miss all of you."

"Will he be staying?" Marta nodded toward the yard,
where they could see Sam surveying his surroundings.

"You mean, will he stay after I'm no longer in danger,
when I don't need a bodyguard?"

"Yes. Will he?"

"I don't know."

"You're in love with him, aren't you?"

Jeannie lowered her head, avoiding Marta's direct stare.
"Am I that obvious?"

"Only to those who know you well and love you dearly."
Marta rose, walked across the living room and sat down on
the sofa beside Jeannie. "Somehow I never pictured you
with a man like Sam Dundee. He's too . . . too—"

"Too much a man."

"Well, yes." Cool, calm, controlled Marta blushed.
"He's quite sophisticated, and very elegant, but . . . Oh, my
dear, he's so big and brutal-looking, despite being so hand-

some. And what he does for a living! A bodyguard. You must know that there's every likelihood he's killed someone at some point in his life."

"Yes, you're probably right." Jeannie covered Marta's hand with her own. "But what you don't understand is that Sam needs me and I have so much to give him. And his strengths are my weaknesses and my strengths are his weaknesses."

"You must be careful not to let him break your heart." Squeezing Jeannie's hand, Marta forced a weak smile.

"Julian's worried, isn't he?" Jeannie sensed the truth as Marta clung to her hand. "I think Julian saw me married to a doctor or a lawyer. Someone local, the son of one of his friends or associates. Perhaps a member of the Fleur-de-lis Society."

"Julian loves you as dearly as if you were his own flesh and blood." Releasing Jeannie's hand, Marta stood and looked down at the floor. "Julian believes you and Mr. Dundee are lovers."

"I'll talk to Julian," Jeannie said. "Sam is taking me to visit him after dinner this evening. I'll make Julian understand how much I love Sam."

"He wants only your happiness."

"Sam makes me happy."

"Has he mentioned marriage?" Marta looked at Jeannie.

"No."

"I see."

"Come back and sit down." Jeannie patted the sofa cushion beside her. "I want to hear about every Howell School child. Give me details on progress and setbacks. How is Cassie Mills? And little Justin Walker? And Missy Suddath? Her mother hasn't taken her out of school, has she?"

"That crazy woman!" Marta sat down beside Jeannie. "She comes inside the school every day when she brings Missy, and looks around to make sure you aren't there. We've told her that you are no longer working at the school."

"I want you to continue allowing her some leeway," Jeannie said. "I know Danette has joined the Righteous

Light Church and thinks I'm a witch, but I don't want Missy to suffer for her mother's ignorance.''

"I've told the staff how you feel and given them instructions to make allowances for Danette Suddath's odd behavior, but I'm telling you, the woman is unbalanced.''

"I wish I could help Danette, but she would never allow me near her. The most we can do is take care of Missy.''

The front door opened, and Sam Dundee stepped into the living room. Jeannie and Marta looked up at him, Jeannie smiling as Marta patted her on the knee.

"There's a beautiful little secluded garden at the back of the house,'' Sam said. "How would you like to have supper out there?''

"My son's ex-wife loved the garden,'' Marta said. "I think it was the main reason they bought this house.''

"Well, it's something to see.'' Sam sat down in the Chippendale armchair to the right of the sofa. "I can see where a woman might find it a selling point when buying a house.''

"I think supper in the garden is a lovely idea.'' Jeannie hoped Marta saw the significance in Sam's suggestion of a romantic supper in a secluded garden. She wanted Julian and Marta to understand why she loved Sam, why she was happy to be carrying his child.

"Well, I need to stop by school and check on things.'' Marta hugged Jeannie, then stood. "I've neglected my job the last few days.''

Standing, Sam walked Marta to the door. She turned to him when he stepped outside with her.

"I'll see y'all at the hospital later this evening,'' Marta said, and walked down the stone sidewalk. She stopped abruptly, turned around and looked Sam in the eye. "She's in love with you, you know. Please, don't hurt her.'' Marta rushed to her car, got inside and backed into the street.

Sam watched her drive away, his back to the porch. He heard Jeannie as she approached him, her cane tapping on the wooden porch and steps.

"You mustn't let what she said bother you.'' Jeannie laid her hand on Sam's back.

"How can I not worry?''

"No matter what happens, you'll never hurt me.''

He turned, looked at her and closed his eyes, the pain inside him shattering in its intensity. How could she trust him so completely, love him so unselfishly, when he'd made no lasting commitment to her? How could he tell her he loved her, when he wasn't sure he was capable of truly loving a woman the way Jeannie deserved to be loved?

"Show me the garden in the backyard." Bracing herself with her cane, she held out her other hand, inviting his touch.

If he touched her, she'd know exactly how he felt. She'd sense his confusion and uncertainty. And she would feel the desperate need burning inside him.

He took her hand in his and led her around the house to the backyard. All the while they walked—slowly, to accommodate her hampered gait—he allowed her to understand how he felt.

She realized he was unaware of how far he'd come in trusting his innermost thoughts and emotions to her. He'd gone from fighting the tiniest link to full acceptance of their joining. As always, she sensed his protectiveness and his possessiveness. A raging hunger. An overwhelming sexual desire. A deep, unrestrained need. And a sweet, tender caring. Gratitude. Unworthiness. Uncertainty. And fear. She picked up on every delicate nuance of his emotions. But she could not connect to the depths of his heart, to that place where the truth of his feelings lay buried so completely that it was a secret, even to Sam.

The garden wrapped around the back of the cottage like an emerald shawl of dense foliage and lush shade. Opening the wrought-iron gate, they entered beneath a clematis-covered arch and walked down a stone pathway leading to a fully enclosed piece of paradise. A concrete table and benches had been placed in the corner of a climbing-rosebush arbor.

"This *is* beautiful," Jeannie said.

"You're beautiful." Sam slipped his arm around her waist, urging her to turn.

She went into his arms, knowing what he wanted, admitting to herself that she wanted the same. He wrapped her in his embrace; she snuggled close, loving the feel of his powerful arms holding her.

"Jeannie?"

Make love to me, Sam. Here. Now. In the privacy of our little garden.

He heard her as clearly as if she'd spoken the words aloud. And the moment he took her lips in an all-consuming kiss of possession, he felt the wild, uncontrollable need within him come alive within Jeannie, too.

Slow and easy, he told himself. Don't frighten her. Don't hurt her.

"It's all right," she said, reaching out to slide first one side of his jacket and then the other off his shoulders.

He let the expensive silk jacket fall to the ground, to rest atop a tiny sculptured shrub. He grabbed her by the waist to support her. She dropped her cane on the stone path. Restraining himself, just barely controlling his need to take her like the savage he was, Sam allowed her to undress him. She whipped off his tie and flung it into the air. Unbuttoning his shirt seemed to take forever. She threw it down beside his jacket, then unbuckled his belt.

Sam sucked in a deep breath. His arousal throbbed painfully. Every muscle in his body strained; every nerve screamed.

"Oh, Sam . . ." Swaying from the force of the sensations she received from his body, she grabbed his forearms.

"You're in charge, angel. We'll do this your way, but I don't think you'll last much longer."

Gulping air, she smiled at him. Perspiration coated her flushed face. She unzipped his slacks and pulled them down his hips. When they hit the ground, Sam kicked them aside. She tugged on his briefs. Taking one hand from her waist, he assisted her in removing the last strip of his clothing.

He stood there, his big body hard, his sex pulsating with life. He felt her longing, knew she was unraveling by slow degrees, just as he was. The passion grew stronger and stronger, becoming raw and uncivilized as it developed.

"Please, Sam," she said aloud.

He pulled her green cotton sweater over her head, loosening her hair. Sliding the pins from her hair, he let it fall free. With shaky fingers, he unlatched the hook on her bra, removed the silken garment and cupped her naked breasts in his hands.

She shivered from head to toe. If he didn't take her soon, she was going to explode. Her sex throbbed painfully. She needed release, needed Sam inside her, giving her all of himself.

"Soon, sweet angel." He kissed each nipple in turn, feeling the spiraling tension in her breasts as it gripped her femininity. She was on fire; he was on fire. Together they would burn themselves out, dissolving into ashes of completion.

Unzipping her slacks, he watched her face. He wanted to kiss her. She was alive in every fiber of her body, on fire with a heat that seared him as completely as it did her. Holding her by the hips, he knelt and slid her green-and-white-striped slacks and beige silk panties down her legs.

He kissed her stomach, burying his face in her warm, soft flesh. He felt her closing off, shutting him out of her thoughts. Why had she done that? he wondered.

She had to keep her secret. Sam's child was nestled there inside her, in her womb, safe and secure. But now was not the time to share her happy news with him. There would be time enough when Maynard Reeves was no longer a part of their lives.

She pushed the thoughts of their child deep into her heart, closing them off from her conscious thoughts. Threading her fingers through Sam's hair, she moaned as he delved his fingers deeply into her body.

She gripped his shoulders, urging him to stand. He kissed her intimately. She shuddered. Sam rose, lifted her off her feet and carried her into the rose arbor. A lush bed of grass and moss beckoned him. Placing her on the ground, he lay down beside her and pulled her on top of him. She stared down into searing blue-gray eyes and had no doubt what joy awaited the two of them. Holding her hips, petting her buttocks with his fingertips, Sam eased her down onto him, entering her with a forceful thrust.

Jeannie cried out with the pleasure of their joining, lowering her head to reach his lips. She plunged her tongue into his mouth; he reciprocated with equal fervor. They devoured each other as he stroked her back and buttocks. Placing her hands on either side of his head, she pushed herself upward until her breasts hung over his mouth, a luscious temptation.

She set the pace, moving with restless need, her own desire so strong she didn't know whether she could handle his, as well as hers. When he took her nipple into his mouth, sucking greedily, the first warning of release clenched her sex. While his mouth toyed with one breast, he lifted his hand to cup the other, then pinched the nipple between his thumb and forefinger. Fulfillment claimed her, rocking her to the core. Sam caught her cries in his mouth as her release rippled through him.

He changed the pace of their lovemaking, increasing the tempo, deepening his thrusts. He was on the verge, and so was she. Together they splintered into shards of unequaled ecstasy, Jeannie sharing his pleasure as he shared hers. Panting heavily, their bodies dripping with perspiration, Sam rolled over onto his side, holding her in his arms, kissing her again and again.

"I love you, Sam. I love you with all my heart."

"Ah, Jeannie...Jeannie...my sweet angel."

Chapter 15

Sam moaned with pleasure. Jeannie smiled at him as she slowly pulled the fork out of his mouth. He chewed the scrumptious bite of blueberry pancake dripping in syrup that she had fed him. They gazed into each other's eyes, silently conveying words of erotic intent as they remembered their night of passionate loving.

Looking at him sitting there in nothing but his slacks, his broad chest bare, Jeannie sighed as her body recalled Sam Dundee's savage possession.

He grinned, enjoying the sight of her, her flawless skin, soft peach lips and warm brown eyes. Tendrils of sun-streaked brown hair curled about her forehead and ears. His body hardened when he thought about her being naked beneath her robe.

Turning his fork sideways, Sam sliced off a piece of his pancake, speared it and lifted it toward Jeannie's mouth. With her gaze focused on Sam, she parted her lips. He slid the morsel into her mouth, watching while she chewed. Laying his fork on his plate, Sam reached across the table and, using the tip of his finger, wiped a trickle of syrup from the corner of Jeannie's mouth. Inclining her head, she captured Sam's finger between her lips and licked off the syrup.

Groaning deep in his throat, he jerked his finger out of her mouth. He knocked over his chair as he stood quickly, then rounded the table and lifted a laughing Jeannie out of her chair. Shoving her breakfast plate, cup and silverware across the table with the back of his hand, he set her on the edge of the table, opened her silk robe and parted her thighs. In one swift motion, he unzipped his slacks and discarded them.

She gripped his shoulders. He took her mouth at the exact same moment he lifted her hips and plunged into her. The joining was instant, jolting both of them with its power. As their bodies united, their hearts and minds entwined, each experiencing the pure ecstasy of their combined loving.

When they reached fever pitch, Sam groaned hot, shameless words to her, and she responded by abandoning herself to the sheer, pulse-pounding glory of their simultaneous twofold release.

She clung to him in the aftermath, kissing his shoulder as he lifted her and carried her to the bathroom. He drew her a bubble bath and slid her into the tub, then tossed her a washcloth.

"I'll clean up in the kitchen while you take your bath." He kissed her on the tip of her nose.

The telephone rang. Jeannie tensed. Sam winked at her, the action meant to reassure her that all was well. He closed the door behind him, leaving her alone.

She eased back, resting her head against the tiled wall. They'd been back in Biloxi five days. Julian was definitely on the road to recovery and would probably be coming home in a couple of days. Despite the possibility of a storm brewing in the Atlantic, heading toward the Caribbean, she hadn't given up her hope that Sam and she could take Julian back to Le Bijou Bleu to fully recuperate.

But she couldn't hide away on the island forever, and Sam had a life in Atlanta. Sooner or later, he would have to leave.

Although no doctor had confirmed her pregnancy and she hadn't bothered with a home test kit, Jeannie knew she was carrying Sam's child. She had been able to link with the baby and experience the first stages of her daughter's existence. She was almost four weeks pregnant now, and she still hadn't told Sam. How could she add to his burden of worry? He would want this child, and he would be even more protective and possessive if he knew. Until the situation with Maynard Reeves was settled, she would wait, keeping her precious secret in the deepest, most private part of her heart.

Sam opened the door, walked in and handed her the portable phone. "It's Marta. She sounds a little odd, but she says everything's all right. She needs to talk to you about one of the students."

Jeannie took the phone in her hand, then waved goodbye to Sam as he went back into the bedroom. "Hello, Marta."

"Jeannie, please don't let Mr. Dundee know what I'm saying to you."

"All right." Jeannie sensed Marta's fear. "Why don't you tell me what's wrong?"

"When Danette Suddath brought Missy to school this morning, two other women came with her." Marta swallowed. "We allowed her free access, just as you'd instructed."

"Are you alone in your office?" Jeannie asked, realizing that something was terribly wrong.

"Yes. They've allowed me to come in here alone. But Jeannie . . . Oh, dear God, they have guns! They're holding the children hostage."

Jeannie heard Marta sobbing. "What do you mean, they're holding the children hostage?"

"During our before-school free time in the cafeteria, Danette Suddath and these two other women pulled their guns, each one grabbed a child, and they're holding the whole school hostage."

"What do they want?" Jeannie asked, but she knew. She glanced at the partially open door, wondering if Sam had gone back into the kitchen.

"They want you, Jeannie," Marta said. "They're all members of the Righteous Light Church. Danette told me that—that they won't hurt any of the children, if you'll come down to the school."

"Call the police, Marta. Tell them what's happened. Sam and I will be there as soon as possible."

"No! I can't call the police, and Sam Dundee must not come here. They said if I called the police or if Mr. Dundee comes with you, they'll start sacrificing the children. That's the exact word Danette used. *Sacrificing.*"

"They want me to come alone?" Jeannie's mind splintered into a dozen different thoughts, the prime one being the question of how she would ever escape from Sam.

"I don't know what to do, Jeannie. If you come down here, they'll turn you over to Maynard Reeves." Marta's voice quavered more with each word she spoke. "I think they're expecting him to come here and get you."

"I understand. I'll find a way to get there. Alone. We can't allow any harm to come to those precious children in our charge."

"There must be some other way," Marta said. "If only—"

"Everything will be all right," Jeannie said. "I'll do what I have to do."

Jeannie punched the Off button and laid the telephone down on the bath mat beside the tub. Closing her eyes, she said a quiet prayer, allowing her mind to relax and her nerves to calm. She would have to lie to Sam, and she would have to trick him. She hated doing it, but she had no choice. The lives of forty-five children were at stake. Innocent, helpless children with physical and mental limitations that made them even more special to Jeannie. She knew so well the pain these children endured, especially their emotional suffering.

"Sam! Sam, I'm ready to get out of the tub now."

Within a minute, Sam was at her side, lifting her out of the tub and drying her with a large, fluffy towel. She wrapped her arm around his neck.

"Why don't you go ahead and enjoy my bubble bath? It's still warm," she said.

"I haven't finished up in the kitchen." He carried her into the bedroom and placed her on the edge of the bed.

"After I get dressed, I'll take care of that." She pulled him down toward her, rubbing her cheek against his. "Go on. You need a bath. You smell like . . . well, you smell."

Sam laughed. "I smell like you and me. I smell like sex."

"Yes, you do. You smell like sex."

"Need any help getting dressed?" he asked.

"You're better at helping me undress." She shoved him away from her. "Now go get your bath. I can dress myself and finish cleaning up the kitchen without your help."

"Your wish is my command." He stripped out of his slacks, which he'd put on again when he returned to the kitchen.

Jeannie watched while he walked to the bathroom. He stopped in the doorway, turned and smiled at her. When he closed the door, she lifted her cane from its resting place against the nightstand and hurried to the closet. She dressed as quickly as she could, dug the keys to her Lexus from her purse and walked out of the bedroom.

Easing the front door closed, she breathed a sigh of relief when it made only a faint clicking sound. She slid behind the wheel, started the engine and backed out of the driveway, holding her breath all the while.

"Please, forgive me, Sam. I have no other choice." She whispered the words aloud, knowing that Sam had already sensed that something wasn't quite right.

When she pulled out into the street, she glanced in her rearview mirror. Sam Dundee ran into the yard, a towel draped around his hips. He screamed her name.

Tears blurred Jeannie's vision as she pressed the accelerator. The Lexus flew down the street and out of Sam's sight.

Children's whimpers and muted cries drifted down the hallway. Jeannie gripped her cane as she walked along the empty corridor. She hesitated at the closed cafeteria doors, uncertain what she would find once she entered, but knowing she was willing to make whatever sacrifice was necessary to save the children.

She flung open the double doors and stepped inside, halting immediately. The children had been divided into three groups. The groups huddled on the floor in three corners of the cafeteria, each group guarded by a woman with a gun. Danette Suddath held her own daughter in front of her as a shield as she brandished a semiautomatic weapon.

"Hi, Jeannie." Missy Suddath smiled, her round face wrinkling in pleasure lines when she saw Jeannie. "My mama's playing a game with us. It's like cops and robbers. Did you come to play with us?"

"Yes, Missy, I came to play with you." Jeannie clenched her teeth, willing herself to stay calm and unemotional for the sake of the children.

"Come on in, Jeannie Alverson!" Danette shouted. "Your days of evil are about to end."

"Suffer not a witch to live!" A plump middle-aged woman with long, straight salt-and-pepper hair tightened her hold on little seven-year-old Amelia Carson, who'd been born marginally retarded. Clasping a small-caliber gun in her hand, she laid it across Amelia's chest.

"I've followed your instructions," Jeannie said. "I've come alone, without the police or Sam Dundee. You have what you want. Please release the children."

"Such concern for these little ones." The baritone voice came from a tall, slender woman who held the third group of children in the far right corner. She lifted six-year-old Justin Walker, blind since birth, up on her hip. Justin screamed. The woman placed her hand, which held a gun, over the little boy's mouth.

Jeannie sucked in a deep breath. "Please, put him down. You're frightening him."

"Hush now, child," the tall woman, who was wearing a frumpy floral-print dress, said. "If Jeannie loves you, really loves you, none of you will need to be sacrificed."

Jeannie couldn't bear the thought of a child being harmed because of her. How could these women threaten the children, when they claimed to be believers in a religion of love and compassion?

"I'll leave with you," Jeannie said. "I'll go with you to Maynard Reeves without protest."

All the teachers had been lined up against the wall on the far side of the cafeteria. Jeannie looked at them, one at a time, hoping to convey hope and love. Marta McCorkle was conspicuously absent.

"Where's Marta?" Jeannie asked.

"Ms. McCorkle is in her office," Danette Suddath said. "She's there to answer the phone and make sure the outside world thinks everything is normal here at the Howell School."

Jeannie sighed with relief. For one split second, she had feared for Marta's life. "My car is outside. The keys are in the ignition. We can walk out of here, and you can take me to Reverend Reeves. Right now."

"We won't need your car," Danette said, forcing her daughter to walk around her classmates sitting on the floor. "Our plans are already made."

"All right." Jeannie walked into the room, slowly moving toward Danette. "I'm prepared to go with you, on your terms."

Missy Suddath took a step toward Jeannie. "Are you a bad guy?" the child asked. "They're calling you ugly names. I don't like you playing bad, Jeannie."

"I'm not really bad. Remember, this is just a game." Jeannie reached out her hand to Missy.

"No! Don't touch her!" Danette jerked her daughter close to her side, the gun she held resting over the child's body. "I won't have you contaminate her with your evil."

"Danette, surely you know I'd never do anything to harm Missy," Jeannie said. "She's been attending the Howell School for four years, and she's made excellent progress. All of us here love her."

"Enough talk." The tall, deep-voiced woman marched around her charges. Justin shivered in the big woman's arms, tears streaming down his face as he sobbed.

"Justin, don't be afraid," Jeannie said. "I'm here in the room with you."

"I don't like this game," Justin said, choking back his tears. "I don't wanna play anymore."

The woman holding Amelia walked toward Jeannie. "The game will end soon," she said. "As long as Jeannie does exactly as she's told."

"What do you want me to do?" Jeannie asked.

"You'll come with us. My friends and I will walk out of the school to the parking area, where our cars are waiting." The woman in the floral-print dress secured her hold on Justin and lifted her gun to the child's head.

Jeannie was thankful Justin couldn't see, that he really didn't understand what was happening. "Yes, I'll come with you. Just put Justin down, and don't harm any of the children."

The tall woman grinned. Jeannie gasped, suddenly realizing that the person holding Justin was a man disguised as a woman. Maynard Reeves!

His grin widened when he looked directly into Jeannie's eyes. She knew he was aware that she'd recognized him.

"Danette will take her daughter with her," Reeves said. "I'll take Justin. Nora will take the little girl with the blond pigtails. And we'll need five or six more children as escorts. All of us will walk out of here together."

"There's no need to take the children. You don't want them," Jeannie said. "I'm the one you want."

"Ah, but there is a need to take the children, at least until we reach our cars. I wouldn't want you changing your mind, or any of your employees in here deciding to call the police."

"You'll let the children go as soon as we get outside?"

"All except Missy and Justin," Reeves said. "They'll go with us. Once I make sure we haven't been followed, I'll release Justin, somewhere you can be certain he'll be safe."

"Don't do this. Please. No one has called the police, and Sam Dundee has no idea where I am."

"I tend to believe you. However, I'm not a person who takes chances." Reeves waved his gun in the air, then pointed it to the door leading to the hallway. "Shall we go?"

Jeannie watched, feeling totally helpless, as Danette and the plump middle-aged woman gathered up six children, instructing them to form a single line beside Reeves. Confused and crying, the children ran to Jeannie, completely ignoring Danette's directions. Kneeling, Jeannie touched each child, placing them in a circle around her. They reached out, laying their hands on her. She absorbed their fear and frustration, and within minutes all six children had quieted.

"Look at the witch's power!" Reeves bellowed, storming across the few feet that separated him from Jeannie. "She controls the minds of the innocent!"

He set Justin on his feet, then pulled the six children away from Jeannie. She reached for her cane, grabbing it up off the floor just as Reeves dragged her to her feet.

Turning to his two faithful helpers, Reeves motioned them toward him. "She controls these children." He pointed at the four boys and two girls Jeannie had soothed with her touch. "They are useless to us. Take only the child you have with you, and go to your car. Wait for me outside." He looked at Justin, who had found his way to Jeannie and was holding on to her leg. "Take his hand, and bring him with you. And don't try any of your witchcraft on him. If you do, I'll have to destroy him when I destroy you."

"Please, don't—"

"Take his hand! Now!" Reeves screamed.

Jeannie lifted Justin's hand, grasping it firmly, then looked to Reeves for instructions.

Reeves placed his arm around her shoulders. "We'll walk into the hallway and through the school to the back door."

Jeannie nodded her agreement. Danette and her cohort left the room, taking Missy and Amelia Carson with them. Reeves stuck his gun in Jeannie's ribs, motioning her forward. With each step she took, Jeannie prayed. The moment she exited the cafeteria and entered the corridor, she felt Sam Dundee's presence. Dear God, how had he found her? And what was he going to do? Had he called Marta? Had she been unable to hide the truth from him?

Danette and the other woman left the building, Missy and Amelia with them. Halting abruptly halfway down the long central hallway, Reeves squeezed Jeannie's shoulder.

"Wait," he said.

Her breathing quickened. She clasped Justin's hand tightly. Whatever happened, she'd need to move at a moment's notice. If ever she had wished she could run, it was now.

"You and Justin will walk out in front of me," Reeves told her. "Just remember that I'll be right behind you, with a gun aimed at the boy."

Jeannie nodded, swallowed hard, squeezed Justin's hand and walked them toward the back door.

Grab Justin. Drop to the floor and roll into the open classroom on your left. Now! She heard Sam's orders as clearly as if he'd spoken. Not hesitating, she obeyed, grabbing Justin around the waist and throwing them both onto the floor.

"What are you doing?" Reeves fired his gun, but a big hand knocked the weapon upward, and the bullet lodged in the ceiling.

"Don't move a muscle," Sam Dundee said.

With her arms wrapped around Justin, protecting him with her body, Jeannie rolled them directly across the hall. Curling her body into a fetal position as she rolled, she tumbled them through the open classroom door. She caught a glimpse of the female-disguised Reeves, Sam Dundee towering behind him, his Ruger pointed directly at the reverend's head.

With his free hand, Sam jerked Reeves's wig off his head. "Looks like you've been caught in the act."

"Let me go, Dundee, or two innocent children will have to be sacrificed."

"What the hell are you talking about?" Sam flung the wig to the floor, then thrust his big arm around Reeves's neck, bringing the man's back up against his chest.

"Ask your precious little witch," Reeves said. "She'll tell you. Two of my disciples have potential sacrifices with them, and if I give the order to destroy these children for the greater good of the Righteous Light Church, they'll shoot them."

"Sam?" Jeannie called out to him silently. "Danette Suddath has her daughter, Missy, but I'm not sure she wouldn't harm her. And the other woman has Amelia—"

"All right, Reeves, let's you and me go outside," Sam said. "If what you say is true, I'll exchange you for the children."

Reeves's maniacal laughter reverberated in the hushed stillness of the corridor. "You give me Jeannie, and I'll give you the children."

Sam didn't hesitate before giving his reply. "No deal."

"Jeannie, Dundee is willing to sacrifice the children to save you!" Reeves shouted. "Is that what you want?"

"Sam?" she said aloud.

"Stay where you are. Trust me to handle this," Sam said.

Reeves taunted her. "Jeannie, I won't hesitate to sacrifice the children."

She didn't reply. Sam gave Maynard Reeves a tight jerk, choking him momentarily, then loosed his hold and shoved him toward the back door.

"Don't try to screw around with me, you son of a bitch." Sam growled the words in a low whisper, meaning them to be heard only by Reeves. "No one's life is more important to me than Jeannie's. You got that? You do whatever you have to do, but if you issue an order to kill those children, I won't have any qualms about blowing your head off."

"Jeannie? Answer me, you witch, you seed of the devil!"

Reeves struggled. Sam pressed his muscular arm into Reeve's windpipe, cutting off his oxygen. He ceased struggling and stood perfectly still.

Sam waited in the hallway for a moment, allowing Reeves to listen to the silence. "What's it going to be?" Sam asked. "Do you and two innocent children die, or do I exchange your life for theirs?"

"Let me go, and I'll send the children in when I reach my car."

"No deal." Sam rubbed the Ruger's barrel up and down the side of Reeves's sweaty face.

"State your terms."

"We'll walk outside. You'll tell your disciples to release the children. As soon as they're within touching distance of me, I'll release you."

"How do I know you'll keep your word?" Reeves asked.

"You don't. You'll just have to trust me, won't you?"

Sam walked Reeves out into the parking lot behind the school. Danette Suddath and an older woman sat inside a dark blue sedan, two children sandwiched between them in the front seat.

"Tell them to let the children out of the car," Sam said.

"Danette. Nora. Release the children."

Once Danette and Nora saw that their beloved reverend's life was in Sam's hands, they opened the car door and ushered the children out, telling them to go to the man with the gun. Missy clasped Amelia's hand, and the two girls walked toward Sam. The moment the girls came within his grasp, Sam shoved Reeves forward as hard as he could, then grabbed both girls up in his arms. Missy and Amelia clung to him.

Reeves ran toward his Lincoln Continental, parked beside Danette's sedan. He started the engine, shifted the gears and roared out of the parking lot. Danette followed him quickly.

Police sirens screamed in the distance. Sam turned around and walked back toward the Howell School. Jeannie stood in the doorway, her eyes swimming with tears. Sam set the two little girls on their feet and pulled Jeannie into his arms. Within minutes the corridor had filled with children and teachers, all of them crying.

Marta rushed out of her office, dropped to her knees and embraced the children closest to her. "Thank God you didn't believe me, Mr. Dundee. I hope you understand why I couldn't risk telling you the truth when you called."

"You saved us all, Sam." Jeannie wrapped her arms around his neck. "I was so afraid, but I knew you wouldn't let anything happen to Missy or Amelia."

"Don't you ever do something like this again." He covered her mouth with his, claiming her, the kiss one of rejoicing and affirmation.

Chapter 16

Sam had been unsuccessful in persuading Jeannie to allow Marta and the teachers to care for the children. Her compassionate heart would not allow her a moment's concern for herself; her every thought was of the frightened, confused boys and girls who crowded around her, seeking comfort. And she gave them comfort, and so much more, in a way only Jeannie could. One by one, she hugged the children, absorbing their anxieties, freeing them from the trauma they had experienced.

With each child's unburdening, Jeannie grew weaker and weaker. Sam sat down beside her, wrapping his arms around her, wanting desperately to give her some of his strength. The moment Marta lifted the last child out of Jeannie's arms, Jeannie turned to Sam, her eyelids drooping and her lips parting on a sigh. She tried to lift her hand to caress his worry-lined face, but she didn't possess enough strength. When she dropped her hand to her side, Sam lifted it, brought it to his lips and kiss her open palm.

"Take care of me, now, Sam." She closed her eyes and fell immediately into a deep sleep.

With Jeannie in his arms, Sam stood and carried her out of the Howell School. Lieutenant Painter met them in the parking lot, halting Sam before he reached the Lexus.

"Is Ms. Alverson all right?"

"She will be after she gets some rest," Sam said.

"I'll need to speak with her as soon as she's able to answer a few questions."

"Give me a call this evening and I'll let you know."

"Tell her that we apprehended Danette Suddath and Nora Dill. And we've put out an all-points bulletin on Maynard Reeves. He finally made a big mistake. We can throw the book at the reverend. He must have lost his mind, taking a school full of disabled children hostage."

"Reeves is obsessed with destroying Jeannie. He's convinced himself and his followers that she really is a witch."

"Tell Ms. Alverson that we'll get Reeves. We've set up roadblocks and are doing an all-out search." Lieutenant Painter glanced down at Jeannie, lying in Sam's arms. "She's for real, isn't she? I mean she actually can take away other people's pain."

"Yeah," Sam said. "She's for real."

He walked away, carrying Jeannie to her car. He opened the door, reclined the seat and laid her down, then closed the door. He got inside, started the engine and drove out into the street. The noonday sun heated the road, creating a shimmering glare. Reaching inside his coat pocket, Sam pulled out his sunglasses and put them on.

She's for real, isn't she? He heard Lieutenant Painter's question echoing in his mind on the drive to Julian's rented cottage. Oh, yeah, Jeannie Alverson was most definitely for real. A real angel of mercy. A real empath who considered it her sacred duty to relieve the suffering of others. A real healer of the human heart.

When they reached the cottage, Sam carried her straight inside to bed. After undressing her, he sat down on the bed and scooted up to rest his back on the headboard, then closed his eyes.

Reeves was out there somewhere, a hunted animal. He would be even more dangerous than before. Now he had nothing to lose. Sam knew what he had to do if the law didn't apprehend Reeves soon.

Reeves had finally crossed the line from mental instability to insanity. Sam had seen it in his eyes. He'd seen that look before, in the eyes of other men, men who had completely lost their hold on reality.

Jeannie moaned in her sleep and turned over, her hands searching. Sam slumped down in the bed, took her in his arms and held her close. Cuddling against him, she returned to a restful sleep. Sam trembled as he held her, the reality of how close he'd come to losing her finally hitting him. He clung to her, stroking her back, dotting tiny kisses over her forehead and cheeks. An ache formed in the pit of his stomach and spread upward, lodging in his throat. Emotions so vast, so forceful that they threatened his sanity consumed him.

Guarding Jeannie was his first priority. Nothing was more important than keeping her safe. *Take care of me, now, Sam. Take care of me, now, Sam.* Her words replayed over and over in his mind. She had taken care of each one of the forty-five students at the Howell School, depleting her energy, putting her own physical and mental health in jeopardy. And then she had turned to him, trusting him completely, never doubting that she was safe in his hands.

He would take care of her, protect her at all costs, but the one thing from which he could not protect her was her own compassionate heart.

Laying her hand on his chest, she wrapped herself around his big body. Sam drew in a deep breath. How had this happened? How the hell had he allowed himself to become captured by a sweet innocent, by an angel whose tender mercy ruled her life? How could such purity be so sensual, such spirituality be so human, such etherealness be so totally erotic?

Six years ago, when he washed ashore on Le Bijou Bleu, Jeannie had done far more than save his life—she had taken possession of his soul. He had never been able to forget her. The sound of her voice. The feel of her comforting hands. The look in her gentle brown eyes.

He had tried to stop thinking about her, willed himself not to remember the powerful connection that existed between them, but deep inside he'd always known that he could not escape the inevitable. Even his niece Elizabeth, when he stayed with her to recuperate from the nearly fatal gunshot wounds, had sensed he was running away from more than his guilt and remorse over Brock's and Connie's deaths. And Elizabeth, who possessed strong psychic powers, had predicted that Sam would return to Biloxi, and to the woman who had saved his life.

He had not allowed Elizabeth to tell him any more of what she'd seen in his future. He hadn't wanted to know, and he still didn't want to know. He felt unworthy, undeserving of being loved by Jeannie. Didn't she know the kind of man he was, the type of life he'd lived? Of course she knew. She even knew he'd been responsible for the death of his unborn child. And yet she loved him.

Jeannie slept the day away, waking with a ravenous appetite for both food and Sam. He made slow, tender love to her, and she blossomed under his loving care, seeming to gain strength from their physical joining. Later he prepared hearty salads, serving them with wine and bread. They ate in the garden again, isolated from the world, nestled in their own tiny piece of paradise. After dinner, she asked him about the morning's events, and he told her everything he knew.

"Don't ever run away by yourself again, the way you did this morning," he said. "I died a thousand deaths when I saw you drive off and knew I couldn't stop you."

"How did you figure out where I'd gone? And how did you know Reeves was at the school?"

"I knew something Marta had said must have triggered your actions." Tilting his head to one side, Sam rested his cheek against the top of her head. "When I phoned the school and spoke to Marta, I could tell something was wrong. She was acting strange. I put two and two together and figured Reeves was involved."

"I know it was foolish of me to go alone to the school." She covered his hands, which lay across her stomach, with her own. Would Sam ever have forgiven her, or himself, if Reeves had killed her and, in doing so, destroyed their unborn child? "I couldn't let Maynard Reeves hurt the students. I did what I had to do. Please understand."

"I understand." He hugged her, encompassing her in his embrace, wishing he could absorb her into himself and keep her safe. "You don't have the capacity to put your needs before those of others. You give and give and give, no matter what the cost is to you."

"You would do the same." Tilting her face, she reached up and kissed him, wanting him to look inside himself and see the truth.

"Not me," he said. "I'm not as strong as you are, angel. I don't have your guts. Besides, the powers that be knew I was the last person on earth who should have the ability to heal the suffering of others. I don't even know how to love."

"That's where you're wrong. You have a great capacity to love. But before you can use that wellspring of goodness inside you, you must come to terms with all the negative feelings keeping that love trapped."

"Oh, Jeannie you don't know me."

"I know you better than you know yourself," she said. "I'm a part of your soul, as you are mine."

He had no response to her statement. Intense emotion gripped him, holding him captive. Jeannie saw the best in him, sensing a goodness he could not see. Dear God, was he worthy of the trust she placed in him? Could he be the man she thought he was, the man she expected him to be? Or would he let her down?

When Lieutenant Painter arrived at eight-thirty that night, he found Sam and Jeannie watching the weather channel on television. The depression that had begun near the Cape Verde Islands, off the coast of Africa, had moved into the Caribbean and was building up speed and intensity. A tropical storm with high winds and heavy rain was expected to hit the islands southeast of the Gulf by early morning.

"Come on in." Sam opened the door and led the lieutenant into the living room. "Jeannie's concerned about the tropical storm headed our way. She has a close friend living on one of the islands in the gulf.''

"Yeah, I hear they think this thing has a good chance of turning into a full-fledged hurricane before she hits the coast.'' Painter nodded at Jeannie when she glanced up from the television and smiled at him.

"Give me just a moment, Lieutenant,'' Jeannie said. "I'd like to hear the rest of this report from the National Hurricane Center. I've already contacted my friend to make sure he's aware of the storm headed his way, but I want to stay updated on what's happening.''

"Sure. I can wait,'' Painter said.

When the report ended several minutes later, Jeannie switched off the set and turned to the police officer. "Thank you for being so patient. Sam has told me that you arrested Danette Suddath and the other woman.''

"Nora Dill. Yes, we arrested them. But members of the Righteous Light Church posted bond for them, and they're out on bail until their trials.''

"Missy hasn't been given to her mother, has she?''

"No.'' Sam walked over and stood behind Jeannie's chair, placing his hand on her shoulder.

"Social services will place Missy in a foster home until after her mother's trial,'' Lieutenant Painter said. "And she'll remain in one if—or should I say when—Danette Suddath is found guilty and sent to prison.''

"Y'all haven't found Maynard Reeves, have you?'' Jeannie reached up, placing her hand atop Sam's on her shoulder.

"I swear, Ms. Alverson, it's as if the man vanished off the face of the earth.'' Shrugging, Lieutenant Painter shook his head. "The best we can figure it, he must have left Biloxi by boat. Since his church is headquartered in New Orleans, the authorities there have been alerted. The feds have pretty well taken over this case, but we're working with them.''

"Too bad someone in his organization isn't willing to turn him in,'' Sam said. "It amazes me how gullible some people are.''

"None of his followers will betray him.'' Jeannie patted Sam's hand. "People want to believe in something, in a higher power, and that's why they can sometimes be brain-washed by a charismatic leader like Reverend Reeves. He feeds on their fears and prejudices, teaching them hatred and intolerance.''

"I want you to know, Ms. Alverson that we've posted a man at the hospital to guard Dr. Howell, and one at the school to make sure the children are safe. And even though you're well taken care of—'' Rufus Painter glanced at Sam ''—we're sending a patrol around the block here every hour.''

Jeannie clasped Lieutenant Painter's hand. "Thank you for all you've done.''

Painter grinned; it was a lopsided, boyish grin. "Yes, ma'am. You're entirely welcome. Just wish we could have done more.''

"I believe we have some business to take care of, don't we, Lieutenant?'' Jeannie asked.

Flushing, Painter cleared his throat. "Yes, ma'am, we do. I've got someone outside ready to take your statement concerning the events at the Howell School this morning.''

"Are you sure you're up to this?'' Sam moved around to the side of her chair, placing his hand on her arm.

"Yes,'' she said. "I have to do all that I can to help remove Maynard Reeves from society, to put him away where he can't harm anyone.''

After the police left, Jeannie tuned in the weather channel for an update on the tropical storm, then contacted Manton again before she and Sam went to bed.

As they lay together, the room dark and quiet except for the moonlight filtering through the curtains and the hum of traffic a few blocks away on the highway, Sam held Jeannie in his arms.

"Stop worrying,'' Sam said. "You told me Manton has weathered storms, and even a few hurricanes, on Le Bijou Bleu.''

"I know. But I can't help worrying.'' Jeannie kissed Sam's naked shoulder. "He's assured me the storm shelter is stocked with the basic necessities to last several days.''

"Manton will be all right. The man has a sixth sense about things. If the storm hits the island, he'll wait it out in the storm shelter."

"Sam?" She lifted her head off his shoulder and looked down into his blue-gray eyes.

"What is it, angel?" He rubbed his hand up and down her arm, from shoulder to wrist.

"I have an uneasy feeling I can't explain. I'm afraid, Sam. I'm so very, very afraid."

He enclosed her in the strength and safety of his arms, lowering her head to the pillow and kissing her eyelids closed. "Julian suffered a heart attack, the students and staff of the Howell School were held captive, a tropical storm is probably going to hit Le Bijou Bleu while Manton's there alone, and Maynard Reeves is out there somewhere plotting your destruction. I'd say something would be wrong with you if you weren't feeling uneasy and if you weren't scared half out of your mind."

"No, it's more than the obvious things."

With her eyes still closed, she snuggled against Sam, absorbing the warmth and force of his big, powerful body. She had noticed that for weeks now she had been able not only to connect with Sam's thoughts and feelings, but also, in a limited sense, to draw strength from him. She knew he was totally unaware when it happened, that he had no idea the link between them grew stronger, more intricate and complicated, with each contact. Mental. Physical. Emotional. Spiritual.

"Everything is going to be all right," Sam said. "Julian will be home in a few days. The children and teachers at the school are safe now. Manton and Le Bijou Bleu will weather the storm. The authorities will capture Maynard Reeves. And I'll take good care of you."

When his lips touched hers, she responded wholeheartedly. When his body covered hers, she arched upward, encouraging his possession. And when he thrust into her moist heat, she welcomed him, clasping him tightly. They mated in a fast, furious frenzy, sharing their pleasure, then fell into a deep, sated sleep.

Jeannie woke early. The morning sky was red, warning of bad weather. She got out of bed, slipped into her robe and set her cane on the floor.

"Come back to bed, angel. It's still early." Sam patted her pillow.

"I want to check the weather and contact Manton before the storm hits and blocks our communication."

"All right," Sam said. "You check the weather and get in touch with Manton, and I'll put on some coffee. Or would you rather have tea?"

"Coffee will be fine."

Sam slipped into a pair of trousers and headed for the bathroom.

A few minutes later, on his way to the kitchen, he paused in the doorway to the living room. The weather forecaster was predicting that hurricane-force winds would sweep the Gulf Coast by nightfall.

"Get in touch with Manton," Sam said. "Make sure he's all right, and that he's prepared to take shelter."

"I wish I could shake this uneasy feeling."

"You'll feel better after you've been in touch with Manton."

"I hope so."

Sam filled the coffee machine with bottled water, then spooned the gourmet blend into the filter. His stomach growled, reminding him his dinner salad had been a light repast for a man of his size. Omelets, he thought, ham-and-cheese omelets.

He was turning an enormous omelet over in the skillet when Jeannie came into the kitchen. Smiling, he looked up from his chore. Pale-faced, wide-eyed, she walked over to him and gripped his arm. She swallowed, then bit down on her lower lip.

"What's wrong?" He turned off the stove and grabbed Jeannie's shoulders.

"I can't get a response from Manton. I've been trying for the last ten minutes."

"Maybe the storm has already hit Le Bijou Bleu."

"No, it's not possible. The storm couldn't possibly hit the island before late this afternoon." Tears gathered in her eyes. She squeezed his arm. "Something's wrong. Bad wrong. Manton would not have left the house this morning. He would have brought the dogs and cats inside last night."

"We'll keep trying to contact him."

"If I don't get a response soon, I'm going to the island."

"No, you're not." Sam jerked her into his arms; her cane hit the floor with a resounding thump. "There's a damn hurricane headed this way!"

"Something has happened to Manton. Don't you understand? I have to go to him."

"If anyone goes, I'll go," Sam said. "I'll have Lieutenant Painter send an officer over here to guard you until J.T. or Hawk can fly in from Atlanta. I'll go to Le Bijou Bleu and make sure Manton is all right."

"No. If he's hurt, he'll need me."

"Dammit, Jeannie, you are not going to Le Bijou Bleu, and that's all there is to it!"

Three hours later, Jeannie docked the cruiser, and Sam lifted her onto the pier. Dark storm clouds swirled overhead. An angry wind gusted around them, blowing windrows of sand along the beach. Faint, almost indiscernible raindrops fell from the sky.

Sam carried her up the steps to the top of the hill. The wind whistled through the trees, whipping the branches.

"Stop!" Jeannie raised her voice to fight the howl of the wind. "Manton won't answer me!"

"What?" Sam shouted, knowing damn well they couldn't stay out here in the violent wind much longer.

"I've called to him repeatedly since we docked, and he isn't responding."

Sam lowered his head, putting his mouth near her ear. "Hasn't there ever been a time when you couldn't connect telepathically with him?"

"Never. Not since the first time our minds linked, when I was nine years old." She clutched Sam's shoulder. "He's hurt. I know he's hurt. He'd have to be unconscious not to hear me, not to be able to answer."

"Calm down, angel. We'll find Manton and take care of him. Whatever's wrong, you'll fix it until we can get him back to Biloxi."

Sam rushed toward the house as heavy drops of rain began falling. They were both drenched by the time he stepped up on the veranda. The front door stood wide open. Sam carried Jeannie inside. An eerie quiet filled the rooms, though the fury of the rain and wind blasted the outside of the house, making the walls tremble.

Not one dog welcomed them; not one cat slinked about their legs. Where the hell was Manton? Sam wondered. What could have happened to him? Had he taken ill? Had there been an accident?

Sam set Jeannie down on the sofa in the living room. "I'll go get you a cane. You search downstairs, and I'll search upstairs."

Jeannie nodded her agreement and waited patiently for Sam's return. He brought her cane and helped her to her feet, then cupped her face in his hands.

"Stay in touch with me, angel." He looked deep into her gentle brown eyes.

I love you, Sam Dundee.

Swallowing hard, he closed his eyes. *My sweet Jeannie.* He kissed her on the mouth, quickly, then turned around and walked up the front staircase. Jeannie began her search in the dining room, then moved into the kitchen.

Manton. Please answer me.

She checked the downstairs twice, thoroughly searching every nook and cranny. She spoke to Sam telepathically, letting him know that she hadn't found Manton. He told her that he'd found nothing upstairs. No sign of Manton or his animals.

Was it possible Manton had gone down into the basement? she wondered. Had he already moved into the storm shelter when something had happened to him? Or could he have gone outside, be somewhere out there now, injured and alone?

The old stables at the back of the house! The animals bedded there, and Manton carried food and fresh water out

to them every day. Perhaps he'd accidentally fallen and hit
his head last night or early this morning.

I'm going out to the old stables behind the house, Jeannie told Sam telepathically. *Meet me out there.*

Wait for me, he said.

Manton's in the stables, Sam. I know it. I can feel it.

He repeated his telepathic message. *Wait for me.*

Jeannie's need to find Manton urged her through the
house and out onto the back veranda. A row of trees in the
backyard arched over in the wind, many of their tops
touching the ground. Bending in the wind, a young sapling
groaned, then toppled over, its roots lifting and falling, finally tearing loose.

Jeannie fought the wind as she made her way off the veranda. The stable doors hung open, creaking as they
slammed open and shut. With the wind stinging her eyes,
Jeannie squinted and gripped her cane tightly. The black sky
emptied heavy rain onto the earth, and the wind roared a
warning. Instinctively Jeannie knew the tropical storm had
graduated to a hurricane, and it was only a matter of time
until its full force hit Le Bijou Bleu.

She made her way to the stables, slipping inside as one big
door swung open. Darkness surrounded her. She felt Manton's presence. He was somewhere nearby, but he was still
unconscious.

Suddenly cold, menacing evil surrounded her. For one
brief second, she forgot to breathe. Her heart stood still.
And in that moment she knew. *Sam!* her mind screamed.
Help me, Sam!

"I've been waiting for you," the voice said.

Jeannie spun around. There in the doorway behind her,
the faint light from outside casting shadows across his
handsome freckled face, stood Maynard Reeves.

Chapter 17

"So nice of you to come out in this bad weather to meet me." Reeves took a step forward, his toothy, charismatic smile spreading across his face.

Jeannie stepped backward, away from the threatening presence. "I'm not alone. Manton's here, and so is Sam."

"I've already taken care of that stupid giant you call Manton."

"What have you done to him?"

"He's sleeping peacefully, him and his dogs. I used a tranquilizer gun to bring your Manton down. I shot him twice, so he'll sleep a long, long time."

Reeves moved toward her. A flash of lightning struck nearby. Jeannie gasped. Reeves laughed. Shards of light flashed through the open doors and the wide cracks in the rotting wooden walls of the old stables. A shiny 9 mm handgun glistened in Reeves's hand.

"Sam will come out here to find me." Jeannie felt something warm and soft curl around her leg. One of Manton's cats.

"Let him come on out. I want him to find us. The witch's guardian doesn't deserve to live. I'll destroy him first, before I punish you for your evil."

Reeves moved closer and closer. Jeannie backed farther and farther into the darkness, her escape hampered by her inability to maneuver without her cane.

Sam! Sam! Hurry. Please hurry. And be careful. Maynard Reeves has me trapped in the stables.

As she backed away from the approaching madman, Jeannie lost her balance. The raging wind battered the old wooden stables. Lightning zigzagged from heaven to earth. Hard, heavy rain pelted the island. Jeannie fell, landing on her backside, her cane hitting the dirt floor, just out of arm's reach.

Reeves hovered, glaring down at her, his smile wide, showing all his teeth. His eyes glowed in the darkness. Jeannie scooted backward. Her heart hammered, rumbling in her ears like a hundred bass drums. The damp earth stuck to her palms as she used her hands to propel herself backward.

Reeves stomped one big foot down beside her hip. She clenched her teeth. He lowered the other foot, straddling her as he bent over, reached out and seized her. She sucked in air. He jerked her up off the floor. She hit him, her hands flailing against his chest. Reeves grabbed her by her hair, pulling her face against his, so close their noses touched. The more she struggled, the tighter he clasped her hair and the deeper his fingers bit into the gun he held pressed against her back.

Reeves licked her face, from chin to forehead. Jeannie closed her eyes, struggling to make contact with her attacker's inner thoughts and feelings. Anger! Hatred! Passion to possess her power! If only she could hook on to his emotions more firmly, she could begin drawing them from him.

"No!" Reeves screamed, shoving her away from him with such force that she fell backward onto the floor, her fragile body hitting the damp earth with a jarring thud. "You will not use your wicked talents to possess me, witch! I will destroy you, and then God will bless me with your powers."

From her position on the floor, all Jeannie could see was the trembling outline of Reeves's body. Even from several feet away, she could feel his rage. His murderous intent swirled around her, more powerful and far uglier than the raging storm assaulting the island.

The metallic taste of fear coated her tongue. A sour, salty bile rose in her throat.

Stay where you are, Jeannie. Don't move. Don't make a sound. Act as if nothing has changed. Sam cautioned Jeannie telepathically as he entered the stables, his footsteps indiscernible, masked by the storm's fury.

Be careful, Sam. Reeves has a gun.

Reeves held the 9 mm in his shaky hand, aiming it directly at Jeannie. He laughed, the sound hysterical and shrill. "Shooting you would be so easy, but not appropriate for you, Jeannie Alverson, spawn of Satan. No, a witch must burn. You will be a sacrifice to the Lord."

Sam Dundee swooped down on Reeves like a hawk clawing its helpless prey. Grabbing Reeves by the shoulders, Sam lifted him and tossed him into the air. Reeves shrieked as he landed against the wall, his gun sailing out of his hand and disappearing in the darkness.

Stay where you are, Jeannie, Sam told her.

A slash of lightning illuminated the stables momentarily. In a split second, Jeannie saw Sam, his face contorted with rage, his Ruger aimed in Reeves's general direction. He fired a shot. Reeves bellowed. When a second and then a third brilliant explosion of lightning hit the island, she saw it glimmer off Reeves's gun, which lay halfway between Sam and him. Reeves grappled for the gun with one hand while he clutched at his bloody shoulder with the other.

Another shot rang out, then another. She had no idea who was doing the shooting or whether either bullet had hit its target. Pushing herself up into a sitting position, she watched while two shadowy figures lunged headlong at each other. She could distinguish which man was which solely from Sam Dundee's massive size. He was a couple of inches taller and much heavier than Maynard Reeves.

The sound of fists hitting flesh reverberated inside the stables. Thuds. Thumps. Knocks. Ragged breathing. Sam Dundee, his back to the outer wall, landed a resounding blow to Reeve's midsection, knocking the breath out of him and laying him out flat on his back.

Sam stood over Reeves, his chest heaving. Jeannie waited for Reeves to stand. He didn't. Another shot rang out. Sam's body jerked from the impact as the bullet ripped through his side. Jeannie screamed.

Reeves lifted his shoulders off the floor, gripping the 9 mm in his trembling hands. "God is on my side! He will help me destroy both the witch and her guardian."

In one quick, practiced move, Sam lifted his leg, pivoted around and slammed his foot into Reeves's hands, plummeting his gun into dark oblivion. Before Reeves had a chance to react, Sam brought his foot around again and knocked his opponent flat on the floor.

The roar of the hurricane force winds shook the stables. The wall directly behind Sam collapsed. Jeannie screamed again. The old timbers fell on top of Sam, knocking him to his knees, then flat on his face, covering his body completely.

The wind roared like a mighty jet plane. Rain poured into the stables, washing over the remains of the toppled outer wall.

"Sam!"

No response.

Sam!

She tried again to contact Sam, but he didn't answer. He had to be unconscious. And with the weight of those heavy old boards crushing his body, he was probably seriously injured. She had to go to him. Help him. Save him.

Lifting herself onto her knees, she felt around the damp dirt floor for her walking stick. Suddenly she saw her cane, lying several feet to her left. Then realization dawned on her. There was light inside the stables, pouring in from outside.

The deafening rumble subsided. The wind stopped. The air became perfectly calm. Jeannie knew enough about tropical storms to know that the island was encased in the eye of the storm, that eerie, calm core in the center of the massive, spiraling clouds and driving rain.

Jeannie crawled on her knees across the stables, clutched her cane and lifted herself up off the floor. She scurried to the pile of heavy boards lying in a heap, completely covering Sam Dundee.

Sam, you're going to be all right. I'll take care of you. I promise.

She had to remove enough of the debris to touch some part of his body, to clasp his hand, to caress his head. Only then could she begin her loving ministrations; only then could she work her magic and save Sam's life. Balancing herself with her cane, she eased down on her knees and laid her cane aside. Finding the intact boards far too heavy to lift, she clawed at the rubble. She saw Sam's hand. She reached for him.

"You're not going to save him!" Maynard Reeves jerked Jeannie off the ground.

She gasped. It couldn't be. Sam had shot Reeves and knocked him unconscious.

Fighting Reeves proved fruitless, but Jeannie fought him all the same. Although he'd been no match for Sam, he was much larger and far stronger than she was. He dragged her out of the stables, through the huge opening made by the wall's collapse. Jeannie hit him repeatedly; he didn't seem to feel her blows.

All the while he tugged her around the house and toward the beach, Jeannie struggled. She could not—would not—allow this monster, who called himself a man of God, to triumph. If he succeeded in getting her off the island, they were both doomed to drown in the storm, and there would be no one to save Sam and Manton. Even if help arrived in a day or two, it might well be too late for these two men she so dearly loved.

Sam. Sam. Oh, my darling, please hear me.

Silence.

Reeves halted at the top of the hill overlooking the far side of the island, where he'd docked his small boat. "I'm taking you straight to the Righteous Light Church, where my disciples are preparing for your sacrifice."

"No!" Jeannie screamed. "Don't you realize we'll be killed if we leave the island?"

"The storm has passed," Reeves said. "God has calmed the seas for my safe passage."

"The storm hasn't passed. We're right in the middle of the eye of the storm. Don't you know what that means?"

"You can't trick me with your lies, witch."

Reeves pulled her into his arms. Jeannie struggled. Threading his fingers through her hair, he cupped her scalp. "When you draw your last breath, the Almighty will bestow your powers on me. He will cleanse them of evil and infuse them with his glory."

Manton. Manton, can you hear me? If only she could rouse Manton. He was in the stables, not far from Sam. If she could make him hear her, she could tell him that Sam needed him. *Manton!*

Jeannie? Manton asked, their link wavering and fragile because of his grogginess. *Jeannie, where are you? Are you all right?*

The stable wall fell in on Sam. He's hurt. Maynard Reeves is trying to take me off the island. I need your help. Jeannie closed her eyes and said a silent prayer of thanks that Manton was alive and conscious enough for the two of them to communicate. *We're in the eye of the storm, and Reeves doesn't realize that we can't sail to the mainland. Sam will die without my help.*

You must overpower Reeves, Manton told her.

But how? she asked. *I'm not strong enough.*

Yes, you are strong enough. Far stronger than you know. Reach inside yourself. Draw strength from the depth of your love for Sam, Manton said. *Concentrate. Focus all your energy on saving Sam, on saving his life.*

Can you help Sam? Jeannie asked. *Are you able to move?*

Not yet. But soon. The feeling is returning to my body. Be strong, little one.

Reeves licked Jeannie's face. She cringed.

"If you won't listen to me, won't believe what I'm telling you about the storm—" Jeannie looked heavenward, wondering just how long they had before the eye passed and the storm's fury consumed the island once again "—then at least consider the possibility that we'd be safer in my cruiser than in your small boat."

Reeves licked her face again. "I can taste the evil in you, but I can also taste the power. The power that will soon be mine."

"We'll never make it to the mainland alive in your little boat."

"Perhaps you're right about taking your cruiser." Gripping her painfully about the waist, Reeves tugged her in the opposite direction, toward the other side of the island.

Manton?

Yes, Jeannie?

I have to find the strength to stop Reeves and save Sam.

Your love for Sam is your strength. No power on earth is greater.

Jeannie focused on the incredible power surging through her body. She had to overpower Reeves; it was the only way she would be free to go to Sam and save his life. Nothing mattered except saving Sam.

She felt the tightening of her muscles, the hardening of her biceps. She could hardly believe what was happening to her. A few times with Sam, she had realized she was absorbing a small fraction of his strength, but nothing this forceful. Manton had been right. There was no power on earth greater than love.

Jeannie grabbed Maynard Reeves by his shoulders, tightening her hands, lifting him off his feet and away from her. He yelped aloud, fear and amazement bright in his eyes.

"Put me down, you demon-possessed witch!"

Jeannie flung Reeves from her. His body landed on a muddy patch of ground several feet from her. Jeannie slumped to her knees, her crippled legs as weak as ever.

Rising into a sitting position, Reeves glared at her. "I am not afraid to fight the devil, for the Lord—" Reeves lifted his arms toward the sky "—will give me the victory." Reeves stood, his once charismatic, boyish smile twisted into an evil leer.

Raindrops hit Jeannie on the face. The wind whistled through the trees. The eye had passed quickly; the storm would be upon them again in a matter of minutes.

Reeves took a step toward Jeannie. She looked to his left, where a row of palm trees swayed in the wind, bending their heads as if awaiting execution. Lightning crackled in the sky, followed by the rumble of thunder. In the distance, Jeannie heard the storm's deadly roar.

Reeves took another step, and then another. Jeannie scooted backward. *Concentrate on saving Sam, on the depth of your love for him,* she told herself.

When Reeves was upon her, Jeannie prayed for help. A bolt of lightning hit the enormous old live oak directly behind Reeves, splitting it apart as if it had been hacked in two by a giant ax. Jeannie watched in horror and fascination as one half of the tree uprooted and toppled, crushing Maynard Reeves in its downward path. He screamed once, then fell silent. Blood oozed from his mouth. His sightless eyes stared off into space.

Jeannie's battle with Reeves had ended. A higher power had indeed decided the outcome.

Jeannie crawled toward the unmoving man lying beneath the weight of the severed tree. She placed her fingers on the pulse point in his neck. She sighed. Maynard Reeves was dead.

Sam! She had to get to Sam. In her frustration, she struggled to connect her mind to Manton's. God had granted her one miracle. Would he grant her another?

Help me. Please help me get to Sam before it's too late.

She crawled away from Reeves, knowing there was only one way to reach Sam. She would have to crawl, on her knees, back to the stables. The rain poured down, drenching her. The wind toppled her, facedown, into the saturated grass. She lifted herself and continued crawling across the vast front lawn, away from the ocean and toward the house.

She'd made her way to within twenty feet of the front veranda when she saw an enormous dark form running toward her. Manton! She stopped, the pain in her knees radiating up her thighs and into her body.

She lifted up her arms. Manton hauled her up, pressing her wet body against his.

I'm still groggy from the tranquilizer, Manton told her. *I'm weak, and my brain is fuzzy.*

I'm so thankful you're all right, she said. *Now, please, take me to Sam. I can't lose him.*

Manton carried her to the stables, depositing her beside the rubble burying Sam Dundee's big body. Manton cleared the boards off Sam. Jeannie laid both her hands on Sam's back. Tears gathered in her eyes.

Manton picked up a piece of splintered board, laid it over his knee and broke it in half, then handed it to Jeannie.

Use this as a cane. We need to get to the storm shelter. I'll carry Sam.

The wind and rain attacked them mercilessly on their trek from the stables to the house. Completely drenched, their skin bleeding from blowing-sand cuts, they went down the dark flight of stairs leading to the storm shelter in the basement, Manton carrying Sam.

The storm must have damaged the generator, Manton said. *We have no power of any kind. Try to find the kerosene lamps and light them. A box of matches will be beside one of the lamps.*

Once inside the shelter, Manton and Jeannie felt their way around in the pitch-blackness. The fronts of Manton's calves bumped into the cot. He laid Sam down gently. Jeannie found the matches, struck one to find the kerosene lamp on the table. She removed the globe, lit the wick and turned to seek out the other lamp. Manton took the matches from her, nodding toward Sam.

Jeannie hobbled over to Sam and sat down on the floor. She lifted his hand, encompassing it in hers. Concentrating totally on making the connection, she focused her every thought on entering Sam's body, on linking herself to his injuries.

Manton lit the other lamp. The two sources of light, situated on opposite ends of the room, cast a soft glow that illuminated the entire twelve-by-twelve storm shelter. Walking over to where Jeannie sat on the floor, Manton placed his hands on her shoulders.

Sam is very weak, she said. Rising up on her haunches, she reached out and wiped away the blood trickling down Sam's bruised and cut forehead. She wiped the blood across her skirt. *He's bleeding, and his ribs are broken.*

I know you want to save him. Manton squeezed her shoulders gently. *But you must not endanger your life and*

*your child's. Sam would not want you to sacrifice yourself
and the child to save his life.*

I cannot—I will not—let him die!

Releasing her shoulders, Manton stepped away from her
and sat down in a chair at the table.

Jeannie knelt over Sam, embracing him. The faint pulses
of his pain seeped into her body. She moaned as the pain
increased, moving gradually out of Sam and into her.

Sam's eyelids fluttered. Still embracing him, Jeannie lifted
her head and looked at his pale, blood-smeared face. He
opened his eyes.

"Hello," she said.

"Jeannie...don't..." His eyes closed, and he drifted back
into a semiconscious state.

She kissed his lips with the utmost tenderness. "Hush,
now, my love. You're going to be all right."

His injuries were extensive, and the bleeding was severe
and life-threatening. She had to stop the bleeding! He would
die if she didn't help him.

The pain doubled her over. She cried out, the sound a
harsh plea for endurance. As spasm after spasm of torturous cramps racked her body, Jeannie balled her hands into
fists and slid off Sam, down the side of the cot and onto the
floor. Her eyes closed. She moaned again and again, biting
her lower lip to contain the sound.

Manton jumped up, rushing to her aid, lifting her into his
arms. She shivered, once, twice, then opened her eyes. *I
haven't finished. Carry me back to Sam. I have to help
him.*

Be careful, Manton cautioned, then complied with her
request and set her back down on the floor at Sam's
side.

She laid her head on Sam's arm where it rested on the
edge of the cot. She lifted his limp hand, brought it to her
lips and kissed each finger. Squeezing his hand, she focused again. Sam's injuries became hers, ripping her apart,
then dissolving as the pain suffused her body. Tears of agony streamed down her face. Anguished moans rose from
her throat.

Exhausted and close to losing consciousness, Jeannie clung to Sam's hand. He opened his eyes and looked at her.

"My God, Jeannie, what are you doing?" Lifting his head off the pillow, he glanced at their clasped hands. He jerked his hand away.

She tried to smile, to speak, to tell him that there was nothing she would not do to save his life. Didn't he know that he was her life, that without him she did not want to live?

He heard her words as clearly as if she'd spoken them aloud. "You're killing yourself. I want you to stop." Sam looked around for Manton and found him standing a few feet away, his eyes filled with tears as he watched Jeannie's suffering. "Why the hell don't you stop this? Keep her away from me!"

Sam tried to sit up, but weakness overcame him and he fell back on the cot. Jeannie reached for him. He slapped her hand away. "Get away, dammit! If I die, I die, but you're not going to die with me."

"You're already stronger. Your injuries have stopped bleeding." With great effort, she rose up on her knees, her body hovering over his. "When the pain returns and the bleeding starts again, I'll have to help you. To keep you alive. We can't get off Le Bijou Bleu until the storm passes."

"If you take my pain into your body, it will kill you," Sam said. "Don't you think I know that? My God, Jeannie, I don't want you to die for me."

Covering her mouth with her hand, she cried silently, her body trembling with her hushed sobs.

"Promise me," Sam said. "Promise me that you—" his eyelids fluttered, and his voice faltered "—you won't do it again."

"I love you," she said.

"Promise me..." He sank back into a semiconscious state.

Jeannie rested, closing her eyes, laying her hand next to his, careful not to touch him. With his injuries temporarily, partially healed, he would sleep, drifting in and out of consciousness. And Jeannie would sleep, restoring her depleted strength, until Sam's pain from his internal wounds returned and the bleeding began again.

Jeannie covered her stomach with the palm of her other hand. Would saving Sam's life cost them their baby? Could she save both father and child?

In the last conscious moments before sleep overcame her, Jeannie pleaded for the strength to endure, and for the blessing of life for Sam, herself and their unborn child.

Chapter 18

Sleepy, exhausted and nearly depleted of her energy, Jeannie held Sam's hand and listened to his uneven breathing. She would have to join with him again. She had no other choice; without her help, Sam would die.

When she called to Manton, he came to her and placed his hands on her shoulders. She drew strength from him. Manton's strength was the only thing maintaining her consciousness and enabling her to continue keeping Sam alive. If only Manton possessed the power to share her pain and suffering ... but he did not. She, and she alone, had to bear the burden.

When I have finished, Jeannie told Manton, *cover me with a blanket and let me rest, but don't move me away from Sam.*

I'll take care of you, Manton said. *And while you rest, I will go upstairs and try once again to contact the mainland. It's daylight now, and the storm passed hours ago. Perhaps someone can get to the island soon and take you and Sam to the hospital.*

Within minutes, Jeannie had made the connection again and began her miracle of healing.

As she withdrew his pain and stopped the bleeding once again, Sam opened his eyes. Jeannie lay in a huddled mass against the cot, writhing in pain. Weak, dizzy and disoriented, Sam struggled over to her.

"Jeannie...Jeannie..."

Drenched in sweat, groaning in agony, Jeannie barely heard Sam calling her name. She tried to respond verbally, but could not, and when she tried to convey her thoughts to him telepathically, she found she lacked the strength.

Sam saw Manton standing over them, and realized the gentle giant was dying inside as he watched Jeannie suffering and knew he could do nothing to alleviate her pain.

Sam reached over and enclosed Jeannie's trembling, pain-racked body in his arms. On some level of consciousness, Jeannie felt Sam's embrace, sensed his concern. He ached with the need to help her, to share her pain, not realizing that the emotional torment he endured was transferred to Jeannie, weakening her all the more. And she could not relate to him what was happening, that his very nearness was creating more pain inside her, draining her of what little strength she had left.

Manton grabbed Sam by the shoulders, pulling him away from Jeannie. Sam hit out at the other man, dazed by the suddenness of his attack. Manton pushed Sam back down on the cot and signed to him. Sam glared up at Manton, wondering what the hell he was trying to tell him.

He watched closely while Manton jabbed his index fingers toward each other repeatedly.

"Hurt?" Sam asked.

Manton nodded, then signed again, thrusting his right index finger under his prone left palm. Sam didn't understand. Manton repeated the procedure.

"Kill," Sam said, realization dawning on him. "Holding her hurts her? Is killing her?"

Manton nodded repeatedly.

"Then do something to help her."

With his hands prone, Manton struck his left index finger with his right index finger. Tears filled his green eyes and streamed down his bronze cheeks.

"You can't." Sam balled his hands into fists.

Sam huddled on the far side of the cot, forcing himself not to touch Jeannie again. While he lay there helpless, watching her endure his pain, he felt as if his life were being drained out of him. He had begged her not to help him, but she hadn't listened. Dammit, why hadn't she listened to him? Why hadn't she done what he'd asked?

He would rather die a thousand times over than see her suffering this way and know he was powerless to help her. Was this his true damnation? Had the guilt and remorse he'd endured for six years been only a preliminary to this final atonement? Was having to watch the woman he loved die by slow degrees his punishment for Brock's and Connie's deaths? For the death of his unborn child?

It wasn't right that Jeannie had to pay for his sins, to suffer because of his crimes. She was innocent, so completely pure and good. *This isn't fair,* his heart cried. An angel of mercy given no mercy herself.

Sam's angry, savage cry pierced the very gates of heaven.

Minutes dragged by, seeming like hours. Eventually Jeannie fell into a deep sleep. Manton drew the blanket up around her and slipped a pillow under her head. Drained and weak, Sam closed his eyes.

When he awoke, he and Jeannie were alone in the storm shelter. A sudden, sharp pang hit him in the chest. His pain was returning.

Sam heard footsteps on the stairs. J. T. Blackwood swept into the room, Manton following him.

"I've got a float plane waiting to take you back to Biloxi," J.T. said. "The storm missed Biloxi and lost a lot of steam before it hit the Louisiana coast."

"Get Jeannie to the hospital." Sam tried to stand, but swayed on his feet and fell backward onto the cot.

"We'll get you both to the hospital." J.T. glanced down at Jeannie, lying on the floor. "What the hell happened to you two? Did you get caught out in the storm? I don't read sign, so I have no idea what this big fellow's been trying to tell me."

"You carry Jeannie out to the plane," Sam said. "Manton can help me."

Sam watched while J.T. lifted a lifeless Jeannie into his arms. When J.T. walked past Sam, Sam reached out. J.T. stopped. Sam let his hand hover over her face, and died a little inside because he didn't dare touch her.

"A wall fell on me," Sam said. "It should have killed me. I'd be dead now if Jeannie hadn't saved my life."

Manton's cats and dogs, who had followed them out of the stables the evening before, now followed them up from the storm shelter into the house. J.T. stepped around the shards of glass from several blown-out windowpanes and stomped through the water puddles marring the wooden floors.

Outside, the sun shone faintly from behind a mass of clouds. The paint on the north side of the house had been sanded down to the bare wood, and several window shutters lay scattered on the ground. A small section of the roof had blown off, and debris was strewn in every direction. Uprooted trees marred the landscape. Huge sandpiles dotted the beach.

Maynard Reeves's body lay beneath the severed trunk of an old oak tree. Manton stopped abruptly when Sam tugged on his arm.

"Not a very pretty sight," J.T. said. "Looks like lightning struck the tree, splitting it in two. Then half of it fell on the reverend."

"He was out of his mind," Sam said. "He thought if he killed Jeannie, he would somehow gain her empathic abilities. He thought God would give them to him as a gift for destroying a witch."

"Well, it looks like a higher power made a judgment call." J.T. glanced down at Jeannie, lying unconscious in his arms. "I'd say somebody up there was watching out for one of his own."

Every muscle in Sam's body strained toward Jeannie; his need to touch her was overwhelming. "Let's get off this island and take Jeannie to a hospital." A sharp, stabbing ache sliced through Sam's midsection. He doubled over in pain.

"Hang on," J.T. said "The plane's right down here."

He led them down the steps to the beach. Lifting Jeannie up high in his arms, he handed her to the float plane's pilot, then turned to help Manton with Sam. Once Sam was seated and Jeannie rested in Manton's arms, J.T. jumped on board and gave the pilot orders to get them to Biloxi as quickly as possible.

Jeannie did not awaken from her deep sleep on the flight to Biloxi. Sam watched her for any sign of recovery, but she lay in Manton's arms, unmoving, looking like a limp rag doll. If only he could hold her in *his* arms, kiss those pale lips, stroke her tearstained cheeks. As pain radiated through his own body, Sam felt himself slipping away. He tried to stay conscious, not wanting to sever that last link—visual contact—with Jeannie.

After surgery, Sam awoke calling for Jeannie. J.T. assured him that everything possible was being done for her, but Sam wanted to see her, needed to know for sure that she was going to be all right. J.T. and an orderly forcibly held Sam down on the bed while a nurse injected him with a sedative.

He awoke again sometime during the night. Glancing around the hospital room, he saw J.T. sitting in a chair, his tan Stetson covering the upper part of his face as he slept.

Jeannie. Where was Jeannie? Was she all right? He had to find her.

Sam took note of the tubes stuck in his body, then dismissed them, sitting up in bed and sliding his feet over the side. Dizziness swirled around inside his head. He took several deep breaths trying to overcome his disorientation. On wobbly legs, he struggled to stand.

J. T. Blackwood clamped his big hand down on Sam's shoulder. "Where the hell do you think you're going?"

"Jeannie." The one word said everything.

"The shape you're in, you can't do her any good," J.T. said. "Stay in bed. The doctors are doing everything they can for her."

"I've got to see her." Sam jerked away from J.T., took three steps and passed out cold.

Sam floated in and out of a drug-induced sleep, realizing that each time he fought them, begging to see Jeannie, they sedated him again. His gut instincts told him something was horribly wrong, but he couldn't fight the sedatives they gave him to keep him calm and allow him to heal.

Three days after his arrival, Sam awoke at midday, his mouth as dry as cotton balls, his eyes gritty and his mind still a bit foggy. Glancing around the room, he saw J.T. first, standing at the foot of his bed. Manton and Julian Howell stood in the open doorway.

"What's going on? Why aren't you with Jeannie?" Sam sat straight up. His head throbbed. He shut his eyes, trying to block out the sudden pain.

Julian Howell approached the side of Sam's bed. "The doctors felt it was necessary to keep you sedated in order to give you a few days to heal." Julian laid his hand on Sam's shoulder. "Every time you woke, you tried to get out of bed and find Jeannie."

"Yeah, I get the picture," Sam slid his legs off the bed, jerked the tubes out of his arms and stood. "I take it that y'all have finally decided to let me see her."

"You couldn't have done anything for her," Julian said. "She's been unconscious since—" Julian swallowed his tears.

"You mean she hasn't woken up yet?" Sam glanced at J.T. "What is it? What are y'all not telling me?"

J.T. exchanged a concerned look with Julian. Sam glanced at Manton. The gentle giant signed to him. He placed his hands on his shoulders, then moved them outward, the action mimicking the smoothing of feathers on the wings.

Angel. One of the first words Jeannie had taught Sam in sign language. His pet name for her.

Sam didn't understand the next word, although Manton repeated it several times, placing his hands palm to palm, then turning both hands over.

"What's he saying about Jeannie?" Sam asked.

"He said, 'Our angel is dying.'" Julian wiped tears from his eyes.

"No, she can't be dying." Sam gripped Julian's thin arm. "I won't let her die!"

J.T. grabbed Sam's shoulder, turning Sam to face him. "The doctors don't know what the hell is wrong. Like Dr.

Howell said, she's been unconscious for days. Her vital signs are growing steadily weaker. They've run every test imaginable on her. They can't treat her, because they don't know what's wrong with her."

"I know." Sam tried to pull away from J.T., but his friend held him fast. "Dammit, I know what's wrong with her. I killed her. In saving me, in healing me again and again just to keep me alive, she used up all her energy. She has nothing to build on. She's depleted her life force."

He realized that J.T. might think he'd gone mad, but he knew Julian and Manton would understand. He looked at Julian. "Tell him I'm right."

"It's possible that's what happened." Julian turned from them, burying his face in his hands as his body shook with sobs.

"She's been drifting in and out of consciousness for the last hour," J.T. said. "She keeps calling your name. Over and over."

"Take me to her, J.T. Please."

Sam Dundee never begged, never pleaded. But he was begging now.

Manton shook his head, stepping in front of Sam, signing furiously. Sam reached out, grasping Manton's enormous hands, halting him.

"I know what you're trying to tell me." Sam patted Manton's hands. "But if she's dying, I can't hurt her, can I? And she's calling for me. I need to be with her."

Manton nodded, agreeing with Sam.

Julian Howell, tears coating his face, his voice shaky, turned around and said, "Take him to her, Mr. Blackwood. She wants him with her. She loves him so."

"He needs to be told before he goes to her," J.T. said.

"Yes, of course he does," Julian agreed.

Fear like nothing Sam had ever known invaded his mind and body, trapping the screaming rage inside him. "What haven't you told me?"

J.T. closed his eyes momentarily, blew out his breath, then opened his eyes and looked directly at Sam. "She's pregnant. Four or five weeks pregnant."

Sam's blood chilled. His nerves burned. His muscles knotted painfully. Jeannie was carrying his child. And they were both dying. Because of him. She had sacrificed herself and their child to save his life.

"No!" The word roared from his body like the cry of a dying animal, his pain more than he could bear.

Sam turned, balled his hands into fists and pounded the wall so hard his hands burst through the Sheetrock. Pulling out his hands, he squared his shoulders and faced J.T.

"Let's go," Sam said.

J.T. walked Sam down the hall to Jeannie's room, Manton and Julian following. She rested on the pristine white sheets, her face devoid of color, her eyes closed. Dressed in a hospital gown, she lay perfectly still.

"I want to go in alone," Sam said. "I can make it without any help."

Sam entered her room, leaving the door behind him open. J.T., Manton and Julian hovered in the doorway. Sam walked slowly over to Jeannie and sat down in the chair beside her bed, then lifted her hand and pressed it against his lips.

"I'm here, angel. I'm right here with you," he told her. "Come on, Jeannie, wake up."

Her eyelids fluttered.

"That's it, come on, wake up." Standing, he clasped her hand to his heart.

She opened her eyes and looked at him. A faint smile curved her lips. "Sam."

Holding her hand, he leaned down and kissed her lips, the touch feather-light. "You've got to fight, angel. You can't let go. You have to live. What would I do without you?"

"You . . . you're . . . all right?"

"I'm fine." He rubbed the back of her fragile hand across his cheek. "You saved my life again." Tears lodged in Sam's throat.

"I love . . . you," Jeannie whispered.

"Please, Jeannie, don't die." Sitting down on the edge of the bed, he lifted her into his arms, kissing her tenderly on her forehead and cheeks. "I don't want to live without you."

"The baby...she's all right." Jeannie brought Sam's trembling hand down across her stomach. "We need you, Sam. Your little girl and I. You can save us."

"How? Dear God, Jeannie, tell me how!"

"You know how...you know..." Her voice drifted away as she closed her eyes and sank once again into an unnatural sleep.

"I don't know!" Sam shouted. "Tell me! I don't know!"

He clasped her to him, holding her against his chest, stroking her back, whispering her name. Tears welled up in Sam's eyes. A drop fell on his cheek. He swallowed hard. Another tear fell, then another, and another. Tears flooded his eyes, ran into his mouth, dripped off his chin.

Sam allowed his mind to delve into Jeannie's, seeking a response when he telepathically called her name.

I'm here, Sam. Help me. Save me. Save our baby. Take care of us.

"How?" he asked aloud, then repeated the question silently. *How?*

You know how.

He held her close, strengthening their physical connection as he kept their mental link intact.

I love you, Jeannie, my angel. I love you. Please don't leave me.

He felt her love invade his mind, conquer his heart and lay claim to his soul. *Don't let us go, Sam. Give us your strength. Take away our weakness.*

"I'll do anything to save you." Clutching her in his arms, holding her weak, lifeless body against the strength of his, Sam trembled with sorrow, crying from the depths of his soul as he had never cried before in his life. Not even when he was a child and his mother died.

"Please. Please. She's suffered so much for so many people. She gives and gives and asks nothing in return. She's saved my life twice, and shown me the meaning of real love. I can't live without her. If she dies, I die."

J.T. touched Sam on the back. "Come on, Sam. Don't do this. You aren't helping her."

Sam eased Jeannie down on the bed, stood up and turned to J.T. "I would give anything, even my soul, if I could do for her what she's done for so many others. If I could just reach inside and take away her suffering, make her whole again, give her all my strength."

"You're asking for a miracle," J.T. said.

"Yes, I know." Sam shoved J.T. away. "I'm not leaving her. She believes I can save her and our baby." Sam clamped his teeth together, choking on his pain, tears pouring down his face.

Sam fell to his knees beside Jeannie's bed in a mirror image of her vigil at his side in the storm shelter on Le Bijou Bleu. He held her hand.

"I love you. Do you hear me, Jeannie? I love you."

Manton and Julian entered the room and stood next to J.T., all three men standing by helplessly. Several nurses stood in the doorway, tears in their eyes.

"Just this once, angel, let someone hurt for you. Let me remove all that suffering inside you. I'm strong enough for both of us, and for our baby. Give me your pain, Jeannie. Do it for us. Do it for... our little girl."

Sam felt the first faint glimmer of pain, a deep, emotional need, and a physical weakness so great that he cried aloud when Jeannie's suffering began slowly draining from her body.

"That's it, angel. Let it all go. Don't be afraid. Our love is more powerful than anything. We can do this. Together."

Her pain swirled around inside him, sharp and jagged, ripping him apart. He moaned in agony. Suddenly he felt her withdrawal.

"Don't, angel. You've suffered far more for me. Love me enough to give me your pain. Please."

She returned to him, allowing him to take more of her suffering into his body and mind and heart. And when the deed was completed, Sam fell to the floor, unconscious, as his soul joined with Jeannie's forever.

Slowly, Jeannie opened her eyes. "Don't touch him. Leave him where he is," she ordered the others.

She eased off the bed, dragging the sheet and blanket with her. She crawled over to Sam, lifting the sheet over them as she put her arms around him.

"Everyone, please leave," she whispered. "He's all right. He just needs rest."

When the nurses tried to enter Jeannie's room, J.T. demanded they leave. "I don't think Jeannie and Sam need any medical assistance right now."

"Mr. Blackwood is right," Julian said. "Jeannie and Sam will be all right. The miracle of love has proven to be more powerful than medical science." Julian gripped Manton's arm, and guided him out the door. The room emptied quickly. J.T. closed the door when he stepped into the hallway.

Jeannie kissed the side of Sam's face, then drew his head into her lap. Placing her hand over her stomach, she smiled, knowing their baby was safe.

Sam's eyelids quivered, and then he opened his eyes slowly. "I'll always take care of you." Lifting his hand, he laid it over hers on her stomach. "Both of you."

"Your love saved us," Jeannie told him.

"*Your* love saved all three of us," he said, then closed his eyes and drifted off into a restorative sleep. When his limp hand slipped off hers, she grasped it and laid it on her stomach.

"Everything is all right, sweetheart," Jeannie told their unborn child. "Mommy and Daddy are here, and we love you as much as we love each other."

Epilogue

They married a month later in the small Congregational church on Beach Boulevard. Sam was devastatingly handsome in a gray striped morning suit, and Jeannie angelically lovely in Miriam Howell's ivory satin wedding gown. They honeymooned on Le Bijou Bleu, putting the horrors of Maynard Reeves's madness behind them.

Seven months later, little Miss Samantha Dundee came howling into the world, after having made her mother and father suffer together through ten hours of labor. But once they held their daughter in their arms, they agreed that they just might give her a brother or sister in a few years.

After enduring the torment of the damned, Sam and Jeannie found heaven on earth. They loved deeply and completely, sharing every joy, every sorrow, every pleasure and every pain. He would forever be her elegant savage, and she his angel of mercy.

Sam didn't take their happiness for granted. As he had

once guarded Jeannie from a world gone mad, he now guarded Jeannie and Samantha, making it his mission in life to surround them with the shield of his loving protection.

* * * * *

COMING NEXT MONTH

INTRODUCING...

A collection of award-winning books by award-winning
authors! From Harlequin and Silhouette.

VALENTINE'S NIGHT
by Penny Jordan

VOTED BESTSELLING
HARLEQUIN PRESENTS!

Let award-winning Penny Jordan bring you a Valentine you
won't forget. *Valentine's Night* is full of sparks as our heroine
finds herself snowed in, stranded and sharing a bed with an
attractive stranger who makes thoughts of her fiancé fly
out the window.

"Women everywhere will find pieces of themselves in Jordan's
characters."   —*Publishers Weekly*

Available this February wherever Harlequin books are sold.

For an *EXTRA*-special treat, pick up

TIME AND AGAIN
by
Kathryn Jensen

In January 1996, Intimate Moments proudly features Kathryn Jensen's *Time and Again*, #685, as part of its ongoing Extra program.

Modern-day mom: Kate Fenwick wasn't looking for a soul mate. Her two children more than filled her heart—until she met Jack Ramsey.

Mr. Destiny: He defied time and logic to find her, and only by changing fate could they find true love.

In future months, look for titles with the EXTRA flash for more excitement, more romance—simply *more*....

IMEXTRA3

INTIMATE MOMENTS®
Silhouette®

CODE NAME: DANGER

by
Merline Lovelace

Return to Merline Lovelace's world of spies and lovers as
CODE NAME: DANGER, her exciting miniseries, concludes in
February 1996 with Perfect Double, IM #692.

In the assignment of her life, Maggie Sinclair assumed
the identity of an assassin's target—the vice president
of the United States! But impersonating this high-
powered woman was child's play compared to
her pretend love affair with boss Adam Ridgeway.
Because Maggie had done a lot of things
undercover...except fall in love.

Don't miss a single scintillating story in the
CODE NAME: DANGER miniseries—*because
love is a risky business....* Found only in—

INTIMATE MOMENTS
Silhouette®